# No Other Help I Know

Rhonda Washington-Nelson

## No Other Help I Know

RiverHouse Publishing, LLC is registered in the United States Patent and Trademark Office.

All **RiverHouse, LLC** Titles, Imprints and Distributed Lines are available at special quantity discounts for bulk purchases for sales promotions, premiums, fund-raising and educational or institutional use.

Imprint: *RiverHouse Publishing, LLC*
www.riverhousepublishingllc.com


ISBN 978-0-9832186-5-4

*Know therefore that the Lord thy God, He is God, the faithful God, which keepeth covenant and mercy with them that love him and keep his commandments to a thousand generations...*
Deuteronomy 7:9

# Acknowledgments

I would like to take this opportunity to thank all those who helped me realize my dream.  It's such a great feeling.  It took a long time, but it was worth the wait.  Many of you touched this project in your own special way.  Paula, Jacky, Terrell and Angelina, thanks for your encouragement but most of all for your truthfulness.  It gave me the courage I needed to forge ahead.

My pride and joy—Sherra, Marcel, Marcus and Mary, thanks for all your support.  Sherra, you were there when the first chapter was written and stood by me until I finished the last.  You hung in there, honey, so...*mmmmmuh.* (That's me kissing your cheek)  Coren, Kylen, Jaylon, Javian, Miyah, Madisen and my baby Morgen.  Love you guys.

We all know it was Edna Davis, looking down from heaven— literally keeping me up at night, until I got that subject-verb agreement just right.  I was so blessed to have her as a mother and one that was also an English teacher... well, she always made me proud.

Most of all, I want to thank my Lord and Savior Jesus Christ for all that He has done.  I give Him the glory for making His Word real in my life.  It's true, I sought His Kingdom and He's added so many wonderful things. (Matthews 6:33)

# Chapter 1

## Monica

The coolness of the porcelain helped her spinning head. Hanging on, she rested it against the base of the badly stained surface longing for the nausea to subside. Twenty minutes later, it had only partially settled. Monica sat shaky and ashen, wedged between the sink and the toilet. Brushing away the tears, pounding her fists into her head, she thought, a one year-old, three year-old, a seven year-old, and in two more months, a newborn—*it's your own stupid fault*. Wiping the spit from her mouth, she sat.

"Mommy, are you okay?" Peaches asked, her small hand tapping gently against the door.

"Yeah, I'm all right," she said stumbling to get up. "I'll be out in a minute. Get yourself a bowl of cereal and head out for school."

"There's not enough milk."

"Well, hurry so you can eat breakfast at school," Monica said, splashing the tepid water from the faucet onto her face.

"Peaches," she called out. "Don't forget to sneak a carton of milk out of the cafeteria for me. The baby's gonna need it."

"Yes, mommy."

What would she do without her, Monica thought? Despite it all, she had turned out to be one of the most polite, well-mannered, mature, seven year olds ever, but...she also had *"the curse"*.

*"The curse"* had run rampant in their family for generations. Not only were they all beautiful, they were all very poor. Monica couldn't recall who'd started referring to their beauty as this, but all she knew, they'd gotten it right. Standing five feet nine, she had curves in all the right places. Long, flowing, curly hair accented her lovely skin along a perfectly oval face. The deep-almost too deep-dimples in each cheek highlighted her signature smile. Men everywhere were instantly attracted—from the rich stockbroker, to the doctor or lawyer. Then out of nowhere, *"the curse"* would show up. The broken promises "curse"…the multitude of bad choices "curse"…life seemingly never giving her a break "curse" and the next thing she knew, she was left empty handed—accompanied only by a truck load of regret. Now, she could see it inching its hateful way into the lives of her girls. One more mess-up and back into foster care they would go. They'd threatened her real good with that when she finally got them back the last time. She was trying to get her life together but knew at this point, she wasn't doing a very good job.

Using the walls to steady her gait, she crept out the bathroom and crawled onto the ledge of her bedroom window allowing the cool breeze against her face to revive her. She watched as Peaches crossed the street. Such a big girl, she thought.

Once she was safely across, she climbed into bed and pulled the sheet over her head. She knew the overwhelming tiredness wasn't normal, but welcomed the remedy the comforting sleep offered.

She'd slept deeply, but almost immediately, something pulled her right out of it.

"Monica! Monica! Wake up, girl! That baby is getting on everybody's nerves in the whole building," Gail shouted as she pounded her fist hard against the metal door.

Monica slowly pulled the thin-flowered sheet around her as she inched her way to stop the hammering. The pounding echoed in the tiny apartment, causing her head to ache.

"Shhh-hh. Gail, tone it down—please," Monica said opening the door. She knew that was next to impossible for her tall, brightly clad, high-spirited friend.

"Put some clothes on, give that baby a bottle and let's go. Jay Jay and Joey are waiting downstairs. If you hurry, we can make a ton of money," Gail said, shaking her head while opening the refrigerator.

Her loud perfume teased at the nausea Monica tried desperately to suppress. *"Okay, okay,"* she said wiping the tears from her baby's face. She looked over at Julia curled up sucking her thumb. She had already cried herself back to sleep.

"That can't be the right time?"

"Oh, yes it is. It's twelve fifteen. Are you coming or what?" she asked, picking at the long acrylic nail.

She knew it was an easy choice—stay and they'd all be hungry or go with Gail and get paid. "Let me throw on some jeans and a top. I'll be down stairs in two minutes."

Monica hated to leave her babies but she knew she had to. She filled the sippy cup with the last of the milk. A couple of draws and the baby was out like a light.

*Good*…Monica thought as she dressed—quietly closing the door.

# Chapter 2

## Peaches

Peaches skipped along trying to get the picture of her mother's pale face out of her mind. She'd watched her through the crack of the bathroom door and saw how sick she was. She tried not to worry but something was telling her she had every reason to. The biggest reason— their mother was starting to leave them home alone again. *Oh, God, please don't let us be taken away like before. I promise I'll be a good girl,* she prayed. The separation from her sisters and mother had placed a gigantic knot in her stomach that seemed to never go away.

She couldn't help but think of Countess and Julia as she scurried along the familiar path. Her baby sisters were her pride and joy. She dressed them in the morning, fed them when there was food, bathed and put them to bed at night. It didn't matter if she didn't have toys or nice things like the other kids in her class, she thought. She had something they didn't have—two *"real"* baby dolls to love.

Peaches picked up the pace, the wind cold on her face as she pushed against it. She was careful to avoid the speeding, yellow taxies whisking pass her.

She watched the other little girls as they clung to their mother's hands. One day, I'll ask mommy to walk me to school for a change, she thought. When she does, I'll make sure we hold hands.

That made her smile.

Later that afternoon, Peaches climbed the back stairs to the tall, aging, high-rise. She reached inside her backpack and found the pink bunny that held her key. After several attempts, the dead bolt finally clicked. Mommy has got to get that thing fixed, she fussed.

It was too quiet inside. She's not home. I just know it.

Tiptoeing, she whispered, "mommy." Again, "mommy." Still no answer. She walked over to the bed and looked down at the sleeping babies.

"Oh, my goodness. They smell awful." Fanning the pungent fumes, she located its source. The baby's swollen diaper and all its content threatened to spill onto the bed. She immediately went into action, gently removing the smelly culprit.

Both girls stirred and finally sat up. Wiping the sleep from her eyes, Countess took one look at her, poked her lip out and whimpered.

"Now, now, don't cry. See…I brought you some milk."

Putting on a fresh diaper, she propped the baby on her hip, and gently guided them into the kitchen.

"Here, let's eat some cereal. I'm glad I could get away with sneaking two milks out this time thanks to Yolanda—she's my very best friend."

She let the water trickle into the milk carton's spout as she bit her lip, determined not to add too much. "There! Now, that should stretch it out so Countess can have some before bedtime."

Wiping the dribble from her chin, they munched on a large bowl of Cheerios in the middle of the living room floor as they watched their favorite cartoons. Taking turns, the babies offered their mouths much like hungry baby robins as she fed them.

Peaches mind drifted to thoughts of her teacher, Ms Conrad. She really liked her and knew she meant no harm when she turned her mother in. Any student that missed school as much as she did had to be reported. That was the rule. That's how the foster people got them the first time. So, she made up her mind she would never miss school unless she absolutely had to.

Countess continued to fuss, turning her head refusing the last bit of cereal.

"I know what'll cheer you up little one," Peaches said. Filling the tub with warm sudsy water, all three got in.

Peaches was proud of herself. At last they were fed, clean and curled up in their mommy's bed.

She finished her homework even though she had a feeling she didn't need to. She'd already made up her mind. She wasn't going to school and leave her sisters alone.

Little did she know, she wouldn't be going for the rest of the week. She was tired. Looking down at the number scribbled alongside the phone, she shook her head and gently placed the phone back in its cradle. She was afraid to call her grandmother. She'd threatened to turn them in to the State the last time she found out they were home alone. "I'll turn you in to the State myself if you ever do that again," she'd yelled at her mommy.

Thank God it was the week-end. She'd already missed two days of school. Another blessing, Miss B across the hall felt generous for a change, letting them borrow milk, bologna and crackers.

She knew something strange was happening, though. Neither Countess nor Julia would eat and slept curled in the middle of their mother's bed most of the day. When she touched them they both felt really hot. There were no more diapers, and Countess' bare bottom was covered only by the thin sheet as she slept. Tapping her fingers, Peaches chewed the corner of her bottom lip and waited.

The sunlight faded slowly giving way to the dark shadows that filled the room. She turned on as many lights as possible. It made her feel safe. Last night she could have sworn she heard someone twist the door knob. In fact, she knew she heard a prowler outside the door. *Maybe whoever it was, was still out there. What if her mother was never coming home?* The thought of her mother's face the last time she saw her made her shiver. *Maybe she's dead?* She had to get help.

Peaches raced to awaken the girls. She shook them as hard as she could with no response. Even she knew arms as limp as that could only mean one thing. Heart thumping, she dashed for Miss B's apartment. This time it didn't take long for the ambulance to arrive.

~~~

Jay Jay braked, slowing the car. "What in the world is going on," he said.

The moment Monica saw the flashing lights, she knew trouble lurked ahead. Her breath came in spurts as she wrapped her arms around her cramping stomach. She picked Miss B out of the gathering crowd, standing with both hands on her hips, glaring. Then she spotted her girls. Peaches screaming—Countess and Julia, with oxygen, IVs and paramedics all around. They were all the center of the gawking and growing crowd's attention.

Jumping out the car before it came to a complete stop, Monica screamed, *"No-o-o, what happened?"*

The stabbing pain in her stomach stopped her in her tracks. Doubled over, she drew air deep into her lungs trying to catch her breath.

"Your babies are dying, girl," Miss B screamed.

The paramedics blocked her as she tried to push one aside to get in the ambulance.

"Hey, you, let me see my babies!" she screamed.

Clutching her stomach, she turned toward the gut-wrenching cries of Peaches.

*"Ma-a-a-ma, Ma-a-a-ma,"* Peaches wailed as she swung wildly at the man trying to push her into the car.

Monica watched helplessly as they finally succeeded in getting her frantic child inside. With a sudden lightness accompanying her twirling head, Monica collapsed, as all of her girls sped away, red lights flashing.

"Ms. Gold! Ms. Monica Gold, I'm starting an IV. You'll feel a stick," the nurse said, gliding the eighteen gauge needle deep into her skin.

"Monica, we need you to try and stay awake. Can you hear me?"

*"Aww…"* she moaned.

Monica felt the familiar pains of childbirth. This time, however, something was tearing her inside. As she slipped in and out of consciousness she remembered hearing something about needing to operate…twins… bleeding …

"Doctor, her blood pressure is dropping," she heard a voice far away say.

*Dying. Now, that's not a bad idea… may be my way out of all this.* Monica's thoughts flickered in and out much like dancing butterflies. The approaching blackness was not only soothing, but offered a strange sense of comfort she'd occasionally dreamed of—a world where nothing seemed to matter.  Whatever the nurse gave her, it was the best feeling she'd had in a long time.  Plunging deeper into darkness's consoling grip, she mumbled… *"No-o-o, I can't leave … I need to live for Peaches…my girls."*

It felt as if she'd just managed to close her eyes when a voice seemingly calling from inside a tunnel called out, "Ms. Gold, please wake up.  Ms. Gold."

When she tried opening her eyes, she was hit with an ache that tore at her stomach.  Wincing from the pain, she felt tangled masses of tubing connected to her body, seeming to flow from everywhere.

"You had complications during your delivery.  You have twins," she heard the nurse say drawing the curtains around her bed.  "They were delivered prematurely–C-section… twin girls."

With her eyes still closed, Monica finally forced out, "My babies, how are they?"

Another unfamiliar voice spoke.  "Ms. Gold that's what I need to talk to you about.  I'm Dr. Troy and I delivered your twins.  They had to go to our newborn intensive care unit and both are in need of very close monitoring.  There is a definite chance neither baby will pull through this."

The words jarred her awake.  Rubbing her throbbing abdomen, she groaned.  The pain in her stomach, however, was mild in comparison to the ache that tore at her heart.

"Ms. Gold?"

"Yes," she whispered.

"There's one last thing we need to discuss.  If you want to see your babies, well… you'll need to speak to someone in our Social Services department about that."

She pushed those words as far away as possible and cuddled into the restful arms of sleep. For now, it was her sole source of comfort.

Things soon changed however, when she was discharged home. There, she sat curled up on the couch in the dimly lit apartment most of the day. She watched the shadow that the lone candle made as it danced its way along the wall. Shaking her head, she tried to get the creepy sound the quietness made out of it. She longed to hear the familiar voices of her girl's laughter and their chatter once again. She'd spent the past eight weeks all alone and wouldn't open the door for anyone. Not even the day Jay Jay, Gail and Joey showed up or when her mother and grandmother tried to get in. She wouldn't answer the door for any of them. *Guilt* was now her companion.

The only people she wanted to talk to didn't want to talk to her. The information Protective Services gave her about her girls was extremely limited. At least she knew her twins were in good hands at The City Medical Center. Most of the tubes were out and they would be moved to a different area for the larger babies shortly according to the nurses. *Miracles,* they called them.

As she wiped the tears that streaked her face, she listened to the persistent voice that had finally convinced her it was the right thing to do. She stared blankly as she stuffed a fistful of pain killers into her mouth. Gagging, she placed the glass of water gently to her lips.

An unexpected knock at the door startled her. She sat with a mouth full of pills, hoping whoever it was would just go away. They kept knocking. Finally, a strong voice penetrated the metal door.

"Ms. Gold, this is Ms. Dire from Protective Services. Are you there?"

My babies! Monica spit the pills into the trash and stumbled to the door. Removing the chains, she opened it only to see a tall, middle-aged woman in a plain blue suit. The voice matched her stature.

"Ms. Gold, are you okay?" Ms. Dire asked, staring at a thin, almost too thin woman with deep-dark, sunken eyes.

"No ma'am, I'm really not okay at the moment," she said, her voice cracking.

"What's wrong, Ms. Gold?

"What's wrong?" she said flatly. "What do you mean, what's wrong? Just look around, in case you haven't noticed. A lady like yourself, weren't you afraid to come up here? By the way, where are my babies?" Monica said staggering. "Nobody will tell me where my babies are? I have nothing! Look at me, I have nothing!" she sobbed.

Ms. Dire reached for her hand. Monica fell into her arms, allowing the flood of tears to spill onto her visitor's nice blue jacket.

Finally lifting her head, Monica gestured for her to come inside.

"Let's talk." Ms. Dire said. She cautiously selected a place to sit on the badly stained sofa. "I came to let you know your twin daughters have done remarkably well, despite the odds. They are going into foster homes in a couple of weeks."

Monica shook her head as the tears fell freely.

"No-o-o, don't cry," Ms. Dire chided. "Just listen to me. Julie and Countess are doing much better too. They had meningitis and the doctors feel they should both make a full recovery."

Monica sat—her hand covering her mouth.

"Do you want your girls home, Monica? You know I can get them back to you, if you do exactly as I say."

She didn't know what to say as she sat facing the only person she'd let into her apartment in weeks.

"Are you listening to me?" Ms. Dire asked.

Monica stared in disbelief. Had a glimmer of hope just floated her way? She wasn't used to anything ever working out for her.

Maybe, it was a thread of hope.

She held on to it with all her might and forced out a few words.

"Help me, Ms. Dire. Please help me get my babies back."

# Chapter 3

## Monica's Girls
### ~Peaches~

Peaches sat in the den finishing the last of the home-work assignment. She was doing extremely well in the school her foster parents placed her. The lessons were a breeze. The teacher had even been trying to be a little more creative when it came to challenging her.

Peaches began noticing another surprising, yet pleas-ant change. All the girls in her class looked up to her, often calling her the smartest in the class. The boys simply teased her.

She didn't understand any of it—why they were all being so nice. The only reason she figured, it had to be the way she was beginning to dress. The Crafts bought her a brand new wardrobe and had her hair fashioned in a style she absolutely adored.

Her foster parents seemed okay, she thought.

"Peaches, are you finished with your homework?" Mrs. Craft asked.

"Yes, ma'am."

"Go and take a bath and get ready for bed, okay."

Peaches filled the tub the way she liked—with warm, sudsy water and climbed inside. She loved taking baths. It reminded her of the girls. She couldn't think about that too much though, it made her feel like crying. She really missed them and longed for the day they'd all be together again. She scrubbed her face forcing back the tears.

When she finished, she looked up.  Jumping, she splashed water onto the floor.

Mr. Craft was standing there.

She tried to cover her nakedness as she watched him glaring down at her.

"Mrs. Craft wants you to get out of the tub now, Peaches."

"Yes sir," she said, reaching for the towel.

Mr. Craft grabbed it and held on.

She tried reaching for it but it was too far away.  She knew she would have to stand.  "Could you hand me my towel, Mr. Craft?"

"Here, come and get it, Peaches.  Mrs. Craft is waiting for us," he said.

He smiled—taking several steps back.

~~~

"Class, continue the lesson on your computers," Ms. Tate said standing as she closed her grade-book.  "Please, *no talking*.  Peaches, may I see you for a moment?"

She led her into the cloak room area, stooped down and stared into her droopy eyes.  "Are you okay?" she asked gently tucking Peaches long braid behind her ear.

"I'm concerned about your grades.  I've never known you to miss this many math problems.  You can do this stuff with your eyes closed, honey.  Is there anything wrong? If there is, you can talk to Miss Tate about it."

Peaches hung her head as the tears quickly formed. She tried hard not to cry.  Big girls just didn't do that, she thought.  She pushed her head up but couldn't stop the tears this time.  "I want my mommy," she whispered.

Miss Tate pulled her close, patting her softly on the back.  "Hey, it's going to be all right."

"No, it's not.  No one understands—it'll never be all right."

Miss Tate knew about Peaches' circumstances.  When the principal assigned her to her classroom, he'd indicated the child came with, as he described it, "a special set of problems."

It seemed her foster parents were very nice and treated her well, but she could tell Peaches was just not handling being away from her mother.  She decided she'd better speak to the principal.  Perhaps they could talk to Peaches' caseworker about how all this was affecting her. In the meantime, she held Peaches and comforted her all she knew.  Girls just need to be with their mothers, she thought.

Peaches considered running away but didn't know where to go.  She was terrified of Mr. Craft and never wanted to be alone with him, especially after the bath incident.

She'd managed to keep her distance, sticking as close as possible to Mrs. Craft.  She was a nice lady, but it was the strangest thing—she seemed just as afraid of her own husband as she was.

"Peaches, would you go in the den and tell Mr. Craft supper is ready?" Mrs. Craft said, trying to balance the hot platter with the towel.

"Yes ma'am."   Peaches walked slowly toward the back of the house where he sat leaning back in his oversized lounge chair.

"Mr. Craft," Peaches said softly.  "Supper is ready."

He didn't respond.

"Mr. Craft…Mr. Craft…"  She moved closer.  "Mr. Craft…"  Still no answer.  Her hand shook as she reached to touch his arm. "Mr. Craft."

He grabbed her by the arm and sat her hard on his lap.

"Mr. Craft, I just wanted to tell you supper was ready and we need to go and eat now," she said, squirming to get down.

"Sit still a moment, Peaches," he said. "I need to talk to you. How do you like staying here with us?"

"It's okay," Peaches said.

"Are you doing okay in school?"

"Yes, sir."

"Would you like to stay here with us for a little while longer?"

Peaches didn't answer. She felt her answer would make him angry and she didn't want to do that.

"Peaches, answer me. Do you want to stay here with us a little while longer?"

"I just want to see my mommy now, Mr. Craft."

"We would miss you if you left us. Do you know that? Think about whether you would like to stay here with Mrs. Craft and me. With us you can have your own room, nice clothes and nice toys. What do you say?"

"Okay," she said fighting to get down. She knew she didn't belong in his lap.

He finally let her go. "Tell Mrs. Craft I'll be there in a minute. I need to freshen up."

She ran as fast as she could to the kitchen feeling as if she'd done something awfully wrong. *That's it.* She was never going to be alone with that old man, again.

She kept true to the promise she made herself. Everywhere Mrs. Craft went, she went. She kept her in sight at all times and was grateful Mrs. Craft never seemed to mind her tagging along.

Then it happened. She'd only managed to take her eyes off her for a few seconds while she finished her homework. Suddenly, Mr. Craft was standing in front of her, jingling the coins in his pocket. Quickly scanning the room, she noticed Mrs. Craft was nowhere in sight.

How could she let that happen? She scolded herself. The trembling started from inside and slowly worked its way out.

"Peaches, Mrs. Craft has gone to the market and will be back shortly."

Jumping up from the table, she dashed towards the door to run after her protector. She knew it was too late, as she watched the car coax down the hill.

Mr. Craft stood in the hallway. She brushed past him and headed straight for her room.

Closing the door, she sat at the desk with a book covering her face. Pretending to read, she held her breath.

Slowly, the door creaked opened. She could feel his presence—the smell of alcohol rushed her nostrils. She clamped her eyes shut, listening to the sound her pounding heart made. Suddenly, the roughness of his hand scraped against her skin. She opened her mouth to scream.

"John—Peaches, where are you?"

It was Mrs. Craft.

"I forgot the check book," she yelled.

Throwing the book aside, Peaches ran out the door and down the steps.

"Hey, slow down young lady," Mrs. Craft said. "Are you okay? You look as if you've seen a ghost. I forgot to ask if you wanted to go with me."

Peaches nodded vigorously, holding tightly to her hand.

## ~Twin A~

"Gerald, do you think they would agree to us adopting Geraldene?" Charlene asked. "Honey, let's not get into that again," he said. "We have to wait and see what the courts say. If they can prove she is an unfit mother, then our chances of adopting the baby are excellent. According to Ms. Dire, it's looking quite promising. The mother is a hopeless junkie."

Charlene and Gerald had been trying to get pregnant for years. The doctors couldn't find any biological reason for them not conceiving. They'd tried everything for eight years. Still no luck. Then Ms. Dire made arrangements for them to get this baby.

Charlene met Ms. Dire at the governor's inaugural ball and they'd become immediate friends. When she shared her infertility story, Ms. Dire suggested foster care with the idea of eventually adopting one of them. Several foster children were brought to their home but she was never really interested in any of them. It wasn't until she'd met this baby that everything changed.

Call it fate, but she'd instantly fallen in love with Geraldene. As soon as the baby came to live with them, she transformed the spacious corner bed room into a nursery. The bright crib with its large pink and white canopy flowing down from its top was placed in the middle of the room. Personalized teddy bears, dolls and a vintage rocking chair surrounded it, adding to the matching decor. Every kind of outfit imaginable for an infant girl filled the walk- in closets. The baby was adorable and even Gerald had to admit how easy it was for him to get attached to her.

He always seemed to worry though, Charlene thought. "What's going to happen if we can't get this particular baby? Don't get too attached to Geraldene," he'd often said.

Well, it was too late. Nothing had ever caused her heart to overflow with love more than this baby did. Besides, she'd already renamed her—Geraldene. It was a combination of her name and his.

"I'm glad we have a meeting with Ms. Dire on tomorrow to discuss the adoption," Charlene said.

"It should be interesting." Flipping the pages of the newspaper, he never looked up. He didn't want to get engaged into that conversation again.

Gerald wasn't crazy about Ms. Dire's style and wasn't so sure of her motives. It was something about her that made him uncomfortable. He had requested the meeting a while ago and she finally found the time to get together with them over dinner.

The next day, they were scheduled to meet at three, and as usual, Ms. Dire was at least an hour late. Gerald stood up as she approached the table. Pulling the chair out, he could feel the moisture already accumulating on his hands. He'd even chosen the small quaint Italian restaurant that had become his favorite, in hopes it would help him to relax. Right now, it wasn't working.

Charlene held the baby up for Ms. Dire to see. They were both wearing coordinating outfits—hats and all.

"My, aren't the two of you pretty," she said, softly rubbing the baby's face.

"Say hello, Geraldene. Say hello," Charlene said in her baby voice, waving the tiny hand.

"I'll have a cup of your hot tea. Decaf," Ms. Dire instructed the server. She took a quick look around making sure he was no longer close by, moved her chair up and said, "now let's get down to business. Geraldene's mother is going through a very difficult time right now. She's not doing well and we all predict it's just a matter of time before she's out on the streets dealing drugs again. We tend to think she doesn't know any other lifestyle and is much more comfortable on the streets than she is raising her children. Let's face it. The mother is a loser and Protective Services has done all they can to help, but Monica Gold refuses to change. This child would be at serious risk if she were to ever be around her again. That's why we're taking Geraldene from her."

"May I get you anything else?" the server asked, approaching.

She took a sip of the hot tea and looked up at him. "Don't come back until I call for you." The server hastily walked away.

Ms. Dire continued. "There's one more small detail I need to discuss with the two of you. I've begun collaborating with a young lady I know will be very instrumental in helping me validate the mother's continual drug involvement." She lowered her voice. "This extra set of eyes will be my assistant and the help I need in proving that Ms. Monica Gold *is* and always *will be* an unfit mother. I gave her money to help us sort these matters out. She actually lives in the same building that Monica used to live in." She paused and took a deep breath. "I hate to bring this up, Gerald, but I'm going to need more cash to assist me with my inside help."

It was Charlene that spoke. "That's fine, Ms. Dire. We'll do whatever it takes to keep our precious Geraldene. Yes we will," she said in that same tiny voice, tickling the baby under her chin.

Gerald was concerned. However, he knew it wasn't the time or the place to share his feelings. He reached in his pocket and pulled out a roll of fifty-one hundred dollar bills.

"Great. This should do it," Ms. Dire said. "I don't think it'll take us too much longer to wrap things up. Gail said she knows Monica is beginning to hang around the old drug gang again and she's ready to help us prove that."

Ms. Dire smiled. "I have a few other pressing matters I must deal with today," she said pushing her chair back. "I need to run." She took her last bite of the Alaskan salmon and stood. "I'll be talking to you guys real soon."

Gerald couldn't wait to leave the restaurant. He'd barely eaten any of his Fiori Fritti and Arista—a first for him. He didn't like Ms. Dire. On the drive home, they rode along in silence. He laid his head on the headrest as the soothing classical tunes piped its way inside the car. It did little to relax him. He knew Charlene would never understand the way he was beginning to feel. He wanted so badly to tell her how wrong the adoption felt. He could have kicked himself. Why hadn't they tried adopting the baby the traditional way? Going through Ms. Dire to bypass all the "paperwork" as she described it, was a mistake. Plus, she had already asked for more money than they'd originally agreed. Who asked her to bring in outside help anyway? That was just another complication. He knew they needed to get out of this situation and the faster they did the better. Charlene would get all hysterical if he tried changing his mind so late in the game, though. She seemed obsessed about getting this child and he couldn't understand that either.

He needed someone to talk to.

"You're quiet. Anything wrong?" Charlene asked glancing over at him.

"No, dear, everything's fine," he said, taking the shortest route home.

"I need to run by the church to see Pastor Collins. He asked me to stop by when I saw him on Sunday."

After they were safely inside, he picked up his cell and dialed his pastor. As usual, he was available.

Gerald knew Pastor Collins had a reputation of being someone you could talk to about anything and walk away feeling better than you did before you came. How was he ever going to tell him he was involved in something potentially illegal? The thought of it made him want to turn around.

Parking in the church's lot, he laid his forehead on the steering wheel. He was tired of feeling guilty and should have been man enough to tell Charlene they were not going to adopt the baby the second Ms. Dire made the offer. That was the problem. He'd never been able to tell her, no. He'd always treated her like a queen and made enough money for her to live like one. Being at home alone most of the time, he guessed that was the main reason she wanted to have a baby right away. Even though he didn't agree, he couldn't tell her no to that either. Once they began having difficulty conceiving, he noticed how obsessed she became about the situation. They had both endured every technique known to science to try and conceive but having children obviously wasn't in the cards for them. Now that she had a baby she was claiming as her own, how was he ever going to take that away from her?

Lifting his head, he realized there was a distinct possibility Charlene would actually leave him if he tried to stop the adoption. Striking the steering wheel, he knew he wasn't willing to take that chance.

Cranking the car and slowly pulling out the lot, Gerald thought he would just have to go along with everything the way it was—Ms. Dire and all. There was no need to talk with Pastor Collins anymore. He knew what he had to do. He had to get Charlene that baby.

### ~Countess and Julia~

Countess and Julia were passed from foster home to foster home. It was hard placing two sickly kids together, but the doctors felt they needed to stay together. They were right. Those two would cling to each other as if they were the only two people in the world. To further complicate matters, Countess was a crier. Ms. Dire finally found a home she thought would take them both for at least six weeks. When she drove up to the small bricked house where an old rusty Chevy decorated the yard, she took Countess and Julia out of the car. Placing them on the sidewalk and walking ahead, she carefully navigated around the toys and trash that littered the walk. The tiny girls held on to each other to keep from falling.

Ann greeted them, swinging the hole riddled screen door open wide. She had three other foster children along with two of her own. She considered herself an expert at making children behave—especially crybabies.

"Ann, I can't tell you how much I appreciate you taking these two off my hands," Ms. Dire said.

"Hurry up you two, you're letting the flies in," Ann said swinging at one. She watched as Julia helped Countess manage the last of the steps.

"Yeah, I don't need them to be here forever, Dire. The extra cash helps. Thanks for thinking about me."

"This is their third foster home. We don't like moving kids around that much. With over a half a million foster kids in the system, they can easily get misplaced."

"Yeah, Yeah. Just leave 'em. Hey, you, wipe your nose," Ann said pointing to Julia.

"You really do have a way with children, don't you, Ann?"

"It seems I always know how to make them behave, Dire. I guess you can say it's a gift."

Ann was a relatively large woman with an even larger attitude. She didn't take any mess from anybody—especially from the children that lived in her home. To make life better for her household, she was willing to tolerate fosters as she frequently called them. The rent on her house, along with the upkeep on the second hand car, was more than she could afford. Extra income was essential. These two fosters, however, came with difficulties, she heard. The younger one cried all the time and shortly she was going to start teaching her that crying around here could get you hurt. She had become an expert at pinching and twisting arms without causing bruising or broken bones. She had something for the older one as well. It got on her nerves asking for some Peaches. I want to see Peaches. Where is Peaches?

Ann thought, I've got a remedy for that too.

It didn't take long for her to prove to the new arrivals how little girls should behave in her home. It was the crying that upset her the most. She knew she had gone overboard and felt the stress of it all mounting. Her decision to phone Ms. Dire about what she had done was difficult.

"Ann, how did the child's arm get broken?" Ms, Dire asked.

"She fell…uh…she's just so clumsy. I think something is wrong with these two kids, Dire."

"That's *Ms.* Dire, please."

"This little one is always falling and crying," Ann said.

"No one else has ever reported a problem of her falling, Ann—just her crying."

"Well, she's clumsy and she fell and that's that!"

"What did the doctors say?"

"Of course they thought I had something to do with it. They questioned me but since this was the first time I'd ever brought a kid in, they dropped it."

"Let's try and be careful and not let this baby get hurt again, Ann."

"I will, Dire. Listen, I don't want to keep these kids not a day longer than the six weeks. My own kids deserve better than to have these brats around 'em."

Ann's children, Justin and Clara were listening in the other room. They were glad their mom had finally made that decision. It wasn't because they didn't like having the kids around. They were just tired of hearing her screaming and beating the two new girls. For some reason their mother got really worked up whenever those two would cry. They had to admit both girls did cry a lot. The older girl didn't cry near as much, only when the little one was getting roughed up.

Justin and Clara felt the least they could do was to keep the girls away from their mother. First, they had to figure out how to keep them from crying.

# Chapter 4

## Monica's Plan

This is some plan, Monica thought. Moving in with mamma and grandmamma—she had to be out of her mind. She'd rather stay in the behavioral-health center where Ms. Dire fought to get her in than to be there. To be honest, it was mamma she couldn't deal with more so than grandmamma. For the past five years, her mother had started attending church and ever since then, it seemed her lifestyle had become increasingly irritating to her. She didn't like her friends, clothes, not even her hairstyles. It seemed nothing about her life met her mother's approval. Of course, not any of her friends were allowed over to the house or even call. She might as well be in prison, she thought. Not that she wanted to talk to Gail, Jay Jay or Joey. It was just the principle.

However, for now…this was the plan.

Monica knew Ms. Dire had gotten personally involved in her case and every time she could, she reminded her of that. "I'm putting my neck on the line for you," she'd often say. Although the behavioral-health center she'd chosen for her had just recently opened and was slightly over-crowded, Ms. Dire had convinced them to take her.

Initially, she'd fought going there, but while in the facility, she found the intense therapy helpful. They were up early in the morning and the staff insisted she eat healthy meals. She had to attend self esteem and personal development classes and as time passed, she began feeling better about herself and a lot more optimistic about the future. Most of all, the classes were helping her to face what she had done to her girls. Her emotions screamed of how incredibly irresponsible she had been. How could she have left them alone? Now that her head was clear, she wanted desperately to make it up to them— to hold them and tell them how very sorry she was. All she needed was another chance to prove she could be the kind of mother five beautiful girls deserved.

Protective Services wasn't hearing any of it at the moment. They felt it was best to keep Peaches completely away from her since she seemed to be adjusting well to her foster parents.

They didn't know Peaches like she did. She was going to adjust well to any situation. She was just that strong—just that smart. Countess and Julia were together and doing well also. The twins were separated, but they both were reported as thriving.

Now that she was beginning to make better decisions, the choice to remove herself from all association with the drug dealing business had been an easy one. Her *only* focus was getting her girls back. She would do whatever it took to make that happen—even if it meant moving in with mamma and grandmamma.

To cope, she took long walks along a trail in a nearby park. She was really enjoying the exercise and could tell her body was starting to respond.

Walking briskly outside, the occasional breeze cooled her dampened skin. She jogged in place waiting for the light to change.

"Watch where you're going, young lady," a male voice called out.

Ignoring the comment, she trotted across the street.

"Hey, Monica, it's me," he said, lightly tapping the horn.

"Jay Jay!"

He pulled the car to the side as she jogged over. She was glad to see him.

"I had my mind on a million things. How 'ya doing?" She tried not to stare but couldn't help but notice her thin, disheveled friend's appearance. Dark circles caressed the lids of his eyes, his lips cracked and dry.

"You still driving this beat-up old hooptie?" she said, playfully kicking his tire.

"What can I say, it gets me around."

"So, what's going on with you, Jays? Are you okay?"

"Yeah, I'm fine. Don't I look fine?" he said, pulling at his collar in his old playful way. "Let's not talk about me. *Whoa...*" He eyed her up and down. "No one has seen you in months, girl. Everybody's been asking about you, wondering how you've been. Wait 'til I tell 'em how good you look."

A delicate smile slowly emerged before she spoke. "You know Jays, this is the first time I actually feel as if my life is going in the right direction. My head is clear, I'm looking for work and my only goal is getting my girls back home with me. Can you believe it? I have five beautiful girls who I haven't seen in months," she said dropping her head.

She couldn't say those familiar words without a smothering sadness descending upon her. "I guess the people will give me some supervised visitations shortly. Word on the street is there's one couple that may want to adopt my baby. I can't let that happen. I need to try and get my girls home soon, Jay Jay."

"You would never give up a single one of those girls, Monica. If no one else understands that, I do. I know how much you love them."

"Hey, get in and let's kick it with the gang for old times' sake," he said swinging the door open. "It'll be good for them to see you. We'll have a blast like we used to."

"Jay Jay, if they even suspect I'm around that group, doing the things we used to do, they would take away my parental rights in a heartbeat. I'd never see my girls again."

"You know I wouldn't let that happen, Monica. Gail really wants to see you. In fact, everybody does. It's been a long time. Look, if I think they are about to do anything you don't like, we'll vamp right out of there. Deal? Deal...? Come on, you know you can trust me."

She was bored at home and felt she owed Gail an explanation for going *MIA*. She slowly got inside.

~ ~ ~

"Hey, Monica!" one of her old neighbors shouted when she walked up. "Where you been, girl!"

"I'm glad I got the chance to see you today," Monica said, continuing her conversation with Gail and ignoring the neighbor's comment.

"Life's treating me well. My kids are growing up so fast I can hardly keep up with them. I love seeing them growing up right before my eyes," Gail said.

*Hmmm*, now that's a strange comment, Monica thought. The cynicism quite apparent.

Despite the offbeat remark, Monica found herself having a really good time "kicking it" with the old gang. She really did miss Gail's animated ways. The girl was hilarious and kept her in stitches.

All heads turned slowly as Joey cruised by in his shinning new, white Mercedes SUV.

"Monica, Joey wants to see you" someone yelled. Hesitating, she turned and walked slowly towards the truck.

"Hey, what's up?" she asked peeking inside the heavily tinted window.

He opened the door. "Come on. Get in."

Everything inside her told her not to. I won't go anywhere with him she promised herself as she slid onto the fresh leather seats.

"Look at you!" he said, drawing closer.

"Let's not start that, Joey," she said pulling away. "I'm trying to get my life together, man. I have too much to lose."

"Let me help you get your life together, Monica" he said, with more sincerity than she'd anticipated. "Everybody in the projects knows what happened to you. There're even bets going around on whether or not you'll ever see those kids again. Guess what? I'm going to help you get your kids back."

"How can you help me, Joey?"

"I have connections, girl. I have big connections now. Look at what you're sitting in. Let me show you something else."

Before she could say no, he sped off. She couldn't help but notice Gail's troubled expression as she whisked by.

The ride was incredibly smooth as he drove for miles to the other side of town. It was amazing to watch the beautiful homes, sprawled on acres of land increase in size as they drove along.

When he slowed in front of one of the largest two story homes she'd ever had the pleasure of being close to, she gasped.

"Joey, tell me you're not living in a house like this!" Monica said, spinning around in her seat.

He swerved the SUV into the triple car garage. "Come on in, and make yourself at home."

Monica took a tour of the entire house while Joey talked on his cell. Climbing the spiral staircase, she leaned over the balcony enjoying the breath-taking, palatial view. Descending the steps, she ventured into the kitchen, plastered in granite and stainless steel. It made the entire space sparkle. Pulling out the tall bar stool from around the island, she sat and took it all in. *Wait a minute. What are you doing here?* she thought. *You've come too far. Joey is into something super illegal and if you get caught with him, it could be history for the girls.*

She quickly slipped off the stool and found Joey in his study. "Can you get off the phone for a sec, I need to talk to you," Monica whispered.

He shot her a look and she backed off.

A whole hour passed when he finally walked in the room. "Let's go chill out in here," he said, directing her to a plush all white sectional facing a 70 inch theater-style screen.

"Joey, I need to leave. I can't stay. It just doesn't feel right."

"What's wrong?" he asked, gazing into her eyes. I'm getting the idea you don't want to be around me anymore?"

"It's that I'm in a very difficult place right now, Joey. When I try to do right, somehow it all turns so very wrong. I need to leave," she said attempting to get up.

Pulling her to him, he reached up and massaged her shoulders. "Listen," he said, "I've really missed you. You wouldn't answer my calls. I tried to come over and you wouldn't let me in. I didn't realize how much you meant to me, Monica. I don't want to ever lose you again."

"Joey, please stop. I need to go," she said removing his hands.

"Marry me, Monica. I know how to make things right for you. The girls…"

The doorbell's chimes interrupted him mid-sentence. "I'll get rid of whoever that is. We must talk tonight."

She sat, stunned.

Suddenly, a male's voice trailed from the door to where she sat. "Are you Joey Phelps," he said in a hoarse, raspy tone. "I'm Sergeant Foley and we need to search…."

Cops! She jumped from the couch, found the back door and twisted the knob. Locked. Heart pounding, she looked around and spotted a side door. She moved quickly, pulled the handle and slipped quickly through. Reaching the edge of the patio, circling the hot tub, she braced herself to run. She'd only taken a couple of strides when she ran smack into the chest of what appeared to be the largest man in the world. She knew then, all her dreams were over.

"Please, this is my first time over here and I don't know anything." Her heart outraced her stammering tongue. She tried forcing his hands away but he was just too strong. "Let me go!" she cried.

"Monica, hush! It's me, Big Man!" He put his wide hand over her mouth, and all but carried her to his car. Pushing her inside, he sped off. Just in time too. The investigators had already begun searching Joey's backyard.

"Here, quit crying. You're okay," he said, handing her his handkerchief.

"What happened?" Monica cried.

"I'll tell you about it later, just calm down for now." Big Man drove around until he noticed her finally resting her head on the back of the seat.

"Are you okay?"

"No, Big Man, I'm not okay. I don't know what just happened, but boy am I glad you were there. Would you take me home? I really need to get home."

~~~

"Mattie, please sit down. Monica is going to be all right. You can't worry yourself about her like that. Where's your faith? Do you honestly believe God is going to fix her situation like we've prayed?" grandmamma asked.

"Yes, mamma, I do, but..."

"Well, if you're going to worry, quit praying but, if you're going to pray, it'll do you no good to worry."

That made her smile. "Mamma, I'm going to pray whether I worry or not. I just don't understand where she could be. She knows that behavioral center wants her home at a certain time if they're going to give her a favorable report."

"I know, I know." Grandmamma wished Monica would come home too as she watched Mattie pace back and forth.

Monica's mother and grandmother had lived together in the tiny two bedroom, white-framed house on Woodstock for years. Despite the deteriorating conditions of the neighborhood, their home was immaculate. The neighbors respected the two women—especially, grandmamma.

"I want so badly for her to get herself together so we can get our grandbabies back," Mattie said. "Those State people just don't understand. We didn't care about being over crowded. They should have given me those kids like I begged them to."

"They know we are struggling over here and they've got to do what they think is best," grandmamma said. "Listen, God wants them to come back to us, I know He does. He's just going to do it His way and in His own time."

"If she messes up this time, we will never see those girls again," Mattie said. "You remember what Jessica told us about the couple trying to adopt one of the twins. I don't know how she gets all her information but she does and she's never wrong. I just don't have a good feeling about them being in the foster homes this time."

Grandmamma didn't have a good feeling either. Jessica had also confided in her. She didn't want to worry Mattie, but word was that they were having trouble locating Monica's other twin daughter. According to Jessica, the agency was all in a stir about it and Ms. Dire was in a lot of hot water as a result. She had given this twin's case to another caseworker and somehow they had miscommunicated. The caseworker was an inexperienced young woman whose caseload was more than she could handle. She was the one who'd actually lost track of the twin.

"I'm going to bed," grandmamma said. "The girl will be all right, Mattie."

Monica finally drove up hours later and noticed her mother peeking from behind the shade.

"Big Man, I still can't thank you enough. One day we'll sit down and talk about all this. Okay? Right now, I think I need to hurry inside."

As she walked towards the door, she took a deep breath. She didn't want to look as frazzled as she felt inside.

Walking through the door, the flurry of questions began. It made her want to duck for cover.

"Monica Gold. Where have you been girl? Do you know what time it is? The rehab people called and we had to make an excuse for you. Do you want to get your girls back? You must not care. Why didn't you just call and tell us you were going to be late!"

Monica's head throbbed. "Mamma, I know I should've called. One of my friends from the rehab center needed me. Uh… she was having a lot of trouble. I just couldn't leave her like that. I'm sorry. Next time, I promise I'll call." She hated lying.

Mattie fell back in the chair. "I'm glad to see you're helping others but from now on just help yourself. I wish I could make things better for all of us," she said brushing the tears aside.

"Hey… you okay?" Monica asked softly, stroking her mother's hair. Even though she felt she was a real pain, she never wanted to be the reason to make her cry.

"Yeah, I'll be all right," she said sniffing.

Monica leaned over and kissed her on the top of her head. Turning, she walked down the narrow hallway passing the bedroom her mother and grandmother shared.

"Good night, grandmamma." Monica knew she'd heard everything. Grandmamma was always listening.

She headed straight for the place that had become another favorite past time.    It was her sanctuary.  She leaned her head on the back of the tub as the hot water penetrated her tensed muscles.   Slowly relaxing, she thought of Big Man.  What a gentleman.

He'd made it big in the drug world but it didn't seem to change him.   Coming from a very large family, Big Man's mother and her grandmother were close friends. Today, she was thankful.  He'd saved her life.

She could feel her muscles beginning to respond as the steamy water chased away the tiredness.   Then she remembered how much Peaches liked bathing with her sisters.   Out of nowhere, all the guilt and all the pain, found its way into the center of her heart.  The gates of her mind opened wide, allowing the thoughts she'd suppressed for years to come pouring out.    Reality looked her square in the face and wagged its finger.  She had no home to call her own, no job—not even a high school diploma.  If she did get a job, it wouldn't pay enough to take care of five children.  She was virtually penniless and knew she would be considered too much of a risk to ever take care of her girls again.  There's no way out of this, she thought.  She was tired of crying as she licked away the salty tears.

From out of nowhere, the paper thin walls seemed to speak.    Through them she heard her grandmother praying.  *"Father, I stretch my hands to thee, no other help I know......"* Grandmamma always prayed out loud.

Monica thought…that's really where I am right now. Maybe, just maybe, God might help me.  She hadn't prayed in a long time.  She felt too much of a sinner for that.  She ached so inside, she was willing to try anything. So, she started out.  She didn't know what to say at first but then began to talk to God like she would a close friend. When she finished, she had to admit, she felt better.

The next morning, Monica thought of the prayer and the feeling that left her wondering if she should try praying again.

"You're awfully quiet this morning. Anything wrong?" grandmamma asked. She sipped her freshly brewed coffee, its rich aroma filling the air.

"Last night I heard you saying your prayers and I thought I would say one as well. You know what? I think God heard me."

"What makes you think He heard?" she said, blowing into the cup before sipping again.

"I don't know. I just have this feeling that He did."

"That's interesting. The other day I told a few of my prayer partners at church about your situation."

"Grandmaaaamma! That's family business for good-ness sakes."

"No, listen. I had to, baby, so they'd know what to pray for. Sometimes when we pray, we need to be specific about what it is we want God to do. You see, I want God to give you back your babies—every one of them. I want you to be able to care of those girls like I know in your heart you want to. To be the mother He intended for you to be."

"How'd you know grandmamma?" she asked fighting the tears. "That's exactly what I want."

"Grandmamma, will you please keep praying for me? I know I've made some serious mistakes and I'm paying for it now. My reckless behavior is the reason I can't see my girls, and it's killing me. If I don't see them soon, I don't know if I'll be strong enough to hang on." She turned her head and allowed the tears to fall. "All I can tell you is that, this time, things will be different. I'll never leave them again—*never.*"

Grandmamma believed every word her granddaughter said. It was her eyes that told the story this time.

"Why don't you spend the day with me, Monica," she said reaching for her hand. "You need answers and I know where you can find them."

"Let me take a rain check this time. Okay, grandmamma? I don't feel like doing much of anything right now." She wiped her eyes. "Plus, Jay Jay phoned and said he really needed to talk with me. So, I'll probably go and try and find him this afternoon."

"It won't take long. I promise. Come with me," grandmamma coaxed.

Monica hesitated.

She tilted her head and looked into her granddaughter's eyes. "Please."

"Grandm-a-a-a-mmma. You know I can't resist you when you look at me that way. Okay! Let me throw on some jeans."

Grandmamma smiled as she drank the delicious cup of coffee, fixed only the way she could.

After Monica's brief conversation with Jay Jay, they were soon on their way. She wasn't the least bit surprised when her grandmother asked her to drive by the church.

"I had a feeling we were coming here," Monica said. "Tell everybody I said hello and to keep praying for me." She parked the car and adjusted her seat, leaning back for a little more comfort.

"There's more to it than that," grandmamma said slowly getting out. "Come on in. This won't take long at all."

Monica sat on the last pew of the church as grandmamma headed for the altar. She watched as their family matriarch walked the long aisle and slowly knelt, bending her arthritic knee ever so gently. Soon, someone began to pray aloud as the sweet melodic sounds of the organ played along in the background. She recognized her grandmother's familiar and powerful voice as she began to pray. *"God, we thank you for Your faithfulness…even when we find ourselves under the strain of these hard trials, You've been so faithful to us. You've always been there to see us through and for that we are grateful. Thank You Father for keeping every one of your promises… Great, is Your faithfulness…"* She prayed on and on. She kept it personal.

Suddenly, a young lady just two rows ahead rose up, went to the altar and fell on her knees. It was obvious she was overcome with emotion and Monica knew she was praising God from the depths of her soul. It did not deter her grandmamma and her other prayer partners one bit. They kept right on praying.

Monica could tell the electrically charged atmosphere was beginning to have an impact on her. It was obvious others were feeling the same way as shouts and praises rang out. Her heart began to respond as the prayers infiltrated it with hope. At some point, she couldn't remember when, she stood on her feet and headed for the altar—the weight of the world seemingly on her shoulders. She was desperate at that point to shed the burden that had become way too heavy. She knew the altar was the only place for that to happen. Monica fell on her knees and leaned her head into her grandmamma's arms.

"You're in the right place," grandmamma whispered, holding on to her granddaughter.

Monica wept great drops of tears when she asked with all her heart, "*Lord, please help me.*" Immediately, she began thanking God over and over for hearing a prayer from someone like her. A few seconds later... her whole world changed. The load she'd been carrying somehow miraculously lifted. She didn't know how and quite frankly didn't care. She just knew that it did. A new-found freedom exploded inside.

Monica was still in a daze as they drove up in front of their home. Nothing could have prepared her for the miracle that had just taken place. An hour ago, she left the house one way and had come home another. She felt different and this time she knew that she was. Mamma noticed it too as they walked through the door. Tears filled her eyes and yet no one said a word.

Grandmamma slipped her shoes off, sat back in her favorite chair and smiled.

Monica instinctively hugged her mother and blew her grandmother a kiss. She wanted to share everything she'd just experienced with someone and she knew exactly who that someone was. Jay Jay.

"Mamma, may I use your car for a second. I promise I won't be long. I need to help an old friend. It's so strange. I must tell Jay Jay what it's like to be completely free."

"Yes, it's all right this time," mamma said. "I really do understand."

# Chapter 5

## Troubling Times

Joey was cleared of all charges. While he was glad they found nothing during the raid, it infuriated him that they had come to his house in the first place. He hadn't been that angry in a long time, watching them as they went through his personal belongings. There was a snitch close by and he was determined he would find out who it was. The traitor would soon feel his wrath and everybody knew it.

It was going to be very difficult for anybody to trap him, he thought. He was way too smart for that. The car washes, laundries and brand new, high-tech music studio kept his money clean.

"Hey, Joey," Mike said. "One of your boys is holding out on us. He's using more than he's selling and he's always short. We've given him chance after chance and we can't make him shape up."

"Who might that be?" Joey asked, never looking up.

"Jay Jay, man. He's our problem boy."

"Give him another chance."

Everybody knew that's exactly what Joey would say.

Highlighting one of the lines in the document he read, Joey swiveled around in his chair. "Yeah, give him another chance," he repeated. "Just rough him up a little, but nothing too rough."

Mike wasn't going to back off this time. "Another thing," he said. "Word's on the street is that Jay Jay was in on the raid at your house."

Joey sat completely still, allowing the silence to speak for him. Clasping his hands, he rolled his thumbs.

"What are you talking about?" he finally said, breaking the silence. "Jay Jay would never do anything like that. He may pull a number of crazy stunts, but he's loyal...know what I'm saying?"

"We have a reliable source that says he did."

"Who?"

Again, the silence hung around like an uninvited guest. No one wanted to be the bearer of that kind of news.

"Please don't let me have to ask again. Who was it!" Joey yelled.

"Gail, man. Gail said it." It was Mike that finally spoke up.

Joey stood and punched the numbers into his cell. She answered on the first ring.

"All I know is that Jay Jay's desperate right now," Gail said. "He was seen being sweated by a couple of cops and spent a long time talking to 'em."

"That doesn't mean he set *me* up," Joey said.

"No, Joey but word is that he left with this Sergeant Foley. I'm sure you've heard of him."

He pushed disconnect and slowly replayed the words...Joey Phelps, I am Sergeant Foley, and I have a search warrant.

More than anything, he knew there was no compromise for loyalty.

"What do you want us to do?" Mike asked.

He turned as he slowly ascended the stairs. "You know what to do."

~~~

Jay Jay had been hustling, doing anything he could to get the drugs his body desperately craved. He'd lost his job and the little money he had saved was now gone. He spotted Gail as she parked her brand new Malibu.

"Girl, it looks as if you could lend me a few dollars. You're looking good," he said approaching her. "Where'd you get that car from?"

"What do you mean where did I get this car from. I bought it," she said walking away. Stopping, she read a text that had just come through. Texting back, she picked up her pace.

"Come on," he said. "Let me in on the deal. I know you're still unemployed and welfare ain't giving no raises."

Ignoring his comments, she kept walking.

"Seriously, Gail. Can you lend me a few bucks? I'm in a bit of trouble and I need some money real bad," he said, trotting to keep up.

"I don't have any to give you." She turned into the beauty supply store and grabbed a basket.

He lowered his voice. "I helped you whenever you and Monica needed it, didn't I?"

She browsed the aisle. "You call that help?"

"Don't go getting brand new on me 'cause things are looking up for you now. Yeah, I call that help. We have to look after each other and I need you right now. If I don't pay off this debt, man, I know something real bad is going to happen," he whispered.

Gail looked up and down the aisle. "Have you asked Monica for help?"

"What are you talking about? You know Monica is keeping her nose clean."

She faced him and drew closer. "I'll tell you what Jays. Track her down, bring her here and we'll see if we both can't help you."

"She's not going to come to The Hole anymore. Gail, you know that. You heard what happened to her at Joey's."

"I know all about that," she said tersely. "I've been spending a lot of time with Joey lately and he tells me everything. Listen up. Go and find Monica or no deal. I promise, if you bring her here, between the two of us, we will find some way to help you out of your mess. Okay?"

"Here, take this and put some gas in that clunker." She handed him a crisp ten dollar bill. "Now go and get Monica! You know where I'll be." She turned, flipped open the lid to her phone and texted feverishly.

He hesitated at first, but his desperation outweighed the guilt he felt when he called her. Just like a true friend, Monica was already on her way. He understood her reluctancy at first when he'd mentioned The Hole, but she had some good news to share.

Jay Jay smiled as he pumped his gas. When the two of them put their heads together, they could wiggle out of almost anything, he thought. They had always been there for each other and even now, Monica was coming to help him out.

He drove around until he felt she had arrived. He was disappointed when he saw Gail standing alone and obviously upset. Slowly getting out the car, he stepped out to face her wrath.

"Gail, calm down, now. Monica is coming. She promised she would."

"Jay Jay, you're wasting my time, man. Where is she?" Gail paced back and forth.

He frowned, staring at her. What was wrong with Gail? Her behavior was becoming bizarre and no, she had not been there for hours. He did not trust her anymore and when given the chance, he was going to talk to Monica about it.

In fact, he had a lot to discuss with Monica. It was time he found out what it took to clean up his life. Whatever she was doing, he wanted the same for himself. He had even written her a letter about it.

"Jay Jay, you've really disappointed me this time. She's not coming, man."

"Just chill out a sec Gail. I know Monica. She'll be here soon!"

Driving down the street, Monica spotted Jay Jay and Gail standing in the same old place she had spent a great deal of her time in. Unlike before, her business with them was completely different. Slowing the car, she stopped at the red light. She watched from across the street as Gail gestured wildly at Jay Jay.

When she pulled off, suddenly, the all too familiar sound of gun fire rang out. It was an endless barrage of blasts that would have no doubt eliminated whatever was in its way. She ducked behind the steering wheel and gripped it tightly. Peeking over it, she ducked again— only emerging once she was sure the firing had ended. The once crowded street was vacant. A lone blood soaked body lay with its face to the ground.

"Oh, no! Who is that?" The shirt looked familiar.

It was familiar!! It was Jay Jay, his bright red blood now spilling onto the sidewalk. She jerked the car into park and threw the door open wide.

*"Get up, Jay Jay, please get up,"* Monica yelled, running to him.

It seemed she ran in slow motion. Falling to his side, she grabbed his lifeless body and turned it over. *"Somebody help him! Please, somebody help him!"* She screamed.

*"It's going to be okay, I'm here, Jay Jay,"* she said rocking him back and forth, staring into blank eyes.

In an instant, she knew her friend was dead. *"No-o-o, Oh God! No-o-o."* She threw her head back and screamed.

The siren's faint wail could be heard in the distance. She thought about her babies and decided she had to leave her friend. She took one last look not wanting to let his bloody body go. Gently, she laid him on the ground and raced towards the car.

Monica's entire body shook as she drove home. Running up the walk, she used her other hand to steady the shaking one that guided the key into the lock. It wasn't working. She took another deep breath and tried again. When she finally managed to get the door opened, she burst into the bathroom, stripped and stepped under the shower. Thank God mamma was taking a nap and grandmamma was in her room. She stood allowing the blast from the cold water to thoroughly soak her body. She shivered violently, but didn't care. She just wanted the sticky feeling to wash away.

The water finally turned hot as she continued to wash again and again, her hair, face and any part she felt the blood may have dripped its way onto.

Cleaning the bathroom, Monica gathered her bloody clothes and placed them deep inside the trash out back. Finding it difficult to breathe when glimpses of Jay Jay's face surfaced, she stumbled back inside and fell onto the bed. It was the smothering feeling gripping her neck that caused her to gasp for air. She drew in deep breaths, squeezed her eyes closed and prayed for all the haunting images to go away.

She hated Joy was in the room. She needed to be alone.

"What's wrong, Monica? It looks as if you've seen a ghost." Joy said.

"Can you leave me alone for a moment, Joy? I really need some time by myself."

Suddenly, Joy's friend Erica burst in. "Have you heard? Jay Jay's dead," she said gasping for air. "He was just shot at The Hole."

Monica placed her face in her hands and sobbed. Both grandmamma and mamma pushed their way into the tiny room.

"Oh my God!" mamma said.

"How can the best day of my life end up like this?" Monica cried. "My best friend is dead. He was murdered right in front of my eyes."

Mamma looked at grandmamma, and neither said a word.

"Let's give Monica a little time to herself," grand-mamma said. "She's had a really hard day. Come on Mattie, and go with me. Leave the girl alone."

"Mamma, but we need to know why she was at The Hole," she whispered.

"Not right now. Do you honestly think she could be saved in one hour and in the next deal drugs? I don't," grandmamma whispered back.

The doorbell rang.

"I've got it." Joy raced to the door. "Hey, Big Man."

"Good evening, everybody," he said as mamma and grandmamma came into the room to see who it was. "I wanted to know if you heard about Jay Jay."

"We just found out. It's awful. Why don't you go and check on Monica," grandmamma said nodding towards the bedroom. "She's really shaken up."

"Yes, ma'am." Taking a deep breath, he walked down the narrow hallway.

Monica looked up through clouds of tears as Big Man stood in the door. "I saw the whole thing. Why did they kill him like that? Like he didn't mean a thing," she cried.

He gently held her in his large arms.

~ ~ ~

Monica quickly learned to pray. She had to if she wanted to rest at night. It was Jay Jay's eyes that haunted her the most and spilled into her dreams as she slept. She had never seen eyes that oozed blood—ones that had no life—a dying friend. She stayed close to home the entire week.

"Grandmamma, Jay Jay's mother called and asked if I'd say a few words at his funeral," Monica said. "I told her I'd think about it and call her back." Monica curled up in the cushioned chair. "They still don't know why or who shot Jay Jay. The investigators are trying to say it was a drug deal gone bad. I know that's not true. Jay Jay would never have told me to come there if he was going to be involved in anything like that. He knew that would jeopardize me and my girls."

They both sat quietly.

"I don't think I can stand up in front of all those people and talk about Jay Jay," Monica finally admitted. "What do you think?"

Grandmamma knew Monica was still pretty shaken up but had confidence that she could do it. "I believe you can, but why don't you go ahead and ask God about it?"

"That's a good idea," Monica said standing.    Later that evening she called Jay Jay's mother and told her she would say a few words at his funeral services.

Monica was nervous the second she entered the church. There were hundreds of people packed inside. Joey, Gail, and Big Man were all there. There wasn't an empty seat in the very large neighborhood church. She'd forgotten just how popular Jay Jay was. Everybody knew him and he knew everybody. When the family came in, her nervousness escalated. She held on tightly to her grandmamma's hand.

"For we know that if our earthly house of this tabernacle were dissolved, we have a building of God, a house not made with hands, eternal in the heavens," the minister recited.    They followed the funeral program and by the time the woman finished singing, I Won't Complain, sobs could be heard throughout the church. Jay Jay's mother was comforted by his older brothers, as his sisters wept.

Monica made up her mind sitting there that she wouldn't get up and talk. She couldn't do it. As soon as she'd resolved that she wasn't going to speak, she heard the minister say, "We'll now have a few remarks from Ms. Monica Gold."

Grandmamma let her hand go and nudged her elbow. She whispered in her ear and encouraged her on.

Although Monica's mind was telling her she couldn't do it, her heart and feet weren't cooperating. She could feel her entire body tremble as she walked slowly towards the microphone. Thankfully, the minister adjusted it for her and when she looked up, all eyes in the church were on her. She slowly and meticulously unfolded the paper that had the notes she'd written.    She cleared her throat.

*"Good morning to each of you,"* she read. *"I stood to share a few things about my friend Jay Jay. He was one of the few people I could truly trust. I've shared just about all of my secrets with him. He could have gotten me locked up if he ever decided to tell 'em."* The slight laughter from the crowd somehow helped to soothe her out of control nerves. Gazing away from her notes, she looked down at Jay Jay and back at the crowd. She laid the paper aside and spoke from her heart. "Jays had a gigantic smile that matched that gigantic heart of his. He never hurt anyone and would go out of his way to help you. Believe me, I should know. He helped me and my girls out so many times. They just don't come any better than Jay Jay you see. I want everybody to know he really was trying to get his life together. He just needed a little more time and a lot more support from his friends." As Monica came to a close she said, "There was one thing I didn't get to share with my best friend. I didn't get a chance to tell him of the wonderful change in my own life. I wanted Jay Jay to know that I've found something better than whatever we thought we had before." The tears glistened in her eyes as she looked at where he lay. "Jay Jay, I wanted you to know, I've found the Lord and at last, I feel complete. Somehow, though, I think you already know and you're happy for me. I'll miss you Jay's. I will always miss you, my friend."

Jay Jay's mother smiled.

Monica felt so much better once the services were over. It was good seeing and chatting with people in the old neighborhood she hadn't seen in a while. It was an even better feeling knowing they were no longer a part of her world.

Exiting the church, she reached for the door and looked into the face of genuine sunshine. He had to be one of the most handsome men she'd seen in a long time.

"I really enjoyed your remarks, Ms. Gold," he said extending his hand. "Hi, I'm Chris. Jay was a friend of mine. I'm going to miss him very much. In fact, all of his co-workers will."

"So, you worked with Jay Jay?" Monica searched his face to see if she was mistaken. Was he truly *that* fine? She politely shook his hand and gently eased hers out, trying to keep from staring.

"I worked with him for over three years. He really loved his job and did it quite well, I might add. It was somewhat complex, but I tried my best to help him maintain his sobriety. He just made it too difficult for me."

"I do understand." *This man had to have the prettiest smile on the planet*, she thought. As they chatted a while, the crowd thinned.

"What if you and I finish this conversation over a cup of coffee?" he offered.

"We-l-l-l... I guess…"

"It's been a very emotional day. We could use a little breather. Perhaps the Expresso café' just a few blocks over? I promise not to keep you too long."

"Let me tell my family where I'm going," she said.

As they walked to his polished black 720 S Mercedes Benz, she tried hard to conceal her surprise. Ever the gentlemen, he opened her door, as they headed for the quaint café.

She ordered an Expresso as they sat at a corner table. She was pleasantly surprised. He was so easy to talk to. Before long, she was telling him about hers and Jay Jay's past. It eventually led to what happened to her children. Tears and all, she told her story.

"Wow. I must say, your life really has been interesting. Now, can I ask you a question?" he asked. Their eyes met. "What's your plan to get your children back home with you, today?"

A thick blanket seemingly covered her thoughts. The only sensible thing she could think of finally came out. "What do you mean, what's my plan?"

"What are you doing *today* to get your children back?"

She searched again for some kind of answer. She confessed. "Well, I guess I hadn't thought about it that way. I really don't have one."

"If you want your kids back any time soon, you need a plan. Once you devise one, then you need to *work* your plan."

She longed to hear more. "If you were in my shoes, Chris, what would you do?"

"I'd start by asking someone like "*wha*", he said pointing to himself, "if I knew of any kind of employment opportunities. Then I would let that children's welfare agency know right away when I found a job. My next step would be to get my high school diploma. That shouldn't take long. All you need to do is prepare yourself to take and pass the test. Then I would…"

"Okay, okay," Monica said. "I get the picture."

"Chris, were you serious about, me…I mean, asking someone like you about a job?"

"Very. What kind of experience do you have?"

"I'm a great typist. I can do all sorts of clerical work. I'm fairly good with computers, too."

"Good, you're hired!"

Monica muffled her scream.

"Shh-h. They're going to put us out of here," he said, smiling, looking around. "You'll be working for my sister. My dad made her COO of our company and she just happens to be looking for a personal assistant. All you need to do is keep up with her calendar, answer calls, and type a few memos and stuff. I don't know—things assistants do."

She threw her head back and laughed.

"Seriously, she's out of the office on business quite a bit. So the office is fairly quiet. You'll have some real big shoes to fill. Her loyal assistant just retired and she was good."

"Thank you so-o-o, so much, Chris."

He liked watching her smile. It had a way of making the whole room brighter.

"By the way, if your dad made your sister the COO, what did he make you?" Monica asked.

"CEO."

~~~

"Grandmamma...mamma, guess what!" Monica said racing inside. "I have a job! I have a good job!"

"Slow down, you're talking too fast. What's this about a job?" mamma asked.

Inhaling and exhaling deeply, she started over. "I met Jay Jay's ex-boss. We had coffee and I shared my story with him. Next thing I knew, he was offering me a job. Jay Jay was always vague about where he worked," she continued. "That boy could get a job when no one else could. Well, come to find out, he actually worked for this huge manufacturing company. They make boats or ships or something like that. It was his ex boss who just hired me. It's not for minimum wage, either," she said dancing around in a circle. "I'm making a decent salary. More than I've ever made in my life. If I do well, and get my GED, he said I'll get a raise in ninety days."

They all held each other, jumping up and down.

"Wait," Monica said, standing completely still. "I need to call Ms. Dire."

She raced to the phone.

# Chapter 6

## Ms. Dire

"Ms. Dire, may I see you in my office, please?" her supervisor asked. Placing the phone in its cradle, she massaged her temples. She'd been expecting that call. The time had come when she would have to face the music about twin B. A baby had been misplaced in the agency and nobody knew where she was. It was a mess and it was all about to hit the fan. She'd searched everywhere for that baby and had confirmed that the child was definitely missing. Considering herself good—if she couldn't find the baby, then nobody could.

Slowly opening the door, she looked into her supervisor's piercing eyes. He nodded, gesturing for her to sit in the single chair that faced him.

"Ms. Dire, we've been investigating your handling of the Gold case and I must say this is quite disturbing. The report states the mother had twin girls and both were assigned to foster homes. It appears one twin went to the Brown family and the other—well, we don't know where she is." He scratched his head. "Do you have any idea where she might be?"

Before she could answer, he pushed back in his chair. "We've got to find that baby and find her real soon, Ms. Dire. If any of this should leak to the press, things could get pretty ugly for us around here. I would have never believed you would be the one sitting in front of me discussing a missing baby of all things. How could you let that happen?"

Arlene Dire relaxed her shoulders. She chose her words carefully.

"I can assure you, the baby is fine, Mr. Brandon. The paper work has somehow gotten switched around, that's all. I'm going to sort this out real soon. You know my record. I will find that baby and make certain nothing like this ever hits the press."

He leaned back in his chair. "We realize that you've done an outstanding job in the twenty years you've been with the agency. Anyone else misplacing a baby like that would have already been fired. "

Good, she thought. It's working. He's finally calming down. She knew it wouldn't take too much to assure her high strung boss the missing baby situation wasn't as bad as it seemed. She considered herself a master in the art of persuasion and it had gotten her out of much worse situations than this.

When she finally left her supervisor's office, having agreed to let him take her to lunch next week, she thought about how much she really did need to find that baby. It was the rest of her retirement money. In fact, all of Monica's girls were. The moment she laid eyes on them, she knew there was something very special about each one of her daughters. Not only were they absolutely captivating in their childlike innocence, they just seemed to deserve much better lives than that junkie of a mother of theirs was providing for them. So, it had become a simple plan. A master piece of a scheme—one she'd toyed around with for years. She knew if she waited long enough, someday it would all fall in place. Her patience had finally paid off. She was going to make certain each one of Monica's girls were given better living conditions, while at the same time, make a whole lot of money for herself.

Each of Monica's girls would be adopted by families she'd grown close to. All nice. All wealthy. That way they would never have to worry about living with a mamma and grandmamma in cramped-up, little run down houses, she thought.

The agency's policies against what she'd planned were stiff and if discovered, could end her career. That was okay. She knew she was way too good for that to happen.

She reminisced about the day she met Monica. When she saw her mental, physical and living conditions, the plan fell in her lap. All she needed to do initially was to gain Monica's trust and then allow her plan to unfold. Surprisingly, that had been the easiest part.

Things were going smoothly, until Twin B. Where in the world was she? That baby was fast becoming a major kink in such a flawless plan.

Working with Gerald and Charlene with Twin A, who they'd given the odd name Geraldene, had already given her some of the cash she desperately needed. Now, all she had to do was assist the Brown's in the actual adoption and her bank account would soon feel its effect. She had the same plan for Twin B if she could ever find her. Thank God the arrangement she'd made with the Crafts was still on target. Oddly enough, they had never seemed interested in adopting any of the previous foster children she'd introduced them to. Once they met Peaches, they immediately took her up on the offer. The only specific requirement the Crafts had ever requested of her, was to have only one foster child in their home at a time—and they always wanted a girl.

She grabbed her keys and headed straight for the hospital where Twin B was delivered. She was determined to track every inch of the baby's hospital discharge process.

When she arrived, she questioned the nurses, doctors, housekeeper—anybody she thought could give her any information about missing Twin B.

"I'm positive," the nurse said. "Here's the paper work right here. I'm sorry your agency has gotten it all mixed up, but I'm the nurse who discharged her. I specifically remember the case worker saying she was in the area and would go ahead and fill out the correct paper work. She had all the proper credentials. See for yourself."

The nurse described her as having short dark hair, glasses and sort of petite.

"This is who signed off on her paper work, a Ms. Prater."

"I've told you, we don't have a Ms. Prater in our agency!" She didn't mean to yell. Calm down, Ms. Dire thought to herself. Losing her cool now would only complicate matters. It was clear the hospital wasn't at fault. The incompetent caseworker was.

# Chapter 7

## Gail

Gail was glad to get Jay Jay's funeral behind her. She was still having difficulty dealing with the gruesome scene that played out in front of her. She'd been so stressed the day Jay Jay was shot, she'd thrown up no less than three times. She remembered feeling as if she had somehow stepped outside of her body, right into a horror movie's final chase scene.

When they'd asked her to arrange the meeting at The Hole with Jay Jay, she had no idea it involved killing him. After running from the gun fire, she drove straight to Joey's. Was he crazy, getting her involved in a mess like this? Smacking the steering wheel as she drove, she couldn't wait to confront him. She may be a lot of things, but she definitely wasn't a murderer. Her only part in the whole ordeal was to set Monica up, not have Jay Jay killed.

Gail had to admit things were not going as planned. She'd tried trapping Monica twice and each time she'd failed.

Plan-one fell through when she made the phone call to Sergeant Foley. That should have gotten her busted at Joey's, but it hadn't.

Now, plan-two, getting Monica to The Hole with Jay Jay for a fake drug deal. Once the police were tipped off and arrived, she was going to finger Monica as the go to person. She planned on singing like a bird. One dealer ratting on another, Monica would deny it, of course, but they were all well known petty drug dealers. The police would easily take her word. All she needed was to help put an arrest record in Monica's file and that would seal the deal with Ms. Dire. Her take—no less than five thousand dollars, a hook up on a section eight house and foster kids of her own to supplement her income. That was her way out of this hell- hole and she was going to make it happen for herself no matter what.

It was an easy yes when Ms. Dire asked for her help. She hated Monica and for good reason. For years their relationship had slowly deteriorated and was now nonexistent. She had had enough of watching her always being the center of attention and seemingly loving it. The most hurtful part she couldn't ignore was her connection with Joey. She'd confided in Monica about how she would love to get to know him. No sooner had she told her that, Monica started dating him. Monica knew she could have had any man she wanted, why did she have to go and take Joey from her? She was no friend. Everybody was saying that her twins were by Joey, and that was the last straw. She had to get her ex-friend and those kids out of her life once and for all.

Then, there was Jay Jay. He knew better, she thought. He should have been more careful. It was still no way to die and she was going to let Joey know that as soon as she could.

When she burst through the door, she could instantly tell by the look on Joey's face she needed to reconsider her plans. He paid no attention to her abrupt entrance, never even looking up. No matter how much she wanted to, confronting him had to wait.

After Jay Jay's funeral, she'd notice a huge difference in his mood. He was cranky and distant.

Even a few weeks after the funeral, he wasn't getting any better.

"Mike, what's wrong with Joey?" Gail asked pulling him aside.

"Give him a few more days and he'll be all right. He has a lot on his mind."

Joey walked around her and said nothing. When he whispered something to Mike the house emptied, giving them the opportunity to be alone.

"Hey, baby. You okay?" she asked rubbing his neck.

"No," he said, pushing her hands away.

"What can I do for you, Joey?" She tried getting him to look at her.

"Nothing." Joey stared ahead.

"Do you want me to leave?"

"He turned and walked away."

Snatching her jacket and placing one arm in, she yelled, "I'm leaving…I'm outta here. I know that's what you want."

He didn't respond but he didn't have to. She could tell by the look on his face what he wanted. Feelings that had been bottled up far too long sprang up like a geyser. "*You had my best friend killed. How dare you involve me in something like that? If you want Monica over here to comfort you, why don't you just tell me? Maybe the two of you can pray together!*"

"Get out, Gail," he said grabbing her by the arm.

"Stop it Joey, you're hurting me. Let me go," she said jerking her arm away. "I'll leave on my own. You don't have to throw me out."

Clutching her purse, Gail threw open the door and jumped into her car. Tires squealing, she sped out the drive.

"I've had enough." Joey's reactions had Monica written all over them. Gail fumed. It was simple, the plans had to change.

Monica shouldn't be such a problem in my life, she thought. She needs to join Jay Jay.

# Chapter 8

## Ms. Dire's Way

Ms. Dire headed to one of her favorite parts of town. The Craft's estate was absolutely breath-taking and she knew Peaches was a very lucky girl. The teacher had called and asked her to check in on Peaches, something about the child's behavior changing.

As she sat in the massive family area overlooking the pool, she continued her interview. The only thing that seemed a little odd was Mrs. Craft. What a strange woman, she thought. She never said a word, only allowing Mr. Craft to do the talking. Peaches on the other hand looked like all little girls should. She was pretty as ever in her crisp pink blouse, matching brown skirt with threads of pink stitching, and all the complimentary hair bows and girly accessories that went along with her outfit. It was obvious they were taking very good care of her.

The only strange behavior worth noting was every time she asked Peaches a question, she would glance at Mr. Craft before answering. She'd been in the business long enough to know that Mr. Craft was probably a controller. He may have even roughed Mrs. Craft up a few times and simply intimidated Peaches. Well, she'd have to get used to that.

Ms. Dire cut her visit short. Everything was fine at the Craft's. Now, it was time for her dreaded monthly visit to check in on Monica Gold. She drove along thinking how much she thoroughly hated going into that neighborhood. She remembered almost not going to see

Monica the first time she had been assigned to her case. The area was well known for drive-bys and infestation of gangs. She knew women like herself were an open target and didn't belong there. It was obvious she stuck out like a sore thumb whenever she walked among people like that.

Ms. Dire drove up to the tiny white framed house. She had barely knocked when Monica greeted her with a gigantic smile.

"Hi, Ms. Dire, come on in," she said. "It's good to see you again. You remember my mother and grand-mother don't you?"

"Yes, I do."

"Here, have a seat. Can I get you some coffee, water or anything?"

"No, thank you, Monica, I'd prefer to stand. I won't be here that long."

"Well, what good news do you have for me today, Ms. Dire? I know you heard about me getting a job. I…"

"Yes I did," she interrupted. "I must say, that is good news, but there is still only one problem. You haven't started working yet," she said peering over her reading glasses. "Plus, if and when you do begin, you have to prove that you intend to keep that job. The agency has had too many cases where moms find employment, only to discover weeks later they are back on the streets and the kids nowhere to be found. I'm sorry but the promise of a job is not good enough. You would need to be on the job for a decent period of time before I could ever consider asking the courts about you getting your children back. Let's face it. You don't even have a high school diploma.    During these difficult times, people with degrees are having a hard time finding and keeping jobs."

Monica hung her head.  She thought about telling her of her experience at the altar or even pursing her GED, but decided against it.  She felt too much of a failure to share that right then.

"Ms. Dire, is there any way I can just see my girls?  I'll take my mother and grandmother along with me if you're worried about me being alone with them.  Please, Ms. Dire.  I need to see my babies.  Especially, Peaches. *Please*," she said softly.

"I'm sorry, Monica, the agency has its rules.  The decision has been made that it's not in the best interest of the children for you to see them at this time.  Don't worry.  They all are doing fantastic.  They've adjusted to their new homes and are stable for the first time.  You know I handpicked these families—some of the finest.  We wouldn't want to disrupt that, now would we, Ms. Gold?"

"I don't know, Ms. Dire.  I think any kid would want to see their mother," Monica said, not attempting to hide the disappointment in her voice.

"I know that's not a fair question for me to ask you.  That's why, Ms. Gold, we're making the decision for you.  Not at this time.  Remember, I've stuck my neck out for these kids."

Reaching for the door, Ms. Dire turned.  "Good day."  She was glad to get out of there.  It was a disgusting place and she hated the way that grandmother stared at her.  That woman was going to be real trouble.  She could always spot the type.  Monica was easy.  She was trying to pull herself up by the boot-straps.  Unfortunately, she just didn't have any to pull herself up with.

As Ms. Dire drove out of the projects, she contacted the Browns.

"Hello, Gerald, this is Ms. Dire. Good news! The agency is submitting a recommendation to the courts to begin your adopting Geraldene."

"That is good news, Ms. Dire. I know Charlene will be thrilled."

"You give Charlene that bit of news and tell her I'll call back in a couple of weeks. Oh, by the way, our inside source told me Geraldene's mother has been linked to a known drug dealer's murder. That should all but seal the adoption for you. The agency is getting tired of dealing with unfit mothers like that. Geraldene doesn't need to be with anyone that chooses the streets over their own child's wellbeing. I'll call you later."

"Thank you Ms. Dire. What a blessing you've been to us."

Ms. Dire had a few other calls to make. For the first time, she had a lead on Twin B.

~~~

"The woman who signed off on the chart in the missing baby's case was Mrs. Prater. She's a brand new case-worker in our department," the receptionist explained. "She was recently divorced and is now using her maiden name, Gaines. When they kept asking for a Prater, the receptionist only knew her by Gaines and of course told who ever phoned no one worked there by that name. By the way, you may want to talk with Ms. Gains in the morning. She's being transferred to your facility and will be working out of those offices starting tomorrow. I hear the case load over there is tremendous and you sure could use the help."

Oh great, Ms. Dire thought. "I'd still like to leave her a message if you don't mind. This is an emergency."

Now, all she needed was for her to phone.

When at last, the call she had been waiting for came, some of the pressure lifted.

"Hello, Ms. Dire, this is Ms. Gaines."

"I'm glad you called." Wasting no time, she got straight to the point. "I need to speak with you about the Gold twins. You discharged Twin B out of the hospital. Can you tell me with whom?"

"I'm sorry but I'm going to need a little more information. Would you give me a moment? I have to get my notes."

"Yes, Ms. Gaines, go and get your notes." Ms. Dire knew she had to be patient with the young, inexperienced caseworker. She was obviously overwhelmed.

"Now, let me see," she said licking her thumb as she flipped through the pages. "Oh yes, I remember this baby."

"Can you tell me who you discharged her home with?" Ms. Dire asked.

"Yes, it was the baby's aunt, a Mrs. Baldwin. I remember it distinctly now. She was standing there, crying in the nursery as she looked at her niece. It was the first time she'd seen her. When I introduced myself, she wanted me to know that she could easily take care of the baby. I assumed it was Ms Gold's oldest sister. She said she lived alone and had helped the mother with her other children in the past. She showed me the proper ID and even had Ms. Gold's mail with her. She also had a letter for Ms. Gold she'd written asking if she could keep the baby. She said she wasn't that close to her sister anymore, but would be willing to help out with this baby.

We talked for quite a while. I investigated the home thoroughly and the aunt validated everything I'd read about Ms. Gold in her file. She knew all about her and seemed very sincere about taking care of the baby. I made another quick house visit, did the paper work and gave the hospital permission to discharge the baby home with this aunt, temporarily. I sent you the paper work Ms. Dire. Didn't you get it?"

"No, Ms. Gaines, I never received any paper work."

"You mean no one has seen or checked on this twin. Oh my God! What can I do to help?"

"First, you must keep in contact with me and only me, Ms. Gaines. Do you understand?" she said emphatically.

"Yes, ma'am, I do."

"Give me your cell number."

"555-3356."

Ms. Dire grabbed her I Hate Monday's coffee mug and took a big swallow of the black coffee. "Give me the address of this Ms. Baldwin."

She heard the tension in Ms. Gaines' voice. She loved making her squirm.

"72821 North East Madison."

That address sounded familiar, Ms Dire thought. As soon as she hung up, she headed for North East Madison. Wait a minute…that was Monica's building. In fact it was her old apartment. The baby couldn't be there. She swung into the parking lot and headed straight for the manager's office.

"We have a waiting list for these apartments, ma'am. Let me see who's living there now." The thin man thumbed through his rolodex while adjusting his glasses. "It's a, Ms. Gonzales. You might want to check back a little later. Many of our occupants get off from work at four and don't get home until around six. They have to ride the bus, you know."

"Thank you. I'll be back."

At six sharp, she went up to the apartment and knocked. A small Hispanic girl with dark curly hair answered. "Is your mommy home?" Ms. Dire asked.

"*Mamá*," the little girl called. "Alguien está en la puerta."

"Hola. Usted necesita ayuda?"

"Do you speak English...*Ingles*?" Ms. Dire asked.
"Si."

"May I come in?" Ms. Dire motioned with her hands.
"Si, Si"

She counted at least six kids, all crammed in the tiny apartment. "Do you know anything about a baby whose last name is Gold?"

"No. No baby aqui."

"Have you seen a baby..." she rocked her arms back and forth as if cradling one.

*"Don't know... No se,"* Ms Gonzales said with a flurry of Spanish following. She threw her hands in the air and opened the door. *"Done no wrong. Bebé no está aquí."*

"I know, Ms. Gonzales, calm down. I know you haven't done anything wrong."

*"Bebé no... sólo las minas"* she said loudly. *"No trouble."* By now the neighbors were starting to peek out their doors. Someone shouted, *"Cut out the noise and leave her alone!"*

Ms. Dire knew it was time to go.

# Chapter 9

## The Unexpected

Monica rose early the next morning. After she and grandmamma had their morning prayer and coffee, she headed for the testing center.

"Fill this out and you can take the test on any of these dates listed," the clerk said pointing to the information on the brochure. Monica had been an excellent student in high school but during her senior year, got pregnant. She still thought she would graduate but the late night partying affected her grades. It was shortly after that, she dropped out. Gail also dropped out right after she did. Jay Jay and Big Man were the only ones to graduate.

"I would like to sign up for the first date available, please."

He asked Monica a series of questions and placed her paper work in the bin. "There, you're signed up," he said, handing her the study guide.

After Monica left the testing center, out of curiosity she took the bus to the company where she would be working. In just two weeks she'd have a real job. Was she dreaming? The massive buildings spread across miles of well-kept grounds in a heavily guarded gated area. Those entering and exiting were presenting IDs as they approached the gate. Chris hadn't told her about needing an ID to get in, she thought. There was nothing she could do about that now. She would just show up and see what happened. She still wanted to pinch herself. Were things really about to turn around for her?

Several buses later, she was home. The house was quiet. A good time to get some studying in.

She had twenty minutes alone when the door swung open.

"Monica, what ya reading?" Joy asked jumping on the bed curling both feet underneath.

"I'm studying. I'll be taking the test next week to get my GED. I'm really not feeling this stuff. I guess it's been too long and I don't understand what I'm reading."

"Here, let me check it out."

Monica was proud of her baby sister. She was a senior in high school and a straight A student. Even though she had "the curse," it didn't seem to be bothering her too much. She would graduate this spring at the top of her class and was even running for Homecoming Queen—a first for their family.

"Tell me what part of this you don't understand."

When Monica pointed it out, Joy patiently explained it all. Before she knew it, she was getting all the answers right. "Gee, thanks, Joy. That made all the difference in the world."

"If you want me to, I'll be glad to tutor you so you can pass that test with flying colors!"

"I'd like that." They started from the beginning and studied for hours.

"I'm exhausted," Monica said closing the book. "Let's pick up again tomorrow."

"Okay, but as soon as I get home from school, I'm going to quiz you on chapters one through five."

"Oh, no-o-o, what have I gotten myself into!" Monica said, laughing as she fell back onto the bed. "Thanks, kiddo…but please be gentle."

Each day after school they studied together. It wasn't long before Monica had completed the entire study guide.

"Now, we are going to start all over beginning at chapter one," Joy said. "You'll take the test at the end of each chapter. Once you've finished answering the questions, hand me your paper so I can grade it. By the way, did I tell you I would be timing you?"

"No, you did not, Professor Gold."

"Student, are you ready?" Joy asked displaying a serious look—attempting not to unleash the huge smile.

Monica nodded.

"Pencil up—go."

Monica dived in, chapter after chapter until she finished. She was exhausted.

"I'll give you your test scores in the morning. Get some rest."

Monica felt pretty confident she'd done well.

The next morning, Joy had placed her scores on the table.

What! Out of fifteen chapters, she'd only passed seven. She had a lot of work to do and only three days to do it.

~~~

Monica opened the well manuscript letter addressed to her and frowned. *Your caseworker came to your old apartment and caused quite a scene. Please call as soon as you can. It's urgent.* It was signed, *Miss B.* Now what? Monica thought. There was a strong possibility she wouldn't be making *that* call. Miss B was mean and nosey and was known for causing trouble. Plus, she didn't have room for any unnecessary drama in her life. She threw the letter on top of the dresser and buried her head in her books. The test was tomorrow.

"Joy, I'm thinking about not taking the test. I'll sign up for it on a later date, when I feel more prepared."

"I think you're ready Monica. You might be nervous, that's all. You made simple mistakes. All you need to do is take your time. You'll ace it."

Monica rested her head in her hands, still not convinced.

"I know that look," Joy said. "Let's retest you on one of the chapters you struggled with. If you pass, go tomorrow. If you don't, then reschedule it for a later date. Okay?" Joy said.

"All right," she said slowly. She began re-taking the practice exam. When she finished, Joy went into the other room to grade it. Slowly and sadly, she emerged. She looked at Monica with remorse and said, "Psych! Do you want me to drive you to the testing center tomorrow or are you going to drive yourself?"

"I passed? You mean I passed?"

"With flying colors!"

Monica wanted a good night's sleep, so she went to bed fairly early. Just as she was about to doze off she thought about the letter from Miss B. She picked up the phone.

"Miss B., this is Monica. I received your letter. What is this all about?"

"I'm so glad you called. You need to come over here tomorrow so we can talk. I've *got* to tell you what's going on."

"Miss B., I have a lot to do tomorrow and I..."

"Listen to me! You need to talk to me, girl. I have some very important information that I know you'll be interested in. It's up to you though. I'm just trying to help. I'll be here all day, you can stop by if you want to—it's your choice."

After Monica hung up, she still wasn't sure if she would go and hear what Miss B had to say. She generally had nothing nice to say about anybody. Anyway, she was convinced it was Miss B that called Protective Services on her in the first place.

Her plan to get a good night sleep was interrupted by a combination of strange dreams. She'd actually dreamed at one point that she had over slept and the testing center wouldn't allow her in to take the exam. "No you can't take this test," the proctor yelled. When she awakened, she had a difficult time falling back to sleep, for fear she'd really oversleep.

She arrived early at the testing center. When they finally opened the doors, she sat next to another young lady who seemed about as nervous as she was. "Good luck," the lady said.

Monica took a deep breath. "Good luck to you too." She was ready to get this over with.

Leaving the testing center, her head throbbed. She had no idea how well she'd done. At one point she thought she knew all the answers. Then she thought she'd gotten them all wrong.

When Joy picked her up, she suggested they grab a bite to eat before heading home. Satisfying the hunger might make her feel better.

"Joy, do me a favor and swing by the projects," she said leaving the restaurant. "I need to see Miss B,"

"Now, why would you need to be talking to Miss B?" Joy asked raising both eyebrows.

"Don't give me that look. I promise I'm just going to see what she wants." Monica told her all about the letter and how strange it all seemed.

"I don't trust any of this, Monica. Do you think we should even go there?"

"I want to see what she has to say. If it gets too crazy or if you feel uncomfortable, we'll leave, no questions asked."

Joy switched lanes as she drove towards the projects. She parked at the bottom of the hill and as soon as they got out, Monica spotted a number of familiar faces.

"Hey Monica, what you doing hanging out over here?" someone yelled.

She waved, grabbed Joy's hand and headed for the elevators. It was stuck on the 9th floor. "Stupid things never work," she said pushing the Up button. "You ready to climb nine flights of stairs?"

"Not at all… and that must be our clue that we need to get out of here." Joy tried pulling Monica back towards the door.

"What if she has some information about my girls?"

That's all she needed to say. Joy headed for the exit sign that led to the stairwell. Opening the door, they began to climb.

"Whew." Monica leaned on the hand rail as she mounted the final step. She took a moment and looked around the old hallway she'd become so familiar with. Seeing her old apartment triggered unwanted emotions. She quickly reached up and knocked on Miss B's door. Nothing. She pounded harder. This time someone eased the door opened and peeked through the crack with the chains still attached.

"Is that you, Monica?"

"Yes, Miss B, it's me," she said rolling her eyes.

"Come on in. I just wanted to make sure." She took her time releasing the five chains that secured the door. "Who's this with you?"

"This is my little sister, Joy. You may not remember her. I can't recall if you two have ever met."

Monica never did have patience with Miss B and didn't want to spend any more time than she had to with her. "Now, would you please tell me what was so important that I had to come here and see you today?"

"Well, all right. Do you mind if we talk in front of her?" she asked nodding at Joy.

"Whatever you say to me, you can say in front of my sister, Miss B."

She stared at them for a brief moment. Puzzled, Monica and Joy looked at each other, shrugged their shoulders, both realizing they had made a huge mistake. Finally, Miss B said, "Monica, I need to tell you something."

"Duh-h-h… I think I've already figured that out. Maybe this was a bad idea Ms. B," she said heading for the door. Monica stopped briefly looking back at the bedroom. "Is that a baby I hear crying?"

"Wait a minute. Please don't leave," Miss B pleaded.

They watched as she walked into the bedroom and came out cradling an infant.

"Is that one of your grandbabies?" Monica asked. "Oh, I forgot, you don't have children. You mean you are babysitting now? You would never keep mine for me even when we lived right across the hall from you."

"It's no to all your questions, Monica," she said softly. "Take a closer look, dear. This is your baby. It's one of your beautiful twins."

"Miss B, what do you mean this is my baby? Please don't joke with me like that!" She reached for the baby.

"I don't joke and I don't play. I wouldn't bring you all the way up here to tease you about something as serious as this."

Monica sat slowly on the first thing she could find as she cuddled the baby, gently kissing her tiny hands. She squeezed her softly, examining her from head to toe. Suddenly, something inside came alive. "I've missed you so much. Oh God, how I've missed you!" Monica said, tears streaming down her face.

"Here, let me hold her," Joy said between gulps of her own tears. "Monica, she's so beautiful. What are we going to do?" she asked.

"I don't know. I really don't know."

"Well, I know," Miss B said. "You're going to take your baby home with you and then try and do everything in your power to get the other girls back."

"No, we have to call Ms. Dire and let her know the baby is here," Monica said.

"I knew you didn't have an ounce of sense in your head," Miss B blurted out. "Don't you know Ms. Dire is trying to take your babies from you? She means you no good, and she's been hanging out with that Gail."

"Miss B, she's a case-worker!" Monica shouted. "She's supposed to be talking to people like Gail." Then it hit her. "How did you get my baby, anyway?"

"Now, now, let's all calm down. Let me explain." Miss B knew she wasn't getting anywhere with Monica becoming increasingly upset. She needed her undivided attention if she was going to help her at all. She started out slowly. "I went to the hospital to see if I could find you because…well… I was concerned and I wanted to see the babies. I took a chance and thought you'd be there. Your mail wasn't being picked up so I got it to give to you just in case you were visiting. When I arrived, the only way they'd let me up to where the babies were, uh… I told them I was your sister. Lord forgive me. The mail really came in handy. Once they saw it, they believed me. Actually, they were happy that someone had finally come to see the baby. When I saw her, that was it. I mean, just look at her. I knew I couldn't let them get her too. So, that's when I started writing you a letter right then and there to ask if I could take care of her until you got yourself together. After I finished the letter, I was surprised when the baby's caseworker showed up. Not Ms. Dire, but another one, a much younger lady. She was obviously frustrated and seemed rushed. We started talking and well, the rest is history."

"I can't believe any of this," Monica said kissing the baby. "I still don't know what to do."

Miss B's eyes rested on the baby. "I know I wasn't the best neighbor and I didn't help you like I should have, but I never hurt you Monica. Never! When you'd leave those babies alone, I'd give them food and look in on them without anybody knowing about it. I'd always check your door to make sure it was locked at night. Your Peaches is a remarkable little girl. She could take care of those babies better than you and I could put together. I really hated you for leaving your children like that," she said sniffing. "I wanted you to do better, but I never turned you in. Please, Monica, you must believe me."

No one said a word. Joy looked at Monica and shook her head. They both stared at the baby.

Finally, Monica asked, "What do you think I should do, Miss B?"

"I'm glad you asked. Don't let those State people take this baby from you. Wait until dark and get her out of here. Ms. Dire is getting too close. When I saw her across the hall the other day at your old apartment causing such a racket, I knew it was time to act."

"They'll figure all this out real soon, Miss B, and they'll come looking for you" Monica said.

"They will have to find me first. I took my screw driver and switched the apartment numbers on all these doors when Ms. Gaines came to visit. By the time Ms. Dire came, I had put them back. That's how she ended up at the Gonzalez's."

"What name did you use when you signed the paper work at the hospital?" Monica asked.

"I used my real name."

Monica's eyes grew wide.

"Calm down, Monica. You'll have to learn to trust me. Ms. Gaines thinks I have moved and she doesn't know where. My name in the office is under an alias. When I had to move in the projects many years ago, I was too proud to let anyone know that I lived here. So, I made up a name. I've lived in this apartment under that made-up name for years. I just go by Miss B, so I can keep a part of my identity. My real name is Miss Beatrice Baldwin," she said proudly. That made Monica smile. She couldn't image Miss B being embarrassed about anything. She kept her apartment immaculate and she always seemed to have an air of superiority about her. Today, she was beginning to see her in a whole new light.

"By the time they figure all this out, I hope you'll have your babies at home. Let me fix you girls some tea and when it's dark, I'll show you how to get out of here."

Monica and Joy knew they were both thinking the same thing. Mamma.

"No, mamma, I don't want you to worry, but Joy and I will be home a little late. No....Mamma...okay...I can't explain why right now. We'll come home as soon as we can. Love you." She hung up and looked up at Joy.

"I'm toast, huh?"

"Yeah, pretty much."

"Hey, it's all worth it. I haven't been in trouble in a long time."

"That's not funny, Joy. Mamma is upset and I don't want her to do anything foolish."

"Was grandmamma home?"

"I heard her in the background while mamma was ranting."

"She'll keep her calm until we get there."

"I hope so."

Monica didn't know if kissing her baby's soft cheeks switched her emotions into overdrive, but she knew something did. A thrill of joy radiated deep inside when she realized something as precious as what she held belonged to her. Then, suddenly, the grim reality of what she'd done to her girls came racing back. Just as fast, a good feeling washed over her when she understood God was actually giving her a second chance. The mixture of the emotions was overwhelming.

"It doesn't matter if we all have to live with mamma, as long as we are together. That's all I want," Monica said. Realizing she'd voiced her thoughts aloud, she bent over and kissed her daughter.

Joy hugged Monica and smiled. She knew her sister was no longer the person she'd grown up with. The one everybody labeled as irresponsible and completely undependable. She was now a remarkable young woman and Joy was convinced, she would soon be an amazing mother.

"It's dark enough outside and a good time for you to leave," Miss B. said. "You are going to have to take the baby out the front doors. You know they lock the back doors at night. Like always, there's going to be plenty of people standing around. Thugs seem to never go to bed. Joy, come over here and put my jacket on. Good, it's too big for you. Monica, take off your jacket. It'll be a good distraction. You'll keep the attention on you and off Joy. Put your shirt in," she instructed Monica. "That's it. I need all eyes on you. Joy, as soon as that group starts coming towards Monica, you head straight for the car. Have the keys in your hands and don't stop. Just get the baby inside."

"Where's the baby going to be, Miss B?" Joy asked.

"She'll be under your coat. Here, put these books in front like this to cover her."

"Oh God, what if it doesn't work Monica? I'm getting scared," Joy said.

"Don't worry. We have a praying grandmother and she's been praying for this very moment. Miss B., do you believe in prayer?"

"Yes I do. I truly believe in the power of prayer." Sticking out her chest, she pointed. "Right down there at The Greater Ebenezer Missionary Baptist Church is where Miss B learned to pray."

"Well, let's pray before we go down so that we can get there safely," Monica said.

She led them in prayer and after Monica finished, Miss B wiped her eyes. "I think your grandmother's prayers have been answered. Everything's going to work out for you, Monica. Now, get going and take care of that baby." Miss B. hugged them all, kissed the baby— again and again.

They headed for the elevator.

Good. For once, the one elevator was actually working. They stepped on with the baby under Joy's bulky jacket as planned. The elevator stopped on the fourth floor and two men got on, chatting. Monica and Joy glanced at each other and stared up at the numbers. The elevator creaked slowly downward. When they finally got off, they looked into each other's eyes for the '*okay*' and then walked into the crowd.

From out of nowhere, Gail walked up. "Hey, girl, I thought that was you. What are you doing over here?"

"I came to check my mailbox," Monica said. "I've been looking for some important mail and I thought it might have gone to my old address."

"That's your little sister Joy isn't it?"

"You know how it is. They love tagging along." As they talked, two other long time acquaintances walked up. Joy walked around them and headed straight for the car. She walked as fast as she could without it being too noticeable.

Finally, Monica caught up with her. "Quick, give me the keys so we can get out of here!"

Gail was heading their way. "Hey, Monica, wait up," she called out.

Joy looked feverishly for the keys. "Oh, my God, I don't know where they are!"

"Think Joy. When was the last time you had them?"

"I took the keys out when we were talking to Miss B in the living room. We held hands and prayed. No-o-o, I laid them on Miss B's table. Oh, Monica, we can't go back up there! We've really messed up for sure."

With the baby wide awake now and beginning to fuss, Gail was only a few feet away. Monica knew then their idea had failed.

"GAIL!," someone shouted. "Joey is up there looking for you."

In a flash, Gail turned and walked back up the hill. It was Miss B.

"I can't believe she left the keys on the table. What was she thinking!" she said racing up to them. "I haven't been out at this time of night in twenty years. Oh my God, I'm going to have a heart attack! Will you two get out of here!"

Jumping into the car, Monica paused for a moment. "Miss B, come here."

She leaned down into the open window. "Now, what?"

Monica kissed her cheek. "Thank you."

"You're more than welcome. Now, *go!*"

Joy and Monica rehearsed the story they would tell mamma as they drove along. It was a known fact, that by now—she was a total wreck. As usual, when Monica drove up, their mamma was peeking from behind the curtain.

"Let me go in first. You follow up close behind," Monica said.

Joy had never experienced so much excitement in one night in all her life. With the baby covered by her coat, she pressed close to Monica as they slowly opened the door. She immediately maneuvered herself around and headed for the kitchen. Mamma and grandmamma now with their backs to her, focused all their attention on Monica.

Both women stood glaring.

"Wait, mamma, grandmamma," Monica said holding up her hand. "I need to explain. I need to show you something."

"Monica, we've tried to trust you, but you keep violating that trust," mamma said.

"Tell me what you're doing," grandmamma said. "You know you can tell me anything. I'll get you all the help you need Monica," she pleaded.

They spoke at the same time, both close to her face.

"I need to know. Are you still dealing drugs, Monica?" mamma asked.

Monica gasped. She slowly walked over to Joy's chair. They stood silently, suddenly aware of what Joy cradled in her arm.

"Whose baby is that!" mamma shouted.

"This is my niece," Joy said as she kissed her cheeks.

"Wait a minute. What's going on Monica?"

"It's one of my twins, mamma."

"Oh, Jesus!" grandmamma said taking the baby from Joy.

Monica sat down and told them the whole story as they passed the baby from one set of arms to the other.

"What are we going to do?" grandmamma asked. "How can we hide a baby? Someone is going to find out."

"I'm not giving my baby away to anyone."

"Calm down, Monica." This time it was mamma who spoke. "We're not giving our baby away to anybody—

that's true. We just have to figure out how we can do this the *right* way."

Grandmamma didn't comment. She stood, went to the sink and filled the coffee maker with water. Soon the familiar aroma of coffee overpowered the room. She knew this was going to be a long night.

"Joy, go and get ready for bed," mamma said. "It's very late, and you need to get up early for school."

"Aw, mom, com'on, let me stay up."

"Let the girl stay up Mattie," grandmamma said. "She's already played a big role in all of this. Here, take your coffee."

They all talked late into the night as Monica cuddled her baby.

# Chapter 10

## Chris and Brooke

"Chris, how could you hire an assistant for me without my permission? What's gotten into you these days?"

"I'm sorry, Brooke," he said, closing the door behind him. "The girl seemed so nice and really needed a job. Do me this one favor and I promise I'll make it up to you." He gave her his infamous sad, puppy-dog face, poking out his lip.

She threw her hand up at him.

"There's one more thing I need to tell you, but I don't want you getting upset." Jumping behind her desk he adjusted her chair so she could face him.

She turned her head to avoid his eyes. "What now?"

"She used to be into drugs....and..."

"No-o-o," she said spinning free from him. "Forget it Chris, this is not going to happen! Have you gone mad?"

"Listen to the whole story, Brooke. She's trying hard to get her children back?" He told Monica's story, about her grandmother, the church experience and all.

Brooke stared.

"I promise." He held up his right hand. "She wants desperately to get those girls back home. You can see it in her eyes. Tell you what, give her a week. If you are still uncomfortable, then let me know and we'll place her somewhere else in the company. Knowing you like I do big sis, you won't let her go."

"*Chris*...I don't know...," she said softly.

Everybody knew how much she loved her brother and would do just about anything for him. Most of all, he knew he could get anything out of her and sometimes took advantage of that. Here we go again, she thought as she felt herself giving in. "If you see something in this woman then…okay, but one week only. I mean it Chris."

"You're the best." He kissed her on the cheek and headed for the door. "I'll call you later."

She trusted his instincts more than anybody's. He was always at the top of his game and everything he touched turned gold. He inherited that from their father. Their dad had done nothing short of a miracle. He'd started out by building small boats. He took such pride in the one he crafted for himself, so much so that an admirer wanted to buy it. When he wouldn't part with it, he built one just like it for the guy. That's when the miracle began. Before the end of the week, he had more orders than he could possibly fill and each time they wanted them bigger and more extravagant. The business literally grew overnight. Then one day their dad reached a point where he couldn't handle it anymore. As fate would have it, she and Chris were graduating from law and architectural schools. Fast forward to the present and now they were considered the dynamic duo of Wall Street. Their company had turned into a billion dollar boating industry. They manufactured boats, yachts, and played major roles in the design and manufacture of cruise ships.

Despite his tremendous success, as Chris grew older, Brooke noticed a definite change in her brother. He'd established multiple foundations to help the inner city youth and they were all flourishing. He'd also given many fathers who were struggling to take care of their families, good paying jobs. The latest incident with Jay Jay was again evidence of his transformation. Jay Jay should have been fired a long time ago, but because of Chris' determination to help him, he hung on with the company longer than he should have. When he'd stopped showing up for work altogether, they had no other choice but to terminate him. She knew Chris felt he'd failed and wasn't used to that. Since Jay Jay's outcome was obviously not a good one, she knew he was reaching out to help this young lady to compensate for the loss. Maybe he would be successful this time.

~~~

She walked up to the guard booth. "Hi, I'm Monica Gold and I'm supposed to be reporting…"

Before she'd finished, the guard dressed in crisp police attire welcomed her inside. "Good Morning, Ms. Gold. We were told you would be starting today. You're going to need to report to the Towers, Room C. They will show you where to get your ID made. It's nice meeting you." He added a check next to her name.

Monica debated long and hard about what she should wear on her first day to work. She decided on the brown tailored suit with her shoes that matched. She'd washed and styled her hair herself. The long silky curls spilled loosely over her shoulders. Her make-up wasn't too much and her nails were nicely manicured. She was confident about how she looked on the outside. It was the inside that was a total wreck. She hadn't reported to work in years.

"Ms. Gold, you need to take the shuttle to the Towers. It's quite a walk from here," the guard said.

When the shuttle arrived, it dropped her off in front of a beautiful office tower accented with a huge fountain propelling water with bursts of rainbows in the air. She wasn't surprised at all when her nerves came pouring in.

Monica walked up to the receptionist behind the mahogany desk. "Hello. My name is Monica Gold and I'm here to see Ms. Blankenship."

"Hi, I'm Tanya." She stood extending her hand. "We've been expecting you," she said. "You can follow me this way." She led her to a conference room with large comfortable chairs surrounding one of the longest tables Monica had ever seen. As soon as she entered, she noticed a portrait of Chris and his family on the wall. She admired the beautiful porcelain vases, tasteful paintings and plaques that decorated the walls. The sterile environment made her uncomfortable, sending her confidence plummeting. She wasn't so sure she'd be able to make it through the first day.

Monica completed pages of paper work, insurance selection forms, confidentiality and disclosure statements and was eventually taken to get an ID made.

"Ms. Blankenship will be back in her office around nine. By that time, you'll be finished processing all your paperwork, and then you can see your new boss," Tanya said smiling.

It was about five 'til nine when she came back in the room. "Ms. Blankenship isn't quite ready," she said. "She'll buzz us when she is. It'll be all right," Tanya said, noticing as Monica fidgeted with her pen. "Ms. Blankenship is wonderful to work for. She runs a tight ship but I'm sure when she met you, she felt you could handle it."

Monica wouldn't dare tell Tanya she had never even laid eyes on the woman who in about fifteen minutes would be her boss. "You know how first day jitters can be," she said, placing the pen delicately on the table. "How long have you been working here?"

"This will be my third year in the Towers—six altogether with the company. It's everybody's dream to work in the Towers, though," Tanya said.

"I made a few enemies when I was promoted. So many people wanted this position. You can't imagine what it was like when they knew your position was available. You can also imagine the disappointment when they found out it had been filled. Everybody is anxious to see who the special person is that got it."

That bit of news sent rip tides of nerves crashing in. Feeling slightly nauseous, Monica prayed for the initial introductions to be over.

Finally, Tanya walked back in. "Come on. She's ready."

Monica took a deep breath as they walked into an office that looked every bit like the pictures she'd seen in magazines.

"Hi, I'm Monica," she said shaking her hand.

Wow! Brooke Blankenship. What a classy woman, Monica thought. She wore a classic cranberry Saint John knit with matching accessories. Earrings, bracelets, necklace, even the shoes coordinated to perfection. Her hair was swept up in a way that made her keen features ever so striking.

Monica was mesmerized and instantly wanted to walk back out the door. Brooke on the other hand—she'd never seen a woman so poised and one who spoke so eloquently.

"I've heard good things about you. May I call you Monica?"

"Yes, ma'am."

"All right then, Monica, tell me about yourself," she said, twirling around, in the leather studded high-back chair.

Monica knew she bore the look of a child trying to say their first Easter speech.

She swallowed hard and cleared her parched throat. 'I've been trained to utilize the computer and I'm fairly familiar with most of the software programs. I'm a real hard worker and follow directions well. I'll do whatever it takes to make your office function the way you want it to, Mrs. Blankenship."

"Call me Brooke."

"Okay."

While Brooke briefly described some of the duties required around the office, Monica tried applying moisture to her lips. Eventually she quit. Her mouth was completely dry.

"Do you think you can handle that?" Brooke asked.

"Oh, yes ma'am. I'll do everything I can— anything I can to make you happy." Monica made every effort to flash her usual bright smile. It was a miserable attempt.

Brooke didn't respond.

Monica's voice dropped as she shook her head. "The truth is, ma'am, I don't have a choice in the matter. I desperately need this job. It will help me in ways you could never imagine. I will do well here if I'm just given a chance. All I need is a chance."

Brooke smiled. "Let me show you your new office."

Brooke understood instantly what the attraction was from her brother. The girl was lovely. She wondered if her beauty came with brains, though. Time will tell, she thought, as she walked ahead.

By the end of the week, she was hopeful. Monica had a knack for anticipating exactly what she needed. She even noticed how a little bit of encouragement caused a chain reaction of self confidence to emerge. In a couple of weeks she had rearranged her calendar to give her more free time. She'd discovered an error that could have easily caused a major contract to be voided. Her politeness and accommodating attitude made the clients feel at ease. She received glowing compliments from them all. It was hard to believe Monica hadn't graduated from high school, Brooke thought. She was obviously a very bright young lady. She was impressed.

It was still too early to let Chris know that he was probably right...*again*. They often pulled a one-up on each other. She had to admit, this stunt of hiring Monica as her assistant really did catch her off guard.

Tanya invited Monica to the cafeteria and this time Monica accepted. She'd been trying to get her to go to lunch ever since she started working there.

"So, tell me... how did you meet the Blankenship's?" Tanya asked.

"A friend told me that the position was available and I asked for the job."

"Your application must have really stood out, huh," she said.

"I'm thankful about it all."

Tanya talked non-stop while Monica ate and listened. Her mind drifted to the girls as she thought about how they loved playing with each other. She knew they would be mesmerized by their twin sisters. It suddenly occurred to her in the middle of one of Tanya's stories, she wanted to leave on time today. Except for her first day at work, she hadn't gotten off at five since she'd started. The first week, she tried to stay as long as Brooke did, but that proved impossible.

"You okay, Monica?" Tanya asked. "It seems as if your mind is a million miles away."

"I hate to leave you, but I need to get back to the office. I have some paper work to finish."

"We've only been gone twenty minutes—enjoy your lunch, girl. We all get a forty-five minute lunch break."

"I've got to get back sooner, that's all. Enjoy your lunch, I can find my way back."

Monica placed her tray on the conveyor and headed back. The walk was enjoyable and a great way to get her daily exercise in. The sunshine felt soothing as she walked the winding path etched in colorful red and pink geraniums.

"Hello, Monica." The greeting caught her off guard. Startled that someone knew her name, she looked up only to stare into Chris' face.

"Oh, my, I didn't know that was you, Chris."

She wanted desperately to conceal her nervousness. "It's good to see you." She let out what she knew was a real goofy laugh. Camouflaging her jitters was proving difficult.

Amazing, she thought, as the sunlight reflected off his tall frame. She had been right. He was a very handsome man.

"I haven't been in the office in a couple of weeks. I just flew in from London and thought I would grab a bite to eat. I'm starving and its lasagna day," he said kissing the tips of fingers. "Our lasagna is the best kept secret in town. Make sure you try it."

She was taken back at how he acted, nothing like the way she'd imagine CEO's to be. She had already heard how he often ate with the employees and even wandered in at night, just to give them a hand. They chatted a little longer.

"Enjoy your meal. I've got to head back to the office," Monica said. "I hope to see you around. Oh, and Chris, thanks again for helping me to work my plan," she turned, smiling.

Chris was happy to finally run into her. He hadn't been able to keep her off his mind. He would love to take her out. He hadn't been on a real date since he'd decided to break off his engagement, but what would a girl like Monica have in common with him, he thought. He'd just have to find out.

~~~

Grandmamma had been awake since dawn. This was the second dream she had of Countess drowning which kept her tossing and turning most of the night. Her phone call to Jessica had been a high priority for the day.

"Hi, Miss Anna, how are you?" Jessica said.

"I'm doing good, baby, doing good. I wanted to know if you've heard anything about Monica's girls. We're getting a little nervous over here and I was wondering what you knew. Monica has made all of us so proud, and it's past time for her to see her girls." grandmamma said.

"I heard she is doing really well, Miss Anna. I'm happy for her. Anyway, this is the little that I know," Jessica said. "I heard they were close to letting the people that have her twin adopt that baby. It's largely because they've somehow tied Monica to Jay Jay's murder. I also heard that Peaches seems to be doing okay, though I really haven't heard much else about her. Now promise you won't get upset, Ms. Anna?"

"Go ahead, Jessica."

"Well, I heard the lady that's got the other two, broke one of the girl's arms. I'm not sure which one, but they say this woman is a known child abuser."

"Is that it?" Grandmamma didn't really want to hear anymore.

"Yes, ma'am that's about it."

"Any news about the other twin?"

"Okay, here goes." Jessica said. "Nobody seems to know where that baby is. It's the strangest thing and it's turning into a real scandal! I didn't want to tell you about that and get you all concerned. Don't worry Miss Anna, I believe the baby is safe but they are getting frantic about it. I'll just be glad when they find her."

"Thanks Jessica." She hung up the phone as she rocked the baby gently in her arms.

~~~

"What a wonderful day this has been," Monica said coming through the door swinging her jacket.

"I can hardly believe my job."

When Joy walked through the door, she kissed her baby sister and swung her around. "You should see my office. It's gorgeous!" She stood in the middle of the living room floor as she described every inch of it, using her arms for emphasis. "Can you believe I have my own office?"

"Dinner's ready," grandmamma called for them. Throughout the entire meal they listened as Monica talked nonstop about Blankenship Enterprise.

"The company is huge. You have to take a shuttle almost everywhere you go. I'm working in one of the prettiest buildings on campus. Fortunately, it's in walking distance to the cafeteria." She chattered on and on.

Grandmamma looked over and noticed Joy's silence.

"Are you okay? You're awfully quiet," she said lightly tapping her fork on her plate.

"I'm okay."

Monica kept right on talking.

"So what happened at school today, Joy?" grandmamma asked, before Monica could start talking again.

"I think I got another *A* on both my Calculus and English Lit tests."

"That's great!"

"Oh. Yeah. I was also voted Homecoming Queen," Joy said under her breath.

They all stopped eating and stared at her.

"What?" Monica squealed.

"I was voted Homecoming Queen," she said matter-of-factly.

Monica put her fork down and sat straight up. "Just when were you going to tell us, young lady?"

"I was going to tell you. I wanted to hear all about your good news first. I'm so happy for you."

Monica stood and gave her sister a great big hug. "Have I ever told you how proud I am of you? I know what it takes to be voted Homecoming Queen. You have to be smart, talented, and it doesn't hurt if you're gorgeous. So, when is the homecoming game and everything?" she said shaking her hands.

"In four weeks. Can you believe that?"

"Don't worry kiddo. By then I'll have my first paycheck, and we'll buy you the prettiest dress ever!"

Grandmamma looked at her granddaughters. "I'm proud of you girls." She pushed aside the thoughts of what she and Jessica had discussed.

# Chapter 11

## Fight Back

*"Are you sure, Peaches? Tell me exactly what Mr. Craft does."* What she heard left her reeling. It was a fact that she had only been teaching for two years but she had grown to love her students and they loved her. Still, she'd never faced anything as horrific as this.

"Peaches, now you listen to Miss Tate very carefully," she said. "I will help you. Trust me. I'm going to get you out of this."

As soon as she stood, she muffled a light scream. She'd caught a glimpse of his tailored gray suit right before staring into his piercing eyes. Mr. Craft stood in the doorway.

"Mr. Craft." She knew the slight quiver in her voice was noticeable.

"I was just about to bring Peaches down to you." Peaches stood frozen in place.

"You look startled, Miss Tate. I didn't frighten you, did I?"

The rest of her nerves unraveled when she heard his sarcasm.

"I became concerned when Peaches wasn't out front after school." With one hand inside his pocket, he jingled the coins.

"I'm sorry. I needed to talk with Peaches about her grades. They seemed to be slipping, and I...uh...I wanted to... I mean... to know if she needed help or some further instructions."

"Shouldn't you talk to her parents about that first, Miss Tate?"

"Well, yes…but I…" She coughed.

"A girl that young doesn't know what she needs, now does she?" The sarcasm dripped from each menacing word.

"I guess not, Mr. Craft. I'm sorry, I should have…" Finally, she gave up. Any attempt at explaining at this point, was futile.

"Try not to let it happen again. Come, Peaches." He grabbed her by the hand and walked out the door.

"Uggh,"…she said, kicking the air when they left. Sitting on the edge of her desk, the redness in both cheeks glistened.

What was she thinking? If she was ever going to help this little girl, she had to do better than she was.

Sheila knew the only person she could confide in was her best friend Angela. She'd help her make sense of it all. They'd been friends since grade school and shared almost everything with each other.

Angela rushed over. "Are you serious? Don't you think you should go to your principal about this?" she asked.

"I thought about that, but we've had several instances where teachers have reported suspected abuse before. For whatever reason, he doesn't take these situations serious enough for me. He's very strict about presenting solid evidence before reporting alleged abuse. Plus, it draws too much attention to the child. Peaches just doesn't need that right now."

"What are you going to do?"

"Perhaps I need to do a little investigating of my own. Then I'll feel more comfortable reporting it. I may even talk with Peaches' mother just to validate some things. The problem is, I don't know where to find her. I don't even know her name."

"You're going to have to ask the child for it."

"I don't think she knows where her mother is. Peaches said she really had a problem and would leave them home for days. This just doesn't sound good."

Sheila sat, resting her head in both hands.

"Do you really believe all that she's telling you about her foster parents?"

"I believe every word of it. The child is very bright, well mannered and has never given me one ounce of trouble. Why would she want to make up something like that anyway? I had to pull it out of her to make her tell me. That's what's wrong with people today. When these babies try and tell us they're being hurt, adults never want to believe them or they dismiss it. Then they grow up to be men and women with severe emotional problems or better yet...serial killers!"

"Calm down. I get your point. Let's sort this out. Does she have grandparents or aunts or uncles who would know where her mother is?"

"I've heard her speak of a grandmother, but that's about it."

"Is there any way we can get the grandmother's phone number?"

"That might be a start. They keep records with the phone numbers in the computer but you need a code for that. Hey, but they also keep backup records in a file cabinet right by the door inside the secretary's office."

"You'll have to get the number out of that file, Sheila."

"How, for goodness sakes?   The secretary is really stuffy.  If I asked her for the number, she'll want to know why, or go and ask Mr. Jonathan if I can have it.  That's not going to work."

"Does "Miss Stuffy" ever take a lunch break?"

"I've noticed her eating with a couple of the other teachers in the cafeteria.  Why?"

"Where is Mr. Jonathan during that time?" Angela asked.

"He's usually roaming the halls if he's not in his office.  What are you thinking, Angela?"

"Sounds like lunch hour may be a good time to go and see if you can get into the file cabinet."

"Angela, look at my hands, they're shaking just thinking about what you're saying."

"All right, then we can just let good old, Mr. Child Molester have Peaches and stand back and watch," she said.

"I know.  Just give me a minute.  Let me digest all of this."

"You can do this.  We don't want to see this little girl hurt any more than she already has been."

Sheila devised her plan.

At her usual time, she took her classroom to the cafeteria guiding them along in a single line.  This time she sat at the table facing the door while she waited for the secretary to come in.  She took large bites of her sandwich, finishing it quickly.

"You in a hurry, Miss Tate?" one of the male teachers asked.

"Yes.  I need to catch up on my paper work.  I'm thinking of leaving as soon as the kids are dismissed today.  I'll see you guys later," she said, leaving the table.

She kept her eyes on the secretary as she walked in, watching her as sat among friends.

Sheila headed straight for the principal's office. Peeking inside—unbelievable, no one was there. Rubbing the sweat from her hands onto her pants, she looked down the hall one last time. Again, no one was in sight. She walked towards the secretary's office where the files were.

"Mr. Jonathan, are you in?" She knocked and looked inside his empty office. Good. She hurriedly walked back to the files and flipped through them until she found her students.

What was Peaches' last name? Gold! That's it. Sheila was determined to beat the nervousness, so she took a deep breath and at last found the file. The grandmother's information had a line through it and the Craft's names written on top. Scribbling the grandmother's number listed as the emergency contact, she closed the file cabinet.

"Excuse me, Miss Tate, may I help you?"

She grabbed her chest, hoping it would keep her heart from leaping out. "Oh, my, you startled me."

"May I help you with something?" the sixth-grade student asked again.

"No. Thank you. I was trying to see if Mr. Jonathan was in his office. Since no one was in the secretary's office I thought I'd just check to see if he was in."

"I was supposed to be watching the office, but I had to go to the bathroom," the young girl explained.

"That's okay. I'll see him later."

"I'll let Mr. Jonathan know you were looking for him."

"No, no! Don't do that. I thought I saw him walking down the hall towards my classroom. I'll talk to him there. There's no need to tell him I was here."

She hurried down the hall.

~~~

"I knew you could do it!" Angela gave her a high five.

"Now, what am I going to do?"

"You're gonna call her, that's what."

"Okay, and then what? I can't just blurt out, hey, I think your granddaughter's in trouble."

"You're right. Let's see… don't give your name just yet," Angela said. "Say something like, I'm Peaches' teacher and I would like to speak to her mother. If she comes to the phone—great! If she doesn't live there, then ask if you could leave your number and have her contact you."

"Angela, what if she asks why I'm calling?"

"Then you tell them her grades are slipping and you wanted to talk to her mother about it. That's the truth isn't it?"

"Yeah, but…this is crazy! I just don't want to get in trouble and lose my job!"

"I know, but what if Peaches loses her life?"

"Hand me the phone." Sheila took a deep breath and dialed the number. Her heart pumped harder when someone answered.

"Hello? I'm Miss Tate." She put her hand over her mouth. She didn't mean to say her name. "I mean…, I'm Peaches' teacher and I would like to speak to her mother. Is she available?"

"No, her mother is at work, this is her great-grandmother. Is Peaches all right?"

"Yes, she is. I just needed to talk to her mother about her grades and a few other things. May I leave my number with you and have her mother call me when she gets home?"

"Okay, go ahead."

"It's 555-8817 and I'll be home the rest of the evening."

"I'll be sure to give her mother the number," grandmamma said.

"Oh God, Angela, I'm so glad we went over what I should say. I almost blew it."

"You did great. Now let's wait to see if she calls."

Sheila got up and fixed them both a snack. She tried reading and watching the news, but little deflected her attention from the potential phone call.

Thirty minutes later, the phone rang. They both jumped.

"Hello... Hello."

"Oh hi," she said, mouthing to Angela—it's her. "I'm glad you called, Ms. Gold. I'm Peaches' teacher and I wanted to go over her test scores with you. I do this with all my parents. I realize you work, and I would be willing to meet you later at the coffee shop, a couple of blocks from the school if you'd like."

"You're Miss Tate, right?" Monica asked.

"Yes," Sheila said, hesitating.

"Have they told you about the circumstances surrounding my daughter right now?"

Sheila debated whether or not to answer that question. She kept quiet and listened.

"My baby is in a foster home but I'm doing everything in my power to get her back home to me. I would love to know about her test scores, but I think the people that can help her the most are her foster parents. You should give them a call."

Sheila shook her head at Angela—disappointed. "Okay, I'll get with her foster parents, Ms. Gold. I appreciate you calling me back."

"Miss Tate before you hang up, may I ask you a favor?"

"Okay..."

"Would it be out of your way if I met you at the coffee shop anyway? You know, just to see Peaches' test scores. I realize that's a lot to ask, but I really want to know how my child is doing in school. I may not be able to help her right now, but someday, when she comes back home to me, catching up won't be so difficult."

Sheila jumped out of her chair. "You bet I can meet you tomorrow. I'd love to go over Peaches' test scores with you!"

The next afternoon and right on time, Sheila sat in the small booth at the noisy coffee shop, sipping on a diet soda. She tapped her foot, looking up at the clock again. Only one minute had passed. She and Angela had discussed again and again what they thought the best approach should be. It had to be one of the craziest things she had ever done in her life, she thought.

Sheila looked up as a very beautiful young lady walked in. Dodging a busy waitress, she noticed her looking from booth to booth, trying to figure out where she was.

She motioned when Monica looked her way.

"Ms. Gold?" she asked.

"You must be Miss Tate. It certainly is nice meeting you." Monica said as she slid into the booth.

"It's pretty easy to see who Peaches looks like," Sheila said smiling. "You have an extremely bright and polite daughter. You should be very proud." Sheila shot into action. "Here, let me show you some of her work." She spread several of Peaches' projects and her latest tests on the table. They went over each assignment in detail.

Monica stacked Peaches work and held the papers close. She pressed them against her tightly as she thought of her daughter. "Miss Tate, I need to ask you an important question. Does Peaches seem to be doing okay? I mean, does she seem happy? I noticed her grades are falling, and I was just wondering if you've noticed anything different about her."

Sheila remembered agreeing with Angela not to get into the conversation of Peaches' troubles too soon.

"Make her talk to you Sheila," Angela kept reminding her. "Don't give out any information until she's told you enough to make you feel comfortable. If you never get that feeling, don't reveal a thing. Remember, you came there just to share Peaches' progress in school. If she doesn't seem as if you can trust her, get out of there as soon as you can."

"What do you mean is she happy?" Sheila finally asked.

Monica sipped some of the water the waitress brought earlier. She swallowed hard and fought back the tears. "Peaches has never made anything but A's, so I was wondering if she seemed… You know what Miss Tate? That may not be such a fair question to ask you. Let me apologize. I probably need to let you know what's really going on with my daughter."

While Monica told her how Peaches ended up with the Crafts, Sheila listened intently. "I'm doing everything in my power to get my child back. I just don't know how to speed that process up. In the meantime I want to make sure she's all right."

Sheila nodded.

"Do you have kids, Miss Tate?"

"No, unfortunately I don't."

"Then I guess you can't understand how it feels to want to hold your baby and look into her eyes and tell her how much you love her, but can't. You may not know what that feels like, but I can tell you this, you never…never… want to experience it." She took a deep breath and extended her hand once again. "Well, thank you for allowing me the opportunity to get all this important information about Peaches. I know you really didn't have to do that, and I'm grateful."

As Monica moved to stand, Sheila reached for her arm. "Wait, Ms Gold. I need to talk to you about something—and please call me Sheila. Will you tell me exactly what you have done to try and get Peaches back home?"

This time Monica started with her experience in rehab and what a wonderful job they'd done for her there. She talked about her new job, awaiting her GED results and adding her plans to attend college. "I've kept my nose as clean as I know how, Sheila. I don't know what else to do. I don't associate with any of the people I used to. I can't understand why Ms. Dire won't let me see my babies. It doesn't make sense, but I've been trying to be patient."

"When was the last time you asked Ms Dire to let you visit Peaches, Monica?"

"It's been about three weeks now. I understood at first why she wouldn't let me see her, but now, there's simply no reason to keep her away. I asked if I could even see her supervised. Just let me see my child."

"She hasn't given you any indication that's about to happen?" Sheila asked.

"No, and it's getting very frustrating." The tears finally inched their way onto her cheeks. "I can't afford an attorney to help me and I don't know if I could find one that would be willing to take my case. Look, I know I haven't been the best mother in the past, but...I need another chance," she sobbed. "I know I can take care of my girls this time, I just know it!"

Sheila gathered Monica's hands into her own. "Listen to me very carefully. What I'm about to say could get me in a whole lot of trouble. I could even lose my job. Do you understand?"

Monica nodded.

"I need to know, if you want my help."

Monica nodded again, placing the napkin to her eyes.

"Quit crying and talk to me," Sheila said.

"I will do exactly as you say if you can help me. Please. Help me see my child," she whispered.

She didn't have a clue how she could help a mother and daughter get back together again under these conditions. It was way too risky and if caught she could seriously jeopardize her career. Realizing all of that, she spoke with confidence. "I promise I will help you see Peaches again."

~ ~ ~

Joy paced the floor as grandmamma held up the white envelop that held the GED results. "She's going to die, grandmamma, if she doesn't pass. I just know she will."

"You were helping her Joy. How do you think she did?"

"I don't know. She did all right when she took her time, but she did poorly sometimes when she was timed. Even when I gave her extra time, she didn't do so well."

"She's getting home late again," grandmamma said looking up at the clock. "That new job makes her work some pretty late hours. I hate she has to ride the bus sometimes and get home after dark. This neighborhood is awful and it's no place for a woman to be walking alone."

When Monica finally came through the door, Joy took one look at her and could instantly tell she had been crying. "Hi sis. How was work?"

"It was a good day. Busy though. I need a real hot bath to relax," Monica said reaching for her baby and heading down the hall.

"Are you hungry, Monica? I'll fix you something to eat," grandmamma said.

"No thanks."

Joy looked at Grandmamma as she eased the white envelop in her apron pocket.

"Joy!" Monica called out. "Keep an eye on your niece for me, please."

"No problem."

Monica settled in the hot water as thoughts of her conversation with Sheila clouded her mind. Peaches grades were slipping and she knew in her heart something was wrong. It was a relief that she had finally found someone who was willing to help her, though. As she laid her head back and enjoyed the sensation of the soothing waters, she replaced all her anxious thoughts with a prayer.

Much later, Monica stretched out on the bed. "You know, someone should bottle a hot bath and a prayer.

That combination could make you a billionaire! Nothing can beat it," she said, slowly closing her eyes.

Grandmamma walked into their room. "Monica, I have something for you." She handed her the white envelop.

Monica looked at it knowing full well what was inside. "You open it, Grandmamma, please."

"No, baby, you open it."

She took a deep breath and tore into the envelope. Reading the first line, she set it down and placed her face in her hands and sobbed. Joy and Grandmamma stood there in silence.

"Monica, I'm so sorry. I'll help you until you know that material backwards and forwards the next time. Please, just don't give up!" Joy picked up the letter to see how badly she'd failed her sister.

"Monica, you passed," she shouted.

"What's all this noise about?" mamma asked coming in the room.

"Monica passed her GED!" Joy said.

"Is that why she's crying?"

Grandmamma looked at Monica. "I really don't know why she's crying. What's wrong? You should be happy."

Finally, Monica looked up. "I can't be happy about anything until I know Peaches is okay."

"What's wrong with Peaches?" they all said in unison.

Monica told them about her meeting with Peaches' teacher after work.

"What are you going to do?" grandmamma asked.

Monica sat up in her bed and looked at each of them. "You know what…it's time Ms. Dire listens to what I have to say. I'm going to demand supervised visitation and if she doesn't let me see my daughter, I'll go over her head. When I get up in the morning, the first person I plan to speak to is Ms. Dire and "no" is not an option."

They all stared. None of them were used to that much aggression coming from Monica.

Grandmamma liked it.

# Chapter 12

## Meeting Number One

Ms. Dire sat stunned. How dare that drug addict call and demand anything of her. Not only was she demanding to see her children, she wanted to see them no later than Wednesday of this week. She'd tried intimidating her by flatly refusing. This time it didn't work. She'd actually threatened to talk to her supervisor—*of all things*. If she hadn't told her she would be able to see Julia and Countess, Monica Gold would have gone straight to her boss. This definitely wasn't the time for that to happen. Her supervisor was asking every other day about the second twin and she still had no leads, except that she needed to talk to a Ms. Baldwin. Things were not going well. Holes were threatening to penetrate her watertight plan.

Who did Monica Gold think she was? She had to stall her until they called her in about Jay Jay's murder. Unfortunately, Gail had led her to believe it would have been much sooner. Calm down, she thought to herself. Things are going to work out. She had sufficiently proven to her supervisor that Monica was an unfit mother and an accomplice to a murder. Just being questioned by the police about a murder and drug deal when she was supposed to be clean, was enough for the agency. In the mean time, she'd play along with Monica and her request to see at least two of her girls.

Ms. Dire picked up the phone. "Ann, I need you to get the two Gold children ready on Wednesday at eleven for me to pick up. They are going to see their mother."

"Is there any way you can arrange it next week?" Ann asked.

"No, it has to be Wednesday. Just have them ready."

"Well, the older child had an accident last week. She fell outside and bruised her eye."

"She fell and only bruised her eye? Is that what you're telling me, Ann?"

"That's right, Dire, and it's the truth!"

"Okay. Just make certain they don't get any more bruises this week. Am I understood?"

"Understood."

Ann shook her head. Somehow she hoped the bruise and swelling would disappear in two days.

"Close that door," Ann shouted. "Come here Clara and help me put these groceries away."

"May I have a cookie mom?" Clara asked skipping inside with the two girls.

"Yeah, but you can only have one. I hate shopping like this and you kids eat up everything in just one day."

Julia looked up and then turned away.

"Don't you even think about asking for a cookie, nor your sister. In fact, get in the bed, both of you."

Clara grabbed Julia and Countess by the hand and led them into the single bed. It was only six p.m. and she knew they could hear the other children playing outside. It wasn't fair, these two were never allowed to have fun. The little ones went to bed way too early and when they did, they would get up just as early. They were forbidden however, to get out of bed before ten. It was becoming increasingly difficult for her to keep Countess in bed and quiet no matter how hard she tried. She did everything she could to keep them safe from her mom, but the girls were hungry and as a result cried. Clara knew most of their meals were a bowl of cereal in the morning and a bowl of macaroni and cheese for dinner. If her mother was in a good mood, she would on occasion give them a hot dog to go along with the macaroni.

One time, the little one must have gotten up without her knowing it, long before the sun rose. She figured her mother was probably going to the bathroom when she spotted her.

"Come here you," she heard her yell. "Didn't I tell you not to get out of that bed? The screams as a result of her beating were so shrill, they woke everyone up in the house. When Julia realized it was her baby sister at the brunt of Ann's rampage, she screamed as well.

"I 'no want my sister to die," she yelled. "Help her, somebody, help her."

~~~

Mrs. Blankenship's office was unusually busy. How was she going to get away to see her babies? Monica thought.

She put the fourth person on hold and pressed the intercom. "Yes, Mrs. Blankenship, I'm on my way."

"Will you be able to stay a little late tonight?" Brooke asked.

"Of course."

"Thanks, we'll need copies made, conference calls connected and business letters delivered by overnight mail. It's going to be a real busy night."

"I'll be here until you think its okay for me to leave," Monica said, stacking the papers in neat piles.

"I'll need to leave a little early for lunch though, if that's okay."

"That'll be fine.  We probably won't get busy again until around three—enjoy."

Monica said a quiet hallelujah.  She knew that was Brooke's way of telling her to take her time.

When she finally got the office under control, she rushed to the car.  She drove to the agency as fast as she could.

"Have a seat," the receptionist said.  "I'll let Ms. Dire know you're here."

Ms. Dire approached her never making eye contact. "Are you ready to see your girls?" she asked, turning towards the family area.

"Yes, I am!"  Please don't cry Monica kept telling herself.

"It will only be for an hour," Ms. Dire said walking ahead of her.  "Right this way."  She swung open the double doors and there they were.  Monica took several deep breaths and fanned away her tears.  Julia and Countess looked up when they noticed her standing in the door.  Monica inched her way to them.

"Hi, my babies… it's mommy," she said softly.  She fell on her knees in between the two tiny chairs and kissed them both over and over again.  When she looked into Countess' eyes it was obvious she barely recognized her but she tried not to let that upset her.  Smoothing her girl's hair with her hands, she pushed back hard on the flood gates that were determined to allow the tears to flow freely.  Getting off her knees, she guided them to the couch and sat them both on her lap hugging them tightly.  She lightly laid her head on their tiny heads and fought hard against the tears. When she looked into their eyes, she forced a smile.

"My girls are so-o-o pretty. Here, turn around and let me look at you. Mommy loves you so much…I miss you…oh-h-h boy, you can't imagine how much I miss you."

Julia stared back at her and then slowly laid her head on her mother's shoulder. "Can we go home?" she asked in her very tiny voice.

This time the emotions won. She hugged them tightly, trying to keep the stream of tears from being seen. She knew they could feel her shake as she cried. Wiping her face on her sleeve, she looked at Julia. "Not today, sweetheart. Mommy's trying to come and take you home real soon. Can you remember that?" She looked deep into her eyes and said, "Mommy is coming to get you, okay?"

"Okay," she said taking her tiny hand and wiping Monica's tears. Countess sat on her lap, sucking her thumb.

"Baby what happened to your eye?" Monica asked Julia.

"I fell down," she said.

"O-o-o-oh. Let mommy kiss it and make it all better. Now, be careful, okay. I love you so much." She read them a story and sang their favorite songs. Monica knew the songs jarred their memories as huge smiles finally lit up their faces. Countess reached up and put her arms around her neck. She could see life slowly easing its way back into her girls.

"Time's up. Come, girls," Ms. Dire said, standing in the door propping it open with her hand.

It couldn't be possible. "May I have ten more minutes with them? Please?"

Ms. Dire looked around the room. "Make it five and wrap it up," she said letting the door swing close.

"Listen, Julia, please take care of Countess for mommy, okay?"

"Okay, mommy," she said laying her head on her chest.

"I want you to be careful and not fall and hurt your eye again," she said kissing the swollen eye.

"I will mommy. I'll tell Ann not to hit it anymore."

Monica sat completely still. "I love you girls so much," she said, turning her head.

Exactly five minutes later, Ms. Dire came in and gathered the girls. They didn't cry, but quietly left with her. Monica hung her head and wept. Even though she felt completely drained inside, she knew she had to fight.

By the time Ms. Dire returned, she'd gained her composure somewhat. "Ms. Dire, what happened to Julia's eye?"

"She fell, Ms. Gold."

"Is that what her foster mother told you?"

"Yes, that's right."

"Well, that's not what Julia said. What about the bruises on Countess? I don't know what's going on with these people who have my children, but I think we need to discuss what it's going to take for me to get them back."

"*Now* is not the time, Ms. Gold."

"Well, when is the time!" Monica shouted.

"Don't you ever speak to me in that tone of voice, young lady. I will not tolerate any more of your disrespect!"

"I'm sorry, Ms. Dire for my outburst but we must talk about me getting my children back. I want them home with me."

"I do understand, but uncontrolled anger is not the way to make that happen."

"I apologize, but can you tell me when I can see Peaches?"

"That's not going to happen any time soon, Ms. Gold."

Monica could feel herself about to explode again. Silently, she asked the Lord for help. A voice even she wasn't familiar with, spoke. "Ms. Dire," she said. "I am no longer asking you to see to my children, I'm demanding it. I have rights and I will utilize them. If I have to get an attorney pro bono, I will."

"Ms. Gold—"

"No! Let me finish. I will fight you and the whole state of Illinois to get my children back. I'm doing what it takes to prove I can take care of them. I've cleaned up my life and I will keep it that way. Now, my kids *are* my life and nothing...nothing will keep them away from me. Do you believe in God, Ms. Dire?"

Stunned, she mumbled, "Yes."

"Well, you're not fighting me, you're fighting Him."

Ms. Dire gasped.

Monica gathered her belongings. "Please call me tomorrow with the time and place where I will be seeing Peaches. Thank you for letting me visit with my girls and I'll be waiting for your call." She turned and walked out, the heels of her shoes banging hard against the concrete floor. Once she was outside, she had a light moment with herself. Pro bono.....where'd she get that word? Working with the Blankenship's was paying off, along with prayer.   She could feel the assertiveness running through her veins.

Monica didn't know what to expect next in life, and really wasn't concerned about that.  It was as if she had no control over anything—such a liberating experience.

She knew God did.

# Chapter 13

## Taking Inventory

Joey realized something wasn't exactly right and had never felt so vulnerable. He'd had one of his best friends taken down and now was having trouble with another. For years, he and Big Man had always had a distant yet respectful relationship. They never crossed each other's boundaries and he couldn't understand what was happening now. They were beginning to feud over the Klondike district. Words had been exchanged and a line drawn in the sand. This was not like Big Man at all. They could usually work things out.

"Mike," Joey whispered. "Go set up a meeting with Big Man to see if we can work this craziness out. We can't let him have that spot. It would take too much out of my pocket and the Vegas connection is getting pretty messed up about it. I can't take that chance."

Mike dropped a bombshell. "Joey, I think you need to talk to Big Man's partner," he said. "They haven't seen Big Man in months. Word is he's just walked away from it all."

"Are you serious?" Joey said.

"He didn't take any money, drugs or nothing, just left empty-handed. Some people want to talk with him though, but he's like Casper. Vanished, man. We're going to have to start dealing with his number two man. A guy named Shine," Mike said. "He wants to talk to you and only you. He asked if you could meet him tomorrow.

Might not be such a bad idea, Joey.   We need to settle this once and for all."

"Tell him I'll meet him all right.  At The Arrow—tell this Shine guy I'll be there."

Joey thought about Big Man.  What in the world was he doing?  It could very well be a set up.  He didn't trust anybody these days.  He'd just have to go and meet this Shine dude and see what the deal was.  He'd go prepared.

His house was soon empty.  The crew was preparing for the meeting on tomorrow.  Joey leaned back, and took in a deep breath.  He realized how tired he was but still wanted some company.  He thought about how angry Gail had been when he all but threw her out.   Unlike Monica who flatly refused to talk to him anymore, she tried everything in her power to please him and he liked that.  Joey knew he could call any girl he wanted and they would come running.  He picked up the phone and dialed.

She hadn't quite made it to the projects when she answered.  Gail swung the car around and headed back to his house.

The next day's meeting was scheduled at five.  He didn't like meeting with these clowns, Joey thought, but knew he had no other choice.  Boy, Big Man had really left him in a squeeze.

When they drove up, they followed the long drive to a secluded building in the back of a large restaurant.  As soon as they stepped out, their cars were searched.

Joey scanned the area.  His eyes focused on the man with dark shades that stared their way.  His arms were wider than the trunk of a tree.  He noticed several other men, one in particular standing against a door with his massive arms folded.

"Mike, you ready?" Joey whispered in his ear.

"Born that way. Let's move."

Joey nodded and his entourage strategically took their positions.

They followed the huge men through several doors eventually to where Shine sat. It was soon very obvious why they called him Shine. He wore all the jewelry one man could possibly own around his neck and on his hands.

"You gentlemen have a seat," he said, his platinum teeth shining.

Joey sat, but Mike continued to stand.

"Gentlemen, we have a situation between us that I'm sure we can work out," Shine began.

Joey listened as he stated the problem that brought them face to face. He'd gotten the problem exactly right. It was the solution that he took issue with.

When Shine finished, Joey leaned back and responded with his trademark cool voice. "Listen, Shine, our territories have been clearly marked for years. When Big Man was here—"

"You ain't dealing with no Big Man. You dealing 'wit me," Shine snapped, sitting up.

Joey had intentionally brought Big Man's name up to see what kind of reaction he'd get. The tension was palpable. He allowed it to settle down a little before he spoke again.

"As I said, we've had our territories marked for years. I didn't move in, *you* did." Joey never blinked. "Now, Shine it seems we do have a problem, as you've so eloquently stated. You also have thrown a solution on the table for us to consider. Now, I'm going to give you mine. No part of my territory will be shared or taken.

We can agree that your boys will be allowed to continue to work Flynn Street, but that's it."

Shine stared hard at Joey. Slowly, a glistening smile crept onto his face, followed by a full outburst of laughter. Placing the tooth pick in the corner of his mouth, he leaned over the desk, instantly cutting off his laughter. "You know that ain't gonna work man. You're cutting me out a whole lot'a cash and I think you need to reconsider the proposal that's already on the table."

"Shine, Shine, Shine. What you're proposing is out of the question," Joey said shifting. "Like I said, we've never had any problems in the past, but I understand what happens when new leadership takes over. Things change, but they just don't change on my territory. So, if you can't agree to what I've offered you, I don't know what else to say. I didn't come with any other solutions. We'll see ourselves to the door."

Mike moved slowly. When Joey stepped, he stepped. Mike was an expert at what he did and was well known on the streets for it. He'd spent a lot of time perfecting his martial arts skills and could take down just about anything that challenged him. He was an expert marksman as well. By the time they turned to leave, two other men had joined the giant of a man that faced them at the door. That was okay, Mike had prepared his boys for that.

They were glad when Joey and his men finally drove away. No one was killed and they all knew that was a miracle.

Joey hadn't realized how early the repercussions would begin after his meeting with Shine. Some of his runners had defected and gone to the other side. There had been several shootings and one of his top dealers was killed. Shine was proving to be more of a challenge than he had imagined.

He was in a lousy mood and didn't want to go to the black tie event he'd been invited to.

"Hurry up, Gail! Let's go," Joey yelled.

"I'm coming, baby!"

Gail trotted downstairs with the worst combinations of colors on he'd ever seen. He never should have invited her to go with him in the first place. She was hanging around more than he liked but even stranger, he couldn't understand why he let her. Her never wanting to leave was beginning to annoy him.

"How do I look?" she said admiring herself.

"Come on, let's get going. The driver has been waiting for over an hour."

As soon as she stepped out, she noticed a dark green Impala driving slowly up the street with the lights out. She grabbed Joey's arm to warn him but he pulled it away never noticing the dark green car. The car screeched towards them. Shots rang out. How many she couldn't tell, but they must have emptied all of their clips. The rubber on the burning tire, smoked and the stench of it filled the air as the car sped away. Instantly, Gail felt a fire burning in her arm and side. She touched the area where it stung the most and pulled back a hand full of blood. *Oh no... Joey, I'm shot. Joey, where are you?* He'd fallen to the ground. "*Oh-h-h...,*" he moaned.

Somehow, Gail managed to crawl inside and dial 911, right before she collapsed.

~~~

Mike looked down at Joey in his ICU bed. The tube connected to the respirator rested gently in the corner of his mouth. "Everything's gonna be fine, man," Mike whispered. "Don't worry, Joey, I've got your back."

Joey eyes met Mike's and he blinked weakly his acknowledgement.

"Get your rest," he said, squeezing his hand. Then he set out to visit Gail. She had been moved out of the ICU earlier that day, and was now in the step-down unit. She was slowly improving following surgery.

"Hi babe, how 'ya doing?" Mike asked walking over to her bed.

"I'm pretty sore," she said as they softly embraced. "Do you know who it was that shot us?"

"Yeah, I have a pretty good idea who did it."

"Good. I've got something real special for them when I get out of here. How's Joey doing?"

"He got hit really badly, Gail." Mike looked down, then back up again. "I have some rotten news I need to tell you."

He held her hand. "I think he's going to be paralyzed from the neck down."

Gail slumped over. Looking up she said, "You mean to tell me he's paralyzed?"

"I'm afraid so."

"Is he going to die?"

"I don't know, Gail. It's looking pretty bad."

She turned over and faced the wall. "I'm sorry, Mike. I just need some time alone."

Now, what was she going to do? She had planned for Joey to be her ticket out of the projects and was going to tell Ms. Dire to take her five thousand dollars and shove it! She had to get in touch with Ms. Dire again and go back to her original plan. Monica had to go down and go down fast.

# Chapter 14

## Personal Assessment

Ms. Dire had been summoned to her supervisor's office once again. Now what, she thought, as she walked down the hall. She knew it was time for her to retire. This was her third boss in the past five years and they were all getting younger and younger. These young brats didn't understand the system like she did. They had once asked her to be a supervisor, but she'd declined. She never wanted to be a part of an egotistical-bureaucratic system that consistently ruined the lives of hard working people like herself.

That's why she needed to speed the adoption process up as much as possible. It was her only way of escape. Frowning, she had to admit, Monica was becoming more of a pest than she'd imagined. It was the phone-call she made to Sergeant Foley that had finally made her smile. Slowing her pace, she recalled their conversation. *"Sergeant Foley, I'm calling from Protective Services. I need to talk to you about some information we've received regarding one of our clients, a Ms Monica Gold. I'm making an assessment on whether or not this mother will be able to care for her children who are presently in foster homes. The agency has some serious concerns about Ms. Gold. We would like to know if she has been arrested or even questioned in relation to a murder that happened during a drug deal."* She held her breath hoping he would respond.

"Well, ma'am, it's not customary that we give that kind of information over the phone." His caller ID showed she was calling from the child agency. That made him feel a little more comfortable about what he would say next. "Since you say kids are involved—you know I have three of my own—I can tell you that she will be questioned about matters of that nature."

"That's all we need to know, Sergeant Foley."

"Ma'am... ma'am, there's something else I think you should know..." she heard him saying as she hung up the phone. He had already given her the only words she needed. She carefully documented them in Monica's file. *The client will be questioned about a murder and drug deal during her probationary rehab period.* She also documented Monica's outburst of anger when she was with her two girls. *Being in their presence caused her undue stress and was exhibited through bouts of anger,* she continued to write. *It is my impression that she is not rehabilitating well and still remains a definite threat to her children.* She sent a copy of her lengthy documentation to Juvenile Court and the agency's attorneys.

She was in a better mood by the time she reached her supervisor's office.

"Did you want to see me, sir?"

"Yes, Ms. Dire," he said motioning for her to come in. "I wanted to let you know we had to get the agency's investigative team involved to help us find the missing twin. I know you've tried hard to locate the baby and I commend you for your efforts. However, it's just taking too long to find her. I've recommended that you continue to be the contact person for the team. They've already asked that I send you to question a Ms. Baldwin. It's only a small lead, but it's something."

"I'll follow up on that right away," Ms Dire said. "I'm glad you called me in here today. I needed to talk to you as well about the twin's mother. Ms. Gold it appears has been in violation of her probationary rehab period. She was also involved in a murder and drug deal during that time. The information I'm getting from the rehab center is that she never asks about her children. When they try to question her about her plans for them, she brushes them off. I have validated this information with the proper authorities' sir. I'm thoroughly convinced she doesn't want to be a mother any more. The good news is that the foster parents who have her girls are extremely interested in adopting them. I've assessed their home environment and it is obvious these are excellent families and would be perfect homes for us to place her children."

"That's a shame about the mother, but as usual, Ms. Dire, you have done an exceptional job of following up on your clients. I would support your recommendation to petition the State of Illinois and permanently remove the children from the biological mother. You may start with the adoption proceedings. I'll be working late tonight. If you complete the paper work, bring it to me for my signature. We can get the adoption process well on its way."

No one would have ever understood what the smile on her face actually stood for. She headed straight for her office and stayed late until all the paper work was complete. She picked up the phone to give Gerald and Charlene a call. When she told him the good news, she heard Charlene's cheers in the background.

Now that it seemed she was making progress again, she was not going to be outdone by not finding Twin B. She headed out to see Ms. Baldwin.

~~~

Miss B recognized Ms. Dire the moment she opened the door.

"Hello, are you Miss Baldwin?" Ms. Dire asked.

"That would be me."

"My name is Ms. Dire and I was sent here from the child welfare agency." She pointed to the ID she wore on her lapel.

Miss B knew exactly who she was. Trouble with a capital T. She wouldn't normally allow a woman of such questionable character inside her home but she had to find out her connection with Gail. She thought about the night she took the keys to Monica when they'd accidently left them on the table. She knew Gail had suspected something and it was nothing she could do about that. She also knew somehow, Gail would share that information with her co-conspirator. So, it wasn't a complete surprise that this woman was standing in front of her.

"Come in and have a seat," Miss B said.

"Thank you but I'd prefer to stand." Ms. Dire looked around and thought this was the last time she would ever come into a roach infested, filthy place like this again.

"I need to ask you a few questions, Miss Baldwin. Is that okay?"

"Sure."

"Do you know a Miss Monica Gold?"

"Yes, I do. She used to be my neighbor."

"When was the last time you saw Ms. Gold."

"Almost two weeks ago when we were both checking our mailboxes."

"Do you keep in contact with her, Miss Baldwin?"

"Unfortunately I don't know where she is right now. I would love to see Monica and the girls."

"Did you know that Ms. Gold's children aren't with her anymore?"

"Yes. I knew she had them taken away from her. I was there the night it happened. I was sure she'd have them back by now. I hear she's doing quite well—staying away from drugs and people like Gail Bonner. The girl she used to hang out with, you know. That Gail is bad news. You might know her. She should have a file in your office."

Watching Ms. Dire's facial expression change was priceless.

"Yes, I know Gail, and that is good news if Ms. Gold is getting her life together." She quickly regrouped. "I'm not here to discuss her case. However, I would like to ask you if you know anything about the baby Ms. Gold recently had?"

"How would I know anything about her baby?" Miss B leaned forward closely examining the ID again.

"It was reported that you had a baby in your apartment recently, and the agency wanted to know if it might be the last baby of Ms. Gold."

"Now, why would I have Ms. Gold's baby? I wouldn't even babysit her kids for her when she lived right across the hall from me. Everybody knows that."

"Miss B, come on… it's been reported that you don't have children or grandchildren. So where would you get a baby from?"

"No, you come on. I can't offer to keep children for women who work so that I can make a few extra dollars, Ms. Dire?"

"Sure you can Miss Baldwin. Just give me the name of the child you were babysitting and I'll gladly drop all of this and get out of your hair," she said walking towards the door.

"The child is Michael Gonzales, and he's a one year old. Is there anything else you need to know about him?"

"No, that will do. Oh, there is one thing you can tell me." She turned to face her. "To save me a little bit of leg work, where does this Michael Gonzales live?"

"Right across the hall, ma'am."

"Thank you. I'll see myself out."

Miss B peeked through the opening as she watched Ms. Dire walk towards the apartment across the hall. She noticed her hesitate and then knock very lightly on the door. She had to be thinking about the last time she went to that apartment, Miss B thought. She smiled when she remembered Ms. Gonzalez's reaction, speaking a little bit of English and a whole lot of Spanish. Ms. Dire was about to knock again and must have had second thoughts considering all the noise inside. She quickly withdrew her hand and hurried towards the broken elevator.

# Chapter 15

## Joy

"Joy, please stop fidgeting," Monica said closing the last clasp on the beaded gown. They found the dress she'd discovered on the internet and it was even prettier in person—a perfect fit. She had gone to Mirrors, a highbrow uptown salon, to get her hair styled and the whole place was in a stir about the way the head stylist fashioned it. Once the makeup was applied and she slipped into the white, form fitting halter gown with jewel-accents, Joy looked like a queen.

"Hurry up girls. We're going to be late. The game starts in forty-five minutes. Let's move it!" mamma said.

"Okay, okay." Monica clipped the diamond pennant around Joy's neck.

"Turn around. There," she said running her fingers down the long curls that outlined her face.

"Oh my goodness, look at you." She was so proud and happy for her baby sister.

As she guided her into the living room careful not to step on the long flowing gown, they all gasped when Joy entered.

"My, my, what a lovely queen," grandmamma said, kissing her lightly on the cheek. "I knew when you were born I picked out the perfect name."

"Are you sure you don't mind watching the baby to-night, grandmamma?" Monica asked grabbing her wallet. "I hate you won't be there for Joy's big night."

"Get out of here and have a good time," grandmamma said nudging them out the door. "Take plenty of pictures and remember every detail. Tell that crazy brother of mine to behave," she said, bellowing out her trademark laugh.

When they arrived at the game, a section had been reserved for their family. Her older sisters and nieces were there. Her aunts and uncles and many of her cousins all showed up to see Joy crowned Homecoming queen. At half time they introduced the royal court. Monica's entire family stood and smiled with pride. Their younger cousins yelled Joy's name while giving each other high-fives. Monica stood, quietly admiring her baby sister. It was obvious why she was selected Homecoming queen. Joy was beautiful…but what about "the curse," she thought. Her sister had that trademark beauty and she was poor, yet she hadn't made the same mistakes she had. At that point, Monica realized, the curse was all but a fallacy. From that night on, she vowed she would never associate their lives with that title again. The generational curse had officially been destroyed.

The principal spoke into the microphone and enumerated one by one all of Joy's accomplishments.

"She has a 4.00 GPA, an honor student, a member of the pom pom squad, President of the Young Students of Excellence Society, Secretary of the student council…" the list went on and on. Monica now understood that while she had been wasting her life away, her little sister had been creating a magnificent one. It saddened Monica when she thought of all the opportunities she'd missed. Sadness turned to elation when Joy came to the microphone. She was articulate and her voice was strong. The entire school cheered and it was obvious she was truly admired.

At halftime, Monica went to get a soda for mamma and herself. As she headed for the concession stand, someone called out, "Hey Monica, over here."

She turned to see several of her old high school friends waving. There were a lot of familiar faces around, because this was her old high school as well. The alumni came in record numbers each year to support the team. She climbed the bleachers to where they sat.

"It sure has been a long time," she said hugging each of them. Monica sat and chatted for a while and then said her good-byes. Another voice in the bleachers called out, "Hey, Monica."

"Hi," she said. She recognized the voice but the cap pulled down over his eyes and the scarf wrapped tightly around his neck made it difficult for her to know exactly who it was. Slowly, the man lifted his cap enough for her to see.

"Big Man!" She climbed the steps and gave him a hug. Sitting down beside him, they briefly reminisced. He told her all about Gail and Joey being shot and who they thought did it.

"Try and get by to see him, Monica. He needs some-one to give him a little spark if he's going to pull through this." Eventually he asked her what he really wanted to know.

"When was the last time you've seen Gail?"

"It's been a while."

"There are some things I think you should know about her."

"What has Gail done now? I must admit, she has been acting a little strange. I thought maybe she was a little upset because I pulled away from the old group."

"It may not be a good idea for us to sit here and discuss this," he said looking around. "We need to talk privately."

"I can't do it tonight because of Joy but I'll be free tomorrow."

"How about I pick you up at seven for dinner?" Big Man said.

"Seven it is." Monica walked back to where her family sat. She thought Big Man looked much thinner than she'd ever remembered. Something seemed strange about him too. Almost as if he was hiding something.

~~~

Big Man had second thoughts about everything in his life. Especially the drugs. He saw what it did to the people he cared for and didn't like the feeling. Growing up in the projects with his mother and eight brothers and sisters, he had to do whatever it took to survive. His mother really struggled trying to take care of all nine kids by herself. She worked a minimum wage job and they were dirt poor. He found that dealing drugs was the answer.

In the beginning, receiving all the money from the drug transactions gave him a rush like nothing else he'd ever experienced. Now, it was starting to get old—very old. The biggest reason, he saw how much it hurt his mother. She would always say, "Man," she left the *Big* off. "Man," she'd say. "You're so much better than that."

Those words haunted him.

He had moved up pretty far in the drug world. They said he had a strategic mind. When he showed them how to carve out a section of the drug business causing them to significantly increase their cash flow, he became their number one man. Even though he was finally making it big, he still wasn't able to help his mother. She wouldn't take one single dime from him. He had offered her money in so many ways. A hand full of cash, TVs, beautiful clothes, even a nice home on the other side of town. She refused it all, always saying, "I'd rather starve than take the devil's money."

Now, things in the drug world were changing fast and he didn't have the heart or desire to keep up anymore. He wanted out.

It started the day he ran into one of his old class-mates. The guy had been elected state representative and was doing quite well. It was no surprise to anyone that he'd turned out so successful. He came from a well–to-do family and his dad had been in politics for years. They never associated with each other in high school but did take a few classes together. Big Man was surprised that he even remembered him. It was his parting words that made a lasting impact on him. "You were one of the smartest guys in school. Even when life threw you a curve ball, Big Man, you'd still knock it out the park. You're a survivor. Go out there and make us proud."

Yep, it was time to do something different, Big Man thought. He did have something to offer and it wasn't in the business of hurting people.

Monica…his thoughts shifted. He had seen her the moment she walked into the stadium. He'd heard her sister was Homecoming queen and figured she would be at the game. That was the only reason he risked going there.  He would have been content just watching her from afar, but when she came so close, he had to say something.  Just looking at her, he could tell major changes were taking place in her life.  All good.

He reminded himself that Monica wasn't the only one whose life had taken a sudden turn. His started the day he walked away from everything.  The drugs, the money, the fast life, he left it all behind.  It was also the time when he began to live again.

All the money in the world hadn't been able to make him happy.  He was miserable inside and wasn't able to figure out why.  When he found himself with his nine-millimeter in his hand most of the day, he knew if anybody rubbed him the wrong way, he would have taken that gun and blown them away.  He'd never considered himself a violent man but he felt at that point, he needed to either kill someone or kill himself.  It really didn't matter which.

It was a rough day, so he decided to visit his mother, to try and clear his head.  She was the only one that could usually help him get his thoughts together.

"I was determined I wouldn't let another day go by without seeing you," he'd said kissing her on the cheek as he walked through the door.

"I'm glad you came to see me, Man.  I was thinking about you and hoping you would drop by.  Can I fix you something to eat?"

"No thanks.  I'm not hungry right now."

"Well, that's a first."

"Where's the remote?" he asked falling back on the couch.  "The playoffs are on and I thought I'd check it out over here."

He could feel her staring at him and wished she wouldn't do that.

"Nothing's wrong is it Man? You're not in any trouble are you, son?"

"Can't I go anywhere and get some peace?" Big Man yelled. He tried maintaining his composure but the tiny beads of perspiration had already begun lining his forehead.

"Now, I know something is wrong," she said. She walked over and grabbed his hands. "Listen, I just…"

He snatched them away and threw the remote, splattering it all over the floor.

"Man, have you lost your mind! What's wrong with you?" she said jumping back.

Big Man stood, vigorously rubbing both hands over his head. Grabbing the keys he raced out the door. He could still hear his mother calling him as he took long strides down the hall.

The speedometer's needle inched its way past 98 mph. He'd driven the Ferrari ferociously, taking the winding curves at dangerous speeds. When he screeched into his driveway, he could hear laughter and music blasting from inside. Cars were everywhere. He backed out and drove around the city. Pulling into an alcove perched on a hilltop, he gazed at the orange crescent glow of the sun casting its hazy shadow over the city. He watched as the ruddy colored globe disappeared over the horizon allowing him plenty of time to think. What happened at his mother's home was way beyond his imagination. He would have killed anybody who treated her that way. How could he have shown her that level of disrespect?

Big Man knew he walked a fine line of having a serious mental meltdown when the unfamiliar track of tears
slowly crept their way down his cheeks.  Suddenly, the
urge to run as far away as possible presented itself to him.
How could he do that and live?  His partners would kill
him for sure.  He wrestled with the thought, twisting and
turning the matter over and over in his mind.  From out
of nowhere, the idea emerged.  Why hadn't he thought of
it before?  They'd said they kept him around and moved
him up in the drug world because he had a strategic mind.
Well, he was going to use that same mind to get himself
out of all this.

By the time Big Man drove back to his house, everyone was asleep.  Little did he know how important his
decision to build a safe room would be.  He followed the
maze leading to the secret place and punched in the code.
He quickly removed all his personal cash, some important
papers and sped away.

That was the last they'd seen him.  He drove to
Memphis, purchased a nice condominium, paid cash for it
and moved in.  He didn't know anybody in the city and
that was the way he wanted it.

~~~

Big Man read the ad in the Commercial Appeal, the
local newspaper and found a data entry position.  He
applied for the job and knew by the second interview the
position was his. Fifteen dollars and fifty cents an hour
was all it paid.  It didn't matter.  For the first time in a
long time, he felt free.  When he got his first paycheck, he
bought a few groceries and the rest he put away.  It all
seemed different, but it all seemed right.

His coworkers were mostly a nice group of people.
One man in particular stood out.  He wouldn't have given

him the time of day, but Logan was a little younger than he was, always upbeat, energetic and highly intelligent. That sparked his interest. He spoke with a passion and wisdom well beyond his years. They started eating lunch together and had many interesting conversations. From politics to religion they discussed it all. Logan possessed many traditional values, unlike himself. His wife was a stay at home mom who chose to home school their two sons. He boasted of their garden they grew out back on the acres of land they owned. Eventually, Big Man began opening up and sharing with Logan a few of his own life's chapters. He had never been comfortable enough to let anybody in on his story. However, it was different with Logan. Talking with him somehow made him feel better. It took him off guard when he offered such solid advice one day. "You're strong and never really needed that lifestyle anyway. You need to tap into the hidden treasure that's been buried far too long, deep inside of you," he said.

It also helped Big Man to confront the reality that he would never be in the drug business again, even if it cost him his life. That was no way for anyone to live. How could he have been so blind? He wondered what caused some people to venture into that way of life while others sought to live the one Logan had so wisely chosen. He wanted to know the answer to that question so he'd be able to share it with his own brothers and sisters one day and anybody else who would listen.

"If you don't want to accept the reason why I believe people choose differently, come to my church on Sunday and see for yourself." Logan offered his take on the subject.

Big Man just rubbed his chin and smiled.

"If you come this one time, I'll never ask you again...deal?" They shook hands.

He'd do it if it meant he'd never have to hear about it again, Big Man thought.

That Saturday, he shopped for a nice suit. As a young boy when his mother made him go to church, she always sent him in the same second hand suit Sunday after Sunday. Even though it was way too big, he could hear his mother say, "always give the Lord your best, son." Now, he'd left hundreds of tailor-made suits lining his closet in his old house, but was glad he didn't need or want any of them. He was more than happy to go and buy a brand new one with the money he'd earned on his real job.

He was actually excited when Sunday finally came. He hadn't been inside a church since he was thirteen years old. Walking inside, he sat on the next to the last pew. He spotted Logan smiling widely. He was the assistant pastor there.

Big Man knew he was in for an interesting time as his entire row swayed with the song the mass choir sang. The men and women to his left and right shouted loud amen's, hallelujah's, and praise the Lord's from the moment he sat down. It reminded him of his mother's and Monica's grandmamma's church. When he would occasionally pick her up from Sunday services, he could hear the entire congregation stomping and praising God from the parking lot. Big Man never understood why people acted like that in church. It was all a mystery to him. Nevertheless, they were acting the same way in this church. The choir director held up one hand bringing the song to an end but the audience wasn't finished. They continued clapping, and shouting, until the leader of the song came back again, singing, *"Prayer, Will Fix it For You."* To his surprise, it loosened him up a little, allowing him to sway along just a bit with his lively row. Finally, the pastor came to the podium to begin his message. The manner, in which he unfolded the text, immediately captured his attention. He could relate to almost every scenario. It was something about the preacher's voice that helped accentuate the story and drew him further in. By the time he was half way into the sermon, he began noticing a feeling that tugged a bit at his emotions. He fought to regain control. He tried by rationalizing that it was just the music in the background, the shouts of the people, along with the message itself that got him a little worked up. It'll all subside in a minute, he told himself. Well, it didn't. In fact, it got worse. He shifted and even fanned himself, trying to shake the uninvited feelings—but couldn't. He didn't know whether to run out the church or sit there to see what would happen next. So, he loosened his tie and sat. By the end of the message, that stirring had transformed itself into a full blown case of conviction that simply just wouldn't go away. He wanted to tell someone how sorry he was for all he had done. The drugs, the violence, the deceit, he didn't care who he had to say it to. He just needed to say he was sorry for all the pain and hurt he'd caused.

Call it perfect timing, but it was at that point the minister, wiping his brow said, "Many of you need a second chance at life. You've done some things you're not proud of. You need a Savior who can wash away every sin you've ever committed and remember them no more. If that's you, I invite you to come to the altar."

His expression must have told the story.

When he made eye contact with Logan, he knew he had come to the place where he could finally let go of the pain he had bottled up for so many years.

He watched as Logan came towards him from the pulpit. It took no effort at all to come out of his pew and meet him halfway as they both walked to the altar together.

# Chapter 16

## Taste of Betrayal

They celebrated late into the night at Joy's favorite restaurant.

When Monica finally got a moment alone with Joy, she pulled her aside. "I'm so impressed with what a wonderful young lady you're turning out to be."

"Now don't get all emotional on me, sis."

"No, Joy, it's true. I was knocked off my feet by what you have accomplished." She wrapped her arms around her. "I'm so proud to have you as my baby sister."

Joy rested her head on her shoulder and smiled.

"So, now that I've gotten all the mushy stuff out of the way, do you mind telling me who that handsome young fellow is that can't seem to keep his hands off you?" Monica asked, nodding his way.

"He's just a friend," her smile now wider than ever. She tried covering her face.

"Don't go getting shy on me now. Come on and introduce me," she said, pulling her towards him.

"I wanted to tell you and mamma about him, but you know how mamma is."

"I know," Monica said. "Hey, but I'm not like that."

"Okay! Okay! Come on," she said walking over to where the teenagers mingled. "Myles, this is my sister, Monica."

They exchanged polite hellos. When a few of Joy's friends grabbed her, racing off to meet a group of friends outside, Monica was left alone with Myles.

"So, how long have you and Joy known each other?"

"Since seventh grade," he said. "She wouldn't give me the time of day back then. Man, she wouldn't talk to me for nothing. I don't know what happened, but one day I tried talking to her and she actually stopped and talked back. It blew me away so badly Monica, I didn't know what to say. I stood there looking real stupid."

Monica laughed. They sat and talked for a while. She liked Myles. He seemed to be a good kid.

Watching Joy laugh and enjoying herself left her with a strange sense of contentment.

Tonight, she was happy.

~~~

Monica stretched after her morning jog. It felt good to finally have a day off, and her plans included nothing but lounging around the house most of the day. After a quick shower, she came in and sat with her grandmamma at the kitchen table. They chatted a moment when Joy joined them.

"Sleepy head is finally up," Monica announced as Joy sat beside her. She reached over and playfully tossed her hair.

"Grandmamma, we had such a good time last night."

Monica tried describing how Uncle Bill acted all night as she bent over imitating him. "He was talking to Joy like this." She cleared her throat. "Hey, hey, hey Joys, come heauh and talk to your ole 'unc."

"You sound just like him. Quit it," grandmamma said, laughing so hard she had to wipe the tears away. Monica kept on mocking him.

She was in a good mood as she joked around, enjoying the laughter and talking about the good time they all had. "The food and music in that place was fantastic,"

Monica said. "Everyone who joined in Karaoke had us in stitches, until Miss Joy here got to the microphone of course. By the time she finished singing, *A Hero Lies in You*, everyone in the restaurant was standing. There wasn't a dry eye in the place."

While they snacked on grandmamma's homemade cookies, Monica glanced around the small room filled with her family. It was a good feeling to be surrounded by them all. She truly understood the importance of taking care of those you love.

"My goodness, the time has gotten away from me," Monica said eyeing the clock. "Joy would you mind watching your niece for a couple of hours tonight?"

"Sure." She let out a gigantic yawn.

Later that evening, Monica dressed for dinner with Big Man. He arrived at seven sharp.

She was quite pleased with his restaurant selection. They were seated right away. After the server took their order, Monica sat anxiously.

"Okay, Big Man, tell me about Gail."

"Hey, that's a little bit too heavy to start the evening off with," he smiled. "Why don't you tell me how you've been, first? We have plenty of time to talk about her."

She never got tired of telling about all the marvelous things that happened to her in the past six months.

"I'm so glad you got your GED. I never did quite understand why anybody with the kind of brains you had would drop out of school. Now, you're enrolled in the community college, that's amazing. I'm proud of you, Monica."

"Enough about me," she said. "Tell me what's been going on in your world."

By the time he'd gotten into the middle of his change of life story their meal had arrived.

"You're the first person I've told any of this to. In fact my mother doesn't even know," Big Man said. "I haven't seen her since the night I left going to Memphis."

She stopped chewing for a moment, and stared at him. "Where are you staying?"

"I still have to be careful whenever I come to town. I stay with family and friends I can trust. Now, that things are really looking up for me, my partners and I are actually drawing up plans to open a fitness center that I'll be running in Memphis real soon. I already have someone who's going to help me grow the business. He's a good friend that works with me and is full of ideas. I can see success written all over it. So, when I come to town, I take care of business and get out of here as fast as I can."

"Are you going to be all right? I mean…are you safe, Big Man?" Monica asked. She couldn't deal with another traumatic event happening to another friend of hers.

"I think so. I've prayed about it and I have a strange sense of peace. I don't understand it all, but for some reason, I feel safe."

Later into the meal he eventually brought up Gail. "Monica, there are some things I think you need to know about her."

She frowned. "What things? I haven't seen or talked to her in months," she said chewing on a small piece of the tender steak.

"That may be, but I need you to listen carefully. For some reason, I think Gail is trying to set you up. I haven't figured out why she's going through all this trouble to trap you, but I know that she is."

"Come on, Big Man. Not Gail."

"Remember the day you came back to the projects and ended up getting in the car with Joey? After you left, I noticed her behavior. She was quite upset and she let everybody know it. "I sent"…he hesitated. "I sent an informant to watch her, just to listen and report back to me anything out of the ordinary. Boy was I shocked at what she found out. After you left, Gail got on the phone to someone in Protective Services. She heard her tell whoever it was that she was "in". She then quickly wrote down a number the person gave her. It was to a Sergeant Foley. She gave Joey's address and said he was a known drug dealer that was in the middle of a major drug deal. I knew the cops had been on to Joey for a few years. So, I went to his house just to see what was going down. Plus, I had a feeling you were there. It was a good thing I did. I parked my car on the next street and from out of nowhere, man, cops were pulling up from everywhere. I didn't know how I was going to get you out of there. I ran around back without them spotting me, and from out of nowhere, there you were. When you ran into me, you scared me as much as I scared you. After that fiasco, I made certain my informant stuck close to Gail. Whoever she's talking to, they're plotting against you, Monica. None of this makes sense to me, though. Does it to you?" Big Man asked.

She sat shaking her head. She'd suddenly lost her appetite.

"I can't believe Gail would do something like that to me. She and Jay Jay have been my best friends for years."

"There's one more thing I need to tell you," Big Man said, folding his napkin.

Monica didn't know if she could stomach anymore. Why did everything in her life have to be so stressful? "Go ahead, Big Man, talk to me," she said.

"My informant said she saw Gail talking with Jay Jay right before he was killed. She couldn't hear their conversation very well but did hear her call your name several times. At the end of the conversation she yelled...bring Monica here."

Big Man could see she was struggling with what he'd said. "I didn't mean to upset you, Monica but I thought you needed to know."

She sat quietly, twirling her finger around a single lock of hair. He didn't say anything else for a moment. He wanted to give her some time. There was more bad news to come.

"I'm not one hundred percent sure what this is all about but I believe every word you've told me. Can we get out of here? I need some air," she said pushing her chair back.

He quickly paid the bill as they went to his car.

"Monica I don't know how to tell you this, but there's one more thing I need to let you in on."

"Go ahead. It can't hurt any more than it already has," she said. "It's all messing with my head real bad, Big Man." She held her breath.

"Well," he said slowly. "I was told they are looking to tie you to Jay Jay's murder."

"WHAT!"

"Gail is bad news," Big Man said. He reached over and held her hand. "I know how disturbing all of this is for you, but you have to know so you can protect yourself."

He understood her silence. However, it was her next statement that surprised him.

"Please take me to see Joey, Big Man. I've got something I need to tell him."

They didn't talk any more about Gail. He knew she had gotten the message.

When they drove into the parking garage, they walked into the doors of the large City Hospital. Joey was still listed in critical condition and somehow Big Man had gotten the okay for them to be allowed in to see him. When they walked into his ICU room, she could tell Joey was showing no signs of improvement. He seemed completely unresponsive. Monica left his room and walked up to one of the nurses.

"Excuse me, may I ask you a question?"

"Sure," she said placing the chart on the desk.

"If I talked to the patient in Room 3, do you think he'd be able to hear and understand what I'm saying?"

"Yes, ma'am, he may be able to hear you. We encourage the family to talk to him as much as possible."

She walked back into the room and bent down very close to Joey's ear. She gently reached for his hand and whispered. "Hey, baby, it's me, Monica. I know this is hard right now but things are going to get better. You've got to fight, Joey. You've got to beat this thing. I know you can do it. I need you to live. Your baby girls need you to live. We need to finish that conversation."

They didn't stay much longer and once outside, she rested her head on Big Man's shoulder. "I really do love Joey as a friend, and I hate what's happened to him. He is the father of my twins and I will always honor him for that, whatever condition he's in. It's so strange, Big Man. The two men in my life—my girl's fathers, have both ended up the same way. The older girls will never know their father because of his untimely death. We married way too early but our plans were to be together forever. It just wasn't meant to be. Now, it seems as if it may be the same for the twins' father."

~~~

After the news Big Man shared, Monica was beginning to feel as if her back was against the wall, yet again. Now, some of what Miss B said the night she went to visit her made sense. The person Gail was conspiring with was her caseworker.

Fighting the hopeless feeling this time was a struggle but fortunately, she knew where to find relief.

"Hurry up," grandmamma said, walking out the door towards the car. Monica was glad she'd insisted they leave early. The church was packed but, they found seats up front. All during service, she turned to see whether or not Big Man had made it. They'd agreed to meet there last night after dinner. She finally spotted him, suddenly realizing what a chance he'd taken coming there. He'd told her some of his old drug cronies were still looking for him to settle up even though he hadn't taken anything from them—not one penny of their money. He'd even signed his house over to Shine along with everything in it. They still wanted to see him. Then she smiled. This was actually one of the safest places Big Man could be. Not a one of them would be inside a church.

The church service began and Monica knew there was something special happening when the minister stood to deliver the message. He outlined the predicament a king called Jehoshaphat found himself in. He faced an enormous army whose mission it was to annihilate him and his people.

By the time the pastor finished preaching the soul-stirring sermon, the entire church was standing. It was the words, *"The Battle Is Not Yours but the Lord's"* that ignited their spirits. She looked back at Big Man and he looked at her. They both understood.

When the services were over she walked to where he sat. "Come with me," she said, gently sliding her hand into his. She led him across the aisle to where his mother stood.

When Big Man's mother looked into his teary eyes, she threw her arms around her son and held him tightly.

Big Man held on, thanking God he was finally holding his mother. "Mamma, I'm no longer the old "Man" you used to know. I'm a brand new person. Nothing in my life is the same," he whispered.

"I know, son. I know."

As they all left the church, Monica noticed a dark green Impala parked down the street. Its engine running.

# Chapter 17

## Revolving Doors

Chris pushed through the revolving doors in the Towers and headed for the private elevator that led to his office.

"Mr. Blankenship, your eight 'o clock appointment is waiting. Oh, by the way, you have five messages from Miss Camille." His assistant, Dorothy followed him into his office.

He sifted through the stacks of paper on his desk. "Did Camille say what she wanted?"

"No, sir, she did not but insisted that you call her back."

Chris was surprised that Camille had waited that long to phone him. Ever since he'd broken off the engagement, she'd vowed she would never see or speak to him again. She had actually taken it better than he thought she would. The last time he tried to call it off, she'd got so upset he didn't have the heart to follow through with it.

Camille came from a well to do family and had been exposed to the best life had to offer. She was polished and exhibited the mannerism of royalty, but somehow, Chris knew she wasn't for him. There was one girl he'd met and dated in college who was completely different. Her name was Pat. That would be the type he'd marry some day.

Pat was a city girl who had worked ever since she was fourteen. They'd met their freshman year and dated until

they were seniors.  Chris instantly knew she was one of
the brightest and most caring women he'd ever met.  She
couldn't walk pass a homeless person without reaching
into her pockets.  The last time they were together, he
told her how much he loved her.  She was ecstatic and
told him she felt the same way.  He had wanted to drive
her back to her dorm.   It was getting dark, but she
insisted she needed to stop by the library to do a last
minute homework assignment.  They agreed that as soon
as she finished, she would meet him at his apartment to
watch the playoff-game with a couple of their friends.

He left her and headed back.  It was getting late when
he called her cell and when she didn't answer he became
concerned.   He called again and again— even left a
message telling her how worried he was and to call right
away.  By the time midnight came the police were involved.  The front desk clerk in the library remembered
her leaving the library around nine.  When they hadn't
found her by two am, Chris phoned his dad.   Both his
parents flew in immediately to support him.

Two days after Pat's disappearance, they found her
battered body on the other side of town, in an abandoned
house.  The coroner placed the actual time of her brutal
death around two or three a.m. the day she went missing.
For years Chris blamed himself.  He should have insisted
that she come home with him.

Even though he'd finally started dating again, he
wondered if he would ever be able to replace Pat.  He was
grateful none the less.  He knew the short time he spent
with her made him a kinder and gentler soul.

Camille was completely different.  She had been extremely nice to him.  The problem was when he noticed
how she treated everybody else.  She had no tolerance for

others, especially people she felt, as she called it, beneath her. The day she yelled at the poor server for accidently spilling water on the table, he knew she wasn't the one for him. From stupid to the village idiot, she'd call the poor guy every name in the book. He couldn't believe how naïve he had been. Once his eyes were opened to who she really was, he'd been trying to call it off for months but didn't want to hurt her.

He glanced up. "If Camille calls again, please tell her I'm not available."

~~~

Monica had two clients on hold when she answered the other ringing line. The office had been that way all morning. Brooke was scheduled to go on a business trip for three weeks and would be leaving shortly. There were last minute details she had to take care of.

Monica juggled the phone lines when she looked into the face of a tall, beautiful woman.

"Good morning, I'm Miss Camille Fields and I need to see Brooke." She walked right pass her into Brooke's office.

Monica put the phone on hold and ran from behind her desk to try and stop her, but it was too late.

"It's okay, Monica, I'll handle it," Brooke said looking up.

Monica exited the office, leaving the door partially opened.

"Hello, Camille. How are you?"

"I'm not doing well as you can see," she said removing her sunglasses and exposing her red streaked eyes. "I've tried to contact your brother but he won't return my calls. I can't believe he's treating me this way. After all, I am his fiancée."

"Camille, you know I never get involved in Chris' personal affairs."

"You can at least tell him to call me, Brooke. We've known each other for years. We're like sisters. I need your help."

She couldn't believe her brother had become involved with a girl like this. She was actually glad when she'd learned he had called off their engagement. It did leave their mother disappointed, again. She desperately wanted her only son to marry and give her grandchildren.

"I haven't eaten or slept in days. I'm so weak." Camille fell back in her chair.

"That's not good. You need to take better care of yourself."

"If you help me out this one time, I'll never ask again. I know I'll regain my strength once I speak to him."

Brook suppressed the urge to laugh. "Maybe I'll talk to my brother and see if he won't call."

The chick needs an Oscar, Monica thought, listening.

"Thank you, Brooke, for being such a dear friend. I just need to talk to Chris. I miss him so much."

"Why don't you go and try to calm down? Maybe you'll hear from him today."

"I hope so. The medication isn't helping anymore," she said, touching her forehead with the back of her hand.

"Go home, Camille. Get some rest," Brooke said.

Swinging her hair, she pranced out the office much like the lead horse in a Christmas parade.

Brooke got up to close the door and smiled at Monica. "I'll tell you all about that one day."

Chris answered his personal line.

"I was just about to call you," he said. "Are you prepared for the Italy account? Anything you need before you go?"

Brooke chuckled. "All is well, but I do need to talk to you about something else. I saw Camille today."

Chris was quiet.

"She really wants to talk to you and I told her I would relay the message. I'm not trying to get into your personal affairs, Chris, but she does seem distraught. If it's really over, tell her so. Okay, now that I've done my good deed for the day, what about you and me having lunch before I leave for Italy?"

"I'll meet you in the cafeteria," he said.

~~~

"What are you going to do about Camille, Chris?" Brooke asked sprinkling the special dressing onto her salad.

"I just want her to go away. I don't want to hurt her, but I don't know how to get rid of her either. She falls apart every time I tell her it's over. I'm afraid of what she might do. She's making this very difficult. If I call Camille, it will only give her some kind of false hope, and I don't want to do that either. What advice do you have for your baby brother?"

"If you really want to break it off then you should tell her so and mean it. She's young. She'll get over it," Brooke advised.

"What part of, it's over between us Camille, you don't think she understands?"

"You're right, but you still have to be firm with her, Chris. Tell her not to call or come by. In fact, tell her you're dating somebody else and hope she finds someone just as special."

"My heart has been telling me to do that for quite some time."

They didn't stay long in the cafeteria. She needed to tie up a few loose ends before her flight. When she returned to the office, Monica had already picked up her jacket from the laundry, sent her parents flowers for their anniversary, and had all the documents she needed for the trip prepared.

"The limousine is waiting for you," Monica said.

Brooke walked slowly to the car. Chris had been right yet again, she thought.

Monica was priceless.

~~~

When she'd finally gotten Brooke off to the airport, Monica took a deep breath. Then the phone rang. She was determined to get home at a decent hour for a change.

"Good evening, Mrs. Blankenship's office," Monica said answering the private line.

"Good evening to you to, Ms. Gold. I was just checking to see if my sister got off to the airport on time."

"Yes, she did." Monica had no idea why she felt a slight sense of nervousness whenever she spoke to him.

"The office should slow down now that she's outta there."

There was an awkward silence between the two before he spoke again. "So, how are things going for you around here?" he asked.

"I couldn't be happier. I can't thank you enough for giving me this opportunity, Chris. This job has truly changed my life."

"This is a great company to work for if I have to say so myself."

They both laughed.

"Well, it's good talking with you… but before you hang up, I was wondering, if you're not busy, would you join me for dinner tonight?   Then you can catch me up on everything that's happening in your life."

"Okay," she finally said.   "I'll be glad to have dinner with you."

Neither could see the smiles spreading across the other's face.

The phone calls slowed once Brooke left the office. At five, Monica was just about to leave, when the phone rang.  She thought about not answering but was glad she did.  It was Big Man, calling with news about Joey.  The doctors had called the family to the bedside, his heart rate was dropping.  They had already removed him from the ventilator.

She headed straight for the hospital.  Joey's sister had given her permission to join them.

When she arrived, they were all gathered around his bed.

"Monica.   I'm glad you could come."   It was his younger sister she'd gone to high school with.  A deep sadness outlined her face.

"I'm so sorry about Joey," Monica said as they embraced.

"Joey would want his friends to say their good-byes," Melody said wiping her eyes.  "Gail is in there too."

Her heart fluttered when she mentioned that name. She knew she wasn't mentally ready to be around Gail. She willed herself to stay calm as she walked with Melody to Joey's bedside.  The cold reality of Joey dying in the hospital bed, took her mind completely off Gail for a moment.  Monica looked down at someone she barely recognized—into the dusky, blue tinged, swollen face of a friend, who was obviously dying.  She immediately turned away, unfortunately into the icy cold stares of Gail.  If she had any doubts, not that she did, they were all confirmed.  Gail's body language spoke volumes.  For whatever reason, she knew the woman that had been her childhood friend, hated her.  Between Joey's looming demise and Gail's chilling presence, it was all too much for her.  She headed for the door.

The moment she walked through it, she heard some-one cry out, "oh, God, no-o-o."

The alarms were ringing, alerting everyone to Joey's monitor.  It displayed a continuous straight line.

# Chapter 18

## Love Child

Gerald and Charlene looked like the perfect couple, standing before the judge. This time Gerald cuddled Geraldene in his arms. Inside the courtroom were both sets of grandparents, Pastor Collins and his wife, several members from their congregation, and Ms. Dire.

The judge gazed down at them. "I am granting you temporary custody of this child. It is also the court's opinion that approval of the first phase of the adoption process has been successfully completed. We will set a court date in one month to finalize the adoption. Go home, Gerald and Charlene and enjoy your baby," he said slamming his gavel.

Thank you your honor. Thank you so much, Gerald thought to himself. He had never seen Charlene so happy.

"Oh Gerald," she said. "We have our little girl. Can you believe it!"

Family and friends gathered around to congratulate them.

Pastor Collins raised his hand and silenced the crowd. "Gerald and Charlene, we would like for you to meet us back at the church. We have a wonderful celebration planned for the three of you."

Gerald watched as Ms. Dire approached. She really did it, he thought. She actually pulled it off.

"Well, Gerald, how do you feel?"

"Words can't describe how much I appreciate all you've done for us. I think we also have a little business matter we need to take care of."

She hadn't expected to get most of the money right then. What a relief it would be to finally have it all in her hands.

~ ~ ~

The phone rang almost immediately after the initial adoption decision was made. It was Jessica telling grandmamma the news.

She put the phone down and placed her face in her hands. Her thoughts were of Monica. Looking up, she was startled to actually see Monica standing in the doorway.

"What are you doing home so early?" she asked opening the door.

"Brooke is on her way to Italy and the office is quiet."

Monica told her all about Joey dying and the news Big Man had given her about Gail.

Grandmamma didn't respond and knew her quietness would soon raise suspicion. She couldn't help it. She just didn't have anything to say.

"You seem bothered, grandmamma. Is everything okay?"

She didn't reply.

Monica instantly sat up. "What's wrong!"

"Jessica told me they awarded temporary custody to the other twin's foster parents. They are trying to finalize the adoption next month. I don't know how Jessica gets all this information, but she always knows exactly what's going on."

Monica felt as if someone had just kicked her in the stomach. She sat back and stared into the ceiling.

"Stay strong Monica, please stay strong."

"I'm trying to, grandmamma," she said tearfully. "It seems the harder I try to get things right for myself, the worse things get. Is God paying me back for all the wrong I did in the past?"

"No, He's not. Some decisions you made just have hard consequences, that's all. Have faith, Monica. God said, He would bring all of your babies home, now believe that."

Grandmamma's words gave little comfort this time.

When they shared the news with mamma, as usual, she fell apart. Joy sat quietly taking it all in.

Monica had decided against having dinner with Chris. He didn't deserve her somber mood. She was about to pick up the phone to call him when it rang.

It was Peaches' teacher.

"I haven't heard from you and I wanted to see if everything was okay."

"There's so much going on, Sheila, I hardly know where to begin." She tried filling her in but it was simply too much to tell. They agreed to have lunch in a couple of days. By the time they'd finished talking, Monica looked at her watch and realized it was too late to cancel dinner.

"I promised Chris I would have dinner with him tonight," she said hanging up the phone.

"That might not be such a bad idea," mamma said. "There's nothing else you can do around here."

"Come on, Monica." Joy sprang up from her chair. "I'll help you get dressed this time for your big date. It'll be fun. You'll see."

It didn't take her very long to dress with Joy's help. She came out and sat down beside her mother.

"You look very pretty, Monica," mamma said. A few moments later, the doorbell rang. Oh boy! This was going to be some kind of night, Monica thought. A driver dressed in all black attire stood there ready to escort her to a beautiful stretch limousine.

The women in her family stood at the door as she walked gracefully towards the car.

The neighborhood came alive as they all watched.

~ ~ ~

Once the limo pulled in front of the huge apartment building, the bellman greeted her at the door.

"Good afternoon, Ms. Gold. Right this way, please."

When the elevators opened, he inserted the key and pushed the button labeled $P$.

"Enjoy your evening, ma'am."

"Thank you," Monica said.

When she finally reached the pent house, Chris' butler welcomed her inside.

"Good evening, Ms. Gold."

She walked through an enormous entryway. The room offered a panoramic view of the city people should have to pay to see.

Chris came around the corner with a killer smile.

"I'm so glad you came. Can I get you something to drink? Freshly squeezed juice, spring water or sodas are a few choices."

"I'll take the juice. That sounds delicious."

He joined her at the window while she took in the view. As they chatted, Monica looked down on a city that housed all of her pain...her hopes and dreams.

When the butler announced dinner, he escorted her to the dining area arrayed in fine china and sparkling crystal. While they feasted on lamb chops, asparagus, rich garlic potatoes and other delicacies, she began to relax.

"How's school?" Chris asked.

"I decided to take only one course to see how well I'd do. The class work has been surprisingly easy so far. It doesn't hurt having a very bright sister at home either. She helps me out quite a bit."

Chris finally brought up the subject they had both avoided. Her emotions were always difficult to hide when she talked about her girls.

"Tell me what's going on, Monica."

As usual, it was easy for her to confide in him. In fact, it felt good to finally release it all.

"I'm amazed at how much you've accomplished in such a short time," he said trying to lighten the discussion. "You are a strong woman and never forget that. Just remember it's going to take all that strength and more to overcome what you're about to face, but you have what it takes to do it. Fight back with "this" he said, pointing to his head. "Don't let anybody just take anything from you that's yours. Not your integrity, your love, peace and especially not your children. If it belongs to you, then it's your choice whether to keep it or give it away. Whatever the case may be, remember, it's yours to decide." Chris wasn't only talking to Monica. He was also talking to himself.

"What if I've done all I can do to hold on to it, but it still gets away from me?" she said softly.

"Then you keep fighting. Nothing is over, even when it might seem as if it is."

"If the courts take my babies from me, I can't fight them," she countered.

"Oh, yes you can fight them. It doesn't matter if they're ages three or thirty-three. One day they'll know you are their mother. Never let go."

She told him about Gail and all that she was conspiring to do. "I can't believe my very best friend is trying to destroy me," she said. "This is not a soap opera we're talking about Chris. This is my life."

"Remember the day we went to the Expresso café and I asked you what your plans were to get out of the situation you found yourself in?"

"Yes."

"Well, I'm asking you again. What's your plan, Monica?"

She thought before she spoke. The advice he had given her at Expresso was priceless. "You're right," she said. "I need a plan."

"Okay, what are you going to do tonight to try and get your babies back home?"

"Now, I'm going to ask you what I did the first time you asked me that question. If you were in my shoes, Chris, what would you do?"

"If I were you, Ms. Gold," he said affectionately. "I would walk right out of here and get prepared for tomorrow. Early in the morning, I'd go to the agency and talk to them face to face. I would ask—no, demand to know the plan they've devised for me to get the children back. I would not leave there without answers."

"If my caseworker isn't there I should..."

"You should talk to someone else about your case. It seems as if you might need to do that anyway."

She flashed her signature smile. "Thanks again, for coming to my rescue."

As they talked, she slid off her shoes and curled her bare feet on the couch. She was relaxed and it showed.

They talked for a long time and when Monica left, Chris stretched out on the couch, his hands underneath his head. He thought of how amazingly beautiful she was. It was rare to find a person that way both inside and out.

The phone rang and instinctively, he answered.

"Hello, Chris, this is Camille."

He almost hung up.

"We need to talk, darling," she said. "I'm downstairs. May I please come up?"

"Camille, now is not a good time for us to talk. I'm really tired and I need to get to bed."

"Why are you doing this to me, Chris? I don't understand. After all we've been through for the last three years? Please talk to me. If you want me to leave, after that, I'll go away."

Everything in him was telling him to leave her downstairs. He couldn't believe she had come over unannounced. She had never done that before. He knew she was desperate. An even scarier thought, she'd just missed Monica. Maybe they'd passed each other and didn't realize it. He quickly dismissed the thought. Knowing Camille like he did, if she suspected anything, she would have caused an awful scene. He had experienced her temper before and it wasn't pretty. "Camille, please let's just—"

"Chris, I must see you!"

Chris knew he should let her stay downstairs until she finally got the message. Regretting it already, he heard himself say, "Tom, would you let Ms. Camille up please."

He knew he was listening.

"Right away, sir!"

Camille walked slowly in when he opened the door. "What's wrong, Chris? We've had spats before and we've always seemed to patch things up. Let's try and start all over. We can put all of this behind us and move on."

Chris walked over to the couch. When he looked down, he stared at one of Monica's earrings. Her hair had gotten tangled in it when she nervously tucked it behind her ear. He liked watching her express herself, always playfully twisting her hair. He picked up the earring and held it tightly.

Suddenly, he realized Camille was talking but had no idea what she was saying.

"Did you hear me, Chris?"

"No, Camille. What were you saying?" Chris followed her eyes. They were locked on the earring he held in his hands.

"I asked you, whose earring is that?"

He didn't respond, but stared back into her cutting eyes.

"I thought I recognized the girl that got in the limo," she whispered.

"Camille, I knew this was a bad idea. Please go home. We'll talk later."

"No, we'll talk now. You will not do this to me, Chris. I've put too much into this relationship. We're about to be married."

"No, we're not, Camille. It's over," he said calmly, almost too calmly. This time not turning away.

The astonishment on her face was a clear indication he'd hit a homerun. He had never been able to talk to her like that for fear of hurting her, but tonight it was different.

"Who is she, Chris?" she asked softly. "At least tell me who has taken my place in just three weeks?"

He shook his head. "Listen Camille, I never meant to hurt you but it's time we move on our separate ways. You are a young, beautiful woman with a lot to offer. It's just that we don't need to be together."

"Don't you talk to me like that. Don't you ever talk to me like that," she seethed through clenched teeth. "I can't believe you've done this to me, but I guess that's the way you are. You love them and leave them don't you, Chris."

"I will see you to the door, Camille."

"That won't be necessary. You won't ever have to ask me to leave again," she said. "I'll see myself out." As she walked towards the door, she hesitated and turned.

"I gave you three of the best years of my life and you threw them away. They must not have meant a thing."

She slammed the door.

# Chapter 19

## Taking Charge

Sheila had agreed she would meet Monica bright and early at the little coffee shop before she went to school. This time Angela joined her.

"I'm going to the agency to talk to Ms. Dire about making arrangements to see my daughter."

"When you talk with Ms. Dire, don't let her give you any excuses about not seeing Peaches. The children will be leaving at noon today. Peaches' foster dad picks her up and he's always on time. She told me that he sometimes takes her to get a snack, otherwise she goes straight home," Sheila said.

"Another thing, don't let them tell you they need a specific time for you to see your daughter," Angela said. "Your caseworker has the right to drop in on the child any time she chooses."

"No need to worry. I'm not going to leave without seeing my daughter today. I'll meet the two of you back here at six, to let you know what happened."

"Oh, and one last thing, Monica, if she refuses to let you see Peaches, I want you to ask for a Mr. Robert Washington," Angela said jotting the name down. "I found out that he works in the same office with Ms. Dire. He'll help you. He's a very nice man."

Monica liked Angela and her take-charge attitude. She smiled, took the name and put it in her wallet. "Thanks. I'll see you two at six."

~~~

Monica walked into the Children's Welfare office.

"I'll ring Ms. Dire's office for you," the receptionist said. "Have a seat, please."

She sat in one of the steel chairs acknowledging the presence of butterflies flickering in her stomach.

"Ma'am," the receptionist said. "Ms. Dire is not in right now. Would you like to leave her a message?"

"No, is Mr…" She pulled the name out of her wallet. "Is Mr. Robert Washington in?"

"I'll check for you." She phoned his office.

"Mr. Washington is with another client at the moment and will not be available for a couple of hours."

Monica remembered grandmamma's prayer and tried to encourage herself. "Okay, may I ask who is in that I can speak to regarding my case?"

"The best person to talk to is your caseworker," the receptionist replied. "She's the one that knows the most about the status of your children."

Monica shook her head. "I know my caseworker is the best person to talk to, but she doesn't seem to be available at the time and I really need to see someone today."

"What's your name?" the receptionist asked.

"Monica Gold."

"Let me see if we can get someone to talk with you, Ms. Gold."

"Thank you," Monica said, adding silently. Thank you, God.

The receptionist finally announced that another caseworker would be out shortly. "She says she's familiar with your case."

Monica thanked her again, as she sat. Twenty minutes later, a petite, young lady came from around the corner and introduced herself.

"Hi, my name is Brittany Gaines."

"Thank you so much for seeing me today, Brittany. I've been trying to get some answers to the questions I have about my kids for quite some time."

"Well, why don't you come this way so we can work on getting you those answers?" She smiled.

Monica followed her through the double doors. She seemed awfully young to be a caseworker, Monica thought. She was used to dealing with women like Ms. Dire—the unfriendly kind. She hoped this lady was sincere.

"Have a seat," Brittany said. "I'm sorry about the delay. I tried to go and pull your file, since you are Ms. Dire's primary client. I wasn't able to find it. Anyway, how can I help you today, Monica?" she said.

"I have been asking to see my children ever since they took them from me. Ms. Dire says she's going to schedule times for us to get together, but she never does. I haven't seen my girls in almost four months. Well, that's not exactly right. She did let me see my middle two girls, but only for an hour."

Monica knew she was rambling and tried a few calming techniques. It was no use—excitement took control.

"I need to know the status of my case. When is somebody going to let me see my girls? When will they tell me what the plans are for getting them back to me? I've done everything they've asked of me this time. I really have. I realized this was my last chance and the agency had an obligation to watch me closer than ever. I can assure you, if you would just talk to the people who know, they will tell you that I've changed. My children will never be in jeopardy again. The agency can monitor me from now on if they want to. Just give me my babies back."

"Whoa…slow down a bit," Brittany said laughing. "Let me make sure I understand what you're trying to say." The strings of her heart tugged a bit. Monica sounded sincere, but so did all the others. She'd witnessed cases, too numerous to count, where kids would go home to parents who vowed they'd changed, only to quickly resort back to the same old life style. It was always extremely painful to go back and take the kids dragging and screaming away from their parents again. That was part of the job she hated. So, whenever she could, she would always avoid those types of scenarios. Even though she hadn't been a social worker long, she understood the agency's policy of keeping children in a safe environment. Even if it meant they had to stay in foster homes.

"Now, let's start all over and tell me what you've done Monica, to turn things around? You know, so the agency can feel comfortable letting your children visit or even come back home to you."

Monica told her everything. She started with her new job, successful rehabilitation, a savings account, taking political science courses, obtaining a GED and even her experience with the Lord. This time, she spoke calmly. She didn't leave out how she'd moved in with her mother and grandmother, was saving towards buying a home, and how she no longer associated with her old friends. Although, she didn't bother to tell her that two of them were dead.

"Well, I must say, Monica, this all sounds quite impressive. It seems as if you've made tremendous progress. Surely, we should be able to let you at least visit your children if all of this is true. Is any of this documented—all the good changes you've experienced in your life?"

"Yes, I can prove everything. May I ask you a question, now Brittany?"

"Sure," she said, writing down her notes.

"Why don't you all know this about me? The agency should know whether or not I'm doing well, don't you think?"

Brittany looked up. "I'm sure Ms. Dire does. She probably has it all recorded in your file."

"No, I don't think so," Monica said. "She hasn't asked me anything lately about my progress or what my plans are. She's never asked whether I'm working or what my new friends at the rehabilitation center have to say about me. I've asked the people there if she came by to check on me. They all say she hasn't."

"If I could just find your file, Monica, I'd be able to tell you exactly where you stand. I promise, as soon as Ms. Dire gets back, I'll give her an update and check to see what she says about your case."

"Do you know when Ms. Dire will be back in the office?" Monica asked.

"When I checked, it says she's signed out for the rest of the day. She won't be back until tomorrow morning."

"Tomorrow is too late. I need to see Peaches today. I've got to see my child. Can you set that up for me?"

Brittany could see the tears forming in Monica's eyes. "Calm down. Everything is going to be all right," she said patting her arm. She didn't understand what it was, but something was telling her that this mother really was sincere.

"I guess it wouldn't hurt for you to visit with her if I'm in the room with you."

"Thank you, thank you, thank you!" Monica squealed. "You'll never know what this means to me."

"Let me see. I wrote down a few addresses of several cases I was working on when I moved to this office. I had so many... I just hope your Peaches was one of them."

Monica held her breath.

"I'm afraid, I don't see it. Wait, you're in luck. Here it is," she said holding up a card. "I remembered starting to write down your children's whereabouts, and got distracted. Thank God Peaches made the list. I'll call the foster parents and tell them I'm on my way to pick her up. You really picked a good day to see your child. They have a half day at school and Peaches should be at home."

Monica sat back in the chair and exhaled.

~~~

"Does Ms. Dire know about any of this?" Mr. Craft asked.

"No, she doesn't," Brittany said. "I am the secondary case worker assigned to this case. I will be coming to get her in the next thirty minutes. Mr. Craft, please have her ready."

That's odd, Brittany thought. It seemed as if he didn't want the mother to see the child. Foster parents generally understood this to be a temporary situation. They know the agency is doing everything in its power to get the child back home into a safe environment. Brittany also thought it strange that the entire file on Monica

Gold was missing. It was against the agency's policy to take them out of the office. If they weren't working on the record, they were not allowed to keep them anywhere but the file room.

She'd searched everywhere that files were supposed to be kept. She even looked on top of Ms. Dire's desk to see if was there.

"Monica, why don't you make yourself comfortable in our family area. I will be back with Peaches shortly."

When she arrived, Mr. Craft extended a cool greeting as she stood in the doorway.

"When will you bring the girl back?" he asked jingling the coins in his pocket.

"We'll be back in a couple of hours. Come on Peaches and go with Ms. Brittany," she said reaching for her hand. "You're going to see your mommy."

As they road along, Brittany looked in the rear view mirror at the pretty little girl that looked exactly like her mother. "Would you like me to stop and get you some ice cream, Peaches?"

"No thank you."

"You don't like ice cream?"

"I like ice cream very much. I just want to hurry and see my mommy."

Brittany smiled. Her gut was telling her she was doing the right thing.

When the doors swung open, Monica looked up. She stood, slowly. She'd waited so long to see her child. Now, the overwhelming emotions left her paralyzed.

Peaches ran and fell into her arms. Monica reached out and picked her up, squeezed tightly and buried her head into her face. She kissed her over and over again.

"I've missed you so much. Oh, Peaches... I'm sorry," she cried.

"Please come and take me home. Please, mommy." The tears fell as she rested her head on her mother's shoulder.

"I know...I know," Monica cried. They both held on tightly.

"Don't worry, mommy's trying really hard to come and get you," she said, finally composing herself. "See that nice lady over there." She pointed at Brittany. "She's going to help us, okay?"

"Okay, just hurry."

Brittany stood, her eyes blurry from her own tears. She knew deep in her heart, this mother really loved her child. If everything she said was true, this could be one of the agency's success stories. There weren't many they could celebrate, but obviously this was one in the making. Maybe Ms. Dire was finally slipping and had failed to keep up with the wonderful progress the mother was making. Brittany made up her mind right then and there she was going to help Ms. Dire with all the children involved. Never mind the debacle with Twin B.

"Excuse me, Monica," Brittany said once she thought it safe to interrupt. "I'll be in my office catching up on some paper work. Enjoy your baby."

"Thank you so much, Brittany." Monica actually stood up with Peaches in her arms and hugged Brittany all at the same time.

When Brittany came back to check on them, Peaches was still sitting in her mother's lap. They had no idea she was standing there. She could hear Monica asking about her school and friends. Monica told her all about the visit with her sisters.

"Your sisters aren't sick anymore. Isn't that great?"

"When can we see them mommy?"

"Soon, honey, real soon."

It seemed the hour went by so fast and Brittany knew they had much more to catch up on. She didn't have the heart to tell her it was almost time to go. She eased the door close.

Brittany sat quietly behind her desk tapping the pencil on her knee. Monica's case had generated a lot of questions. Where was her file? She needed to read it so she could make sense of what was going on. Rising from her desk, she headed to get some answers.

"Excuse me, sir, do you have a moment?" Brittany said walking into her supervisor's office.

"Come on in. I was just wrapping up my paper work."

"I have a quick question," Brittany said. "Do you recall one of Ms. Dire's cases involving Monica Gold?"

"Wait a minute. That name sounds familiar."

"Perhaps this might ring a bell. The missing twin."

"Oh, yes. How could I ever forget the missing twin?" He turned in his chair and shook his head. "Now, that's another sad case. The mother will probably lose all of her children this time."

"What's the problem with Ms. Gold," she asked trying everything in her power to remain calm.

"According to Ms. Dire's documentation, she's still running drugs, hanging out with the same old crowd, and may even be involved in a murder."

The hairs on Brittany's arm stood up. "Are you certain we're talking about the same young lady?"

"I'm very sure about this case. In fact, the agency has already been to court to begin the adoption procedures for two of her children - Twin A and… What's the other child's name? It sounds like a fruit."

"It wouldn't happen to be Peaches would it."

"Yes! That's it. Peaches! Those two will probably be adopted in a couple of weeks."

Brittany turned away. She knew the paleness in her face was evident.

"Thank you for your time," she said. She walked straight to where Monica sat.

"Quick," she said waving at her. "Let's go."

"What's wrong?" Monica asked as she held on to Peaches.

"We have to go somewhere where we can talk. I need to ask you more questions and I need you to tell me the truth, Ms. Gold. Do you understand?"

"I have been telling you the truth! What is wrong with you? I have nothing to hide?"

Brittany led them to her car and buckled Peaches into the booster seat. She turned up the radio to drown out her voice.

"Monica, please tell me that everything you've told me you've done to try and get your children back is true."

"I promise. *Everything* I've told you is true. Why do you doubt me? If you don't believe what I've told you, check it out for yourself. What did they say to you back there in that office?"

"I shouldn't be telling you this but I need answers, now. Were you involved in a murder?" she asked lowering her voice even further.

Monica looked at Brittany long and hard. *"A what!"*

"Sh-h-h. A murder, Monica. Were you involved in a man named Jay Jay's murder?"

"Oh, my God," Monica said. She told Brittany the whole story about going to meet Jay Jay and seeing him killed in front of her.

"I hadn't gotten out of the car when he was gunned down. I promise, Brittany! I'd just left church with my grandmamma when all of that happened." Then she told her all about Gail.

Brittany's head was spinning. It was all too confusing. What had she gotten herself in to? She wanted to believe this girl. She seemed so genuine, but she had no reason to doubt Ms. Dire, either.

"Let' go and drop Peaches off so you and I can talk."

When they pulled into the circular drive, Monica held Peaches closely once again.

"I want you to listen to me. I'm doing everything I know how to get you back home with me. I'm never going to stop trying to get you home as soon as I can. Do you understand mommy?"

"I can't go back in there... *please*."

"I know, honey," Monica said, stroking her hair. "Will you please be the big girl that I know you can? I'm going with Ms. Brittany now to try and work something out to get you home with me. I promise."

The Crafts were standing on the porch as they drove up. Peaches gripped her mother so tightly Brittany had to pry her fingers away. She tried consoling her but Peaches ran into the house, wailing.

Brittany felt it was just best to drive away. Monica buried her head and wept.

"Monica, everything is going to be all right."

"When, Brittany? When will anything ever be all right again," she sobbed. "That's my baby and they're not treating her well in that place. Look at her! She's thin, she's not doing well in school. She needs me."

"Did Peaches tell you she wasn't doing well in school?" Brittany asked.

"*Yes!* She said she's starting to make C's and she doesn't know why. Something about the man in the house making her feel strange. I tried to find out more, but she just wouldn't tell me. All I know is there's something wrong. You can tell it too. You've been trained to do that kind of stuff!"

Brittany had no comment. She didn't like Mr. Craft's behavior either but confessing that right then would have only made matters worse.

She tried changing the subject. "Monica, I have a lot of catching up to do with your case. If everything you say is true, then we have to figure out why Ms. Dire doesn't know these things. Then, we have to figure out how to get your kids home."

The diversion worked.

~~~

Sheila and Angela were on their third cup of coffee when Monica walked in. They immediately noticed her puffy, red streaked eyes.

"What happened?" they asked simultaneously.

Monica told them of her emotional visit and all about Brittany. "She seemed as if she wanted to find out the truth."

"What if she believes Ms. Dire?" Sheila asked.

"We'll cross that bridge when we get to it," Angela said. "For now, we have to concentrate on making certain that when she calls to check on Monica, the right person is there to answer all her questions. What about your job? Will your boss be available to talk to Brittany?"

"Oh, no," Monica said. "She's out of the country and I'm taking off for the next few days. Tanya is standing in for me. I wouldn't want her to answer any questions."

"Then you have to direct Brittany's call to someone else. Who can she talk to, Monica? Think!"

"She can talk to the president of the company. He will tell her what she needs to know. I'll arrange that."

"Good. Now, what about the people at the rehab center?" Angela asked.

"You don't have to worry about them. They're my friends," Monica boasted. "They are extremely proud of me. In fact, one of my counselors is a member of my church. She can vouch for me in both places."

"Call and warn them that an extremely important call is coming her way."

They sat for hours discussing what they thought might happen. All three were tired, yet had a growing sense of excitement about tomorrow.

Monica finally pulled up in front of her house. As usual, mamma had assumed her customary position. She was peeking out from behind the curtain.

# Chapter 20

## Pastor Collins

Pastor Collins agreed to meet with Gerald after church. He knew something was bothering him and wasn't surprised when he requested the meeting. Gerald was a gentle and caring man. He'd never heard anything but good things from other members in the congregation about him.

"Have a seat, Gerald," Pastor Collins said.

"No, I won't be staying long," he said. "Charlene and the baby are waiting for me."

"Have a seat." Pastor Collins placed his hand on his shoulder.

"My wife is taking Charlene home with her today. In fact they're on the way to the house, as we speak. She's made her a delicious meal and will drive her home later. When you asked to see me today, I thought we would need a little time to talk."

Gerald sat in the chair beside Pastor Collins.

"I don't know where to begin."

"Just start from the beginning," he said, coaxing him along.

"Pastor, what I'm about to tell you, I realize will be confidential."

"You know it is, Gerald. Hey, not only am I your pastor. I value our friendship. You can talk to me about anything."

He paused. "I'm not excited about the adoption. I believe it's because we're not going about it the traditional way and I don't know how to fix it. I don't want to take something that precious from someone without knowing it's all legitimate and right." He suddenly felt extremely tired. A wave of guilt washed over him as he told the details of the adoption.

After he'd finished, hesitating, he glanced up to take in his pastor's reaction. The tension in his shoulders disappeared when he saw a look filled with compassion on his face.

"I need your help."

"I know. Listen man, let me first talk to you as your pastor. Then, I want to talk to you as a friend. I'm going to tell you exactly what I know you need to hear. I won't hold back. Everything you do must be done in a manner that will allow you to sleep well at night. Even if we sometimes veer outside the boundaries of common sense, God's grace reaches out and pulls us back in. Let me remind you of a story I'm sure you're familiar with. It goes something like this… "In II Samuel, Nathan the prophet came and told David the story about a rich man and a poor man. The rich man owned plenty of sheep while the poor man had only one small ewe lamb that he cherished and raised from birth. For the sacrifice, the rich man offered the poor man's lamb."

Gerald knew the story well.

"Put yourself in David's place. You're right. You can't take something that precious away from someone and rest well at night. Remember how David felt when he was confronted with what he'd done? "

Gerald kept his head down.

"Talk to me," Pastor Collins said. "Man to man, we have to tell each other the truth. As your friend I'm obligated to do that. You're going to have to tell Charlene how you feel."

Gerald finally spoke. "I've tried to. She just won't listen."

"Have you sat her down and told her anyway?"

"Well, not exactly," he acknowledged.

"You owe Charlene that. You love her and she deserves to know the position you believe this is placing the two of you in."

Gerald knew Pastor Collins was right and wasn't surprised at the advice he'd given.

"You know what? I'm going home to talk with Charlene, right now."

"Why don't we go and grab something to eat before you do that," Pastor Collins said reaching for his jacket. "The women have probably finished eating by now."

"Sounds like a good idea. Maybe talking it out a little more will help."

Gerald arrived home just as Charlene was about to give the baby a bath.

"Hi, honey." She turned kissing him.

"Andrea told me that you and Pastor Collins had some business to take care of. It was so nice of her to invite Geraldene and me to dinner. After we ate, we sat and chatted for a while. Mommy stuff of course. We haven't been home too long. Did you get any supper?"

"Pastor Collins and I went to grab a bite to eat." He paused. Then he forced it out. "Charlene, I need to talk to you about something."

"Is everything okay?" She smiled.

"Everything's fine. We just need to talk." Why did she have the face of an angel, he thought.

"Okay, I'll put Geraldene to bed and make us some tea."

"That sounds good. Let me get out of these clothes."

He was trying to stay upbeat but didn't know if he could manage to keep it up. His insides were in knots. It had been helpful talking things over with Pastor Collins at dinner. He had a feeling what he was about to say, was going to change their lives forever.

He replayed over and over the kind remarks Pastor Collins had said earlier. He called Charlene, a good woman. *"Once you talk to her Gerald, she will understand that you should go about adopting Geraldene the right way."*

He hoped Pastor Collins was right. He loosened his tie and breathed in deeply.

"Honey, the tea is ready," she called from the kitchen.

"Here goes."

He watched as she poured him a cup of the herbal brew, gently resting the porcelain tea pot down.

"Now, what do we need to talk about?" she asked.

He never would have blurted out his next statement if he hadn't been so nervous. "Charlene, it's the way we're going about adopting Geraldine."

As soon as he said those words, the frown appeared slowly replacing her happy demeanor.

"What about the adoption, Gerald?"

"We need to reconsider this whole adoption thing. I'd like for us to try and go about it in a completely different way. The right way."

"We are going about it the right way."

He heard the tension in her voice.

"I don't understand what you are talking about. We've come so close, please don't go ruining everything."

Gerald took a deep breath and reached for her hand. She pulled away. He didn't let that bother him. He continued.

"Charlene, I know this is difficult because it's hard for me, but you must listen to what I have to say. We can't adopt Geraldene this way. We need to hire an attorney and go through the biological mother. Carolyn is one of our best friends. She'll be glad to take the case."

"Ms. Dire or Carolyn, what's the difference? Ms. Dire is taking care of the legal part. Anyway, it's quite simple. We're dealing with an unfit mother and she doesn't want the baby for goodness sake. This is not as complicated as you're making this all out to be."

"Think about it," he said. "If it were that easy, why are we having to pay the amount of money we're dishing out?"

"Is that what this is all about Gerald? Money? We'd be paying Carolyn that amount or more! This is crazy! Ms Dire is helping us avoid all the bureaucracy to get Geraldene to us. Don't you see, honey. You're putting too much into this adoption thing," Charlene pleaded. "Let's just allow Ms. Dire to do her job, please."

"No, Charlene. We need to make certain everything is legal about the adoption. We'll let Ms. Dire keep the money and use our own attorney the rest of the way. Then we can make certain that everything is done the way it should be."

"Gerald, I can't believe you're doing this," Charlene said tearfully. "We're weeks away from getting Geraldene forever and now you're about to ruin it."

"How can I ruin it, Charlene? If everything is the way it should be, we'll get Geraldene anyway."

"What if it isn't? Then what, Gerald?"

"Are you worried too," he asked softly. He knew it was a question she wasn't prepared to answer.

"Tell me, why you don't want to go about it the way I've suggested?" Gerald asked. He tried to control the edginess now evident in his own voice.

"Well, because, I think…" she shook her head. "No. I don't know why. I just don't want to start all over."

"I'm not asking us to start all over, Charlene. I'm asking that we let Ms. Dire know we can handle it from here. Let her move on and help other clients. Then we can get Carolyn involved and adopt Geraldene the right way"

She sat completely still, her eyes focused downward. Gerald didn't know if he'd gotten through or not. He tried getting her to look up so he could at least get a feel for what she was thinking. "Charlene, talk to me, baby."

She slowly lifted her head. Her thoughts were clear when he stared into her eyes.

He'd lost.

"Gerald. Humph," she said with a smirk. "I will not allow you to do this to me."

He strained to hear when she spoke.

"You and nobody else will take Geraldene from me. I'll do whatever I have to do to keep my baby. I hope you understand that?" She stood and walked away.

The look in her eyes set off an alarm. One of defiance mixed with anger—a look he'd not seen before. He was thoroughly convinced Charlene would stop at nothing to officially make Geraldene their child. The next morning was proof.

The clock's ringer buzzed at its usual time and Charlene was nowhere to be found.

At his wits end, he decided to phone Pastor Collins. "I hate to be a nuisance, but have you or Andrea seen Charlene?"

"No, we haven't. What's wrong?"

"I woke up around six this morning and she wasn't in bed. I can't remember her getting up during the night. She took the baby with her."

Pastor Collins looked at the clock. It was ten a.m.

"She usually lets me know everywhere she goes. I've called her parents and several close friends, but they haven't seen her either. I'm worried because of how things ended last night," he said, his voice dropping.

"You want to tell me how things ended, Gerald?"

"After I brought up the subject about the adoption, I wasn't expecting her to get that upset. So much so, I eventually told her I would back off and let her have it her way. I'd never seen her quite like that. She kept saying, she couldn't trust me anymore."

Pastor Collins felt guilty. He thought he knew Charlene better and actually believed she would come around to Gerald's point of view.

"Do you think you need to call the police?"

"Not yet. I believe she's gone somewhere to cool off and think things over. Her clothes are still there and so are the baby's."

"That's good news. I'm on my way over."

When he hung up, Gerald paced the entire length of the long den floor. Charlene's behavior had him concerned. After their discussion last night, she left the table and sat in the den until two in the morning. He had tried convincing her to come to bed, but she sat there with her arms folded like a spoiled child. He was still awake when she finally came into the bedroom around three. He guessed he'd slept so hard, he didn't hear her when she left.

What had he done? He would never forgive himself if upsetting her about the adoption caused them harm. His wife and baby were the most important people in his life.

The phone rang and he answered it seconds into the ring. He was disappointed. It was his secretary. About twenty minutes later, Pastor Collins arrived.

"Have you heard from her?"

"Not yet. Thanks for coming over."

"I couldn't keep this away from Andrea. She sensed something was wrong so I told her we'd talk about it later."

"That's okay," Gerald said. "She and Charlene have become pretty close and she may have confided in her anyway."

"Why don't you try her cell phone one more time, Gerald?"

He sped dialed her number and the phone rang and rang.

"She always answers her cell phone," Gerald said.

"Try this," Pastor Collins said. "Check to see if she used an ATM today."

"Good one."

The latest transaction was at six-thirty-eight this morning, at a bank not too far from their home.

~~~

Charlene headed north. She didn't know exactly where she was going but knew she had to get as far away from Gerald as possible. About fifty miles outside of the city, she drove into a Hilton and checked into a suite. Later that morning she went shopping. Returning back to the hotel, she showered and put on her new suit. While the baby napped, she had the opportunity to think about the mind-boggling conversation she'd had with her husband. The thought of it made her angry all over again.

*Gerald.* She wondered why she even married him in the first place. He wasn't her type but she knew he would be an excellent provider. They'd met their junior year in college and she'd only gone out with him to make her old boyfriend jealous. When he showered her with dinner, gifts, and expensive jewelry, she started to like having him around. In the spring of the year when they married, it didn't take long for her to recognize that something was missing in their relationship. A couple of marital counseling sessions later, she felt better. Shortly after that, she began telling Gerald she wanted to have a baby. Even though he wasn't ready, it didn't take too much to convince him how happy it would make her. As the months passed and they'd had no success, she all but panicked. When the months turned into years and still no baby, Gerald took her to the islands to help take her mind off it all. When they returned, as fate would have it, she met Ms. Dire and agreed to become a foster mom. Then Geraldene came along and Ms. Dire came up with the idea of them adopting her. The money she'd suggested they give her initially came as a surprise, but it had all been worth it.

Charlene knew she could always get Gerald to do exactly what she wanted. So persuading him to get involved with Ms. Dire's plan, even the money had been easy. The only thing he had ever managed to get her to go along with since their marriage was to join his church. Although, that didn't take much convincing, she really enjoyed going there. The people were very nice and when Geraldene came, she finally felt as if she truly fit in.

She closed her eyes and relaxed on the King sized bed. It was going to be a long day. A quiet and peaceful one for her.

Later that afternoon she decided enough time had passed. He'd probably worried enough, she thought. She picked up the phone and called him.

"Gerald, please don't talk. Don't say a word."

She spoke so softly he had to strain to listen. He on the other hand, wanted to yell and tell her to come home… how worried he was… how much he loved her, but he sat quietly.

"I am thinking about leaving and taking Geraldene with me to start our lives over again. Just the two of us. I don't really want to do that but I feel you've given me little choice."

He tried to speak, but she'd threatened to hang up if he did.

"You did all the talking last night so now it's my turn to tell you exactly how I feel. I will never let anyone take my baby away from me. I hope you understand that? There will be no more discussion about whose child Geraldene is."

With the long pause, he felt it was safe to speak. "Okay. I understand. Just come home."

"I can't come back to you unless I think it's safe to do so, Gerald. You must promise me that you'll never bring up the adoption in that manner again."

"Charlene, please come home. You'll never have to worry about that."

"Promise me, Gerald?"

"I promise."

"Thank you, darling. I love you very much. I knew you would finally see things my way. Everything is going to be fine. You'll see. We have each other, and most of all we have our Geraldene. I'm on my way home."

"Drive safely, Charlene. It's getting dark," he said. When he hung up, he looked at Pastor Collins and shook his head.

Pastor Collins thought it wise to give Gerald some space. He went into the kitchen and grabbed them both a bottle of water. He had a lot of experience counseling his parishioners but this case caused him great concern. His friend could potentially be involved in something illegal. Later, he walked up to Gerald, watching him as he held his head down. "Tell me what you're thinking," Pastor Collins said.

"Do you really want to know?" he said, looking up. "Man, I'm thinking of throwing it all away. Possibly, walking out and never looking back. I don't know what to do about Charlene. I'm going to be miserable with or without her. If I stay with her, I can't let her go on with the adoption this way. If I try and stop her, she's going to leave me. You see, it truly is a no win situation."

"I understand what you must be feeling but you can't run away from trouble," Pastor Collins said. "I know this is difficult but you're going to have to do what's right. You must face this challenge like all others and that's with every bit of integrity and courage that you have."

"I promised her I wouldn't bring up the adoption again. I just wanted her home."

Pastor Collins sat quietly. "As head of your home, you have to make a decision about what it is, you really want."

"I want a lot of things," Gerald said. "I want to go about adopting the baby the right way. I want Charlene happy. I want Geraldene as my daughter so that I can give her a loving home. Most of all, I want all of this to be over."

"Gerald."

"Yes."

"What does God want?"

~ ~ ~

Gerald was relieved when he saw the black Range Rover pull into the garage. He stood in the door to greet them.

Humming and swinging the shopping bags, Charlene swished past him pecking him on the lips as she went inside.

Unbuckling and taking Geraldene out of the Whinny the Pooh car seat, he gently kissed the sleeping baby on her tiny cheek. He was glad Pastor Collins left before Charlene arrived. They needed to be alone to sort things out.

"Are you hungry?" Charlene asked, placing the bags on the counter.

He watched as she bustled around the kitchen, admiring the fresh sea bass she liberally coated with her special seasoning. What was she thinking? She'd been missing for over twelve hours. They were involved in something that could potentially send them both to jail and she was cooking fish!

He walked into the den to answer the ringing phone. He picked it up and over-heard Charlene say, "Oh, hi, mom."

"Did you find your keys?" her mother asked. He'd forgotten to tell Charlene that when he called her parents, he used missing keys as his excuse to track her down.

"Gerald didn't tell me his keys were missing," Charlene said.

"That's odd. Where did you go all day? I called you a couple of times and Gerald said you weren't home," her mother said.

"I've been shopping and now I'm fixing Gerald's dinner."

Gerald continued listening.

"Is everything all right over there, Charlene?"

"What in the world could be wrong, mother?"

"I don't know. Sometimes I get a strange feeling you're not telling me everything."

"Gerald, Geraldene and I are all as happy as we could ever be. Why don't you and dad come over for dinner and see for yourself? I'm preparing more than enough for all of us."

"No thanks. I just finished cooking for your dad and me."

As Gerald hung up the phone, all his fears were confirmed. Charlene was acting as if she truly believed nothing was wrong.

The aroma from the fish penetrated the den where he sat alone. Charlene walked in.

"Honey, I missed you so much today," she said.

She curled up in his lap.

"I really do love you and I'm glad we've agreed to never bring up the adoption in that way again. You and Geraldene are my life and I would do anything for the two of you. Thank you for making me so happy and being the best husband a wife could ever have."

Gerald looked at his wife and knew he could never hurt her. If adopting Geraldene was the only thing he had to do to keep her happy, then he'd have to do that. He vowed to himself he would never bring up the adoption again.

~~~

Pastor Collins was concerned. He'd waited on Gerald to call and let him know how things turned out with Charlene and the baby. The phone call never came. When he saw them the following afternoon at Bible study, he and Charlene were all smiles. As he chatted with several of his parishioners, he kept Gerald in sight. Finally, getting his attention, he motioned to him. If Pastor Collins hadn't felt he knew Gerald better, he could have sworn he was trying to avoid him. He made his way across several pews.

"Hi partner, how are things?"

"Hey there, Pastor," Gerald said, squeezing Charlene, his arm wrapped tightly around her waist. "I've been meaning to get back with you from the other day. You know how hectic things can get. I really got tied up at work."

"I understand." He looked at Charlene, and smiled.

"All is well. Charlene and I really enjoyed Bible study tonight. Didn't we honey?"

"We always enjoy Pastor's teachings," she acknowledged.

Gerald fiddled with his tie. "Well, it's time for us to get going. We need to put the little one to bed."

"All right, Gerald. You guys be blessed." He watched as they walked away, arm in arm.

When the church was empty, Pastor Collins sat on the bench alongside his wife as she played the last chorus of *Amazing Grace* on the newly purchased organ.

"Andrea, did Charlene seem a little strange tonight?"

"No, in fact, she seemed happier than ever. She did mention that they wanted us to be there next week when they go to court for the adoption. After this court appearance, they only need to meet the judge in his chambers to sign the final papers. Gerald even seemed happier to me than usual."

"I know," Pastor Collins said. "That's what has me so concerned."

"What do you mean?"

"Has Charlene shared with you anything about the adoption?"

She looked puzzled. "Does this have anything to do with the day she went missing? What's going on, honey?"

"Gerald and Charlene have gone around the traditional adoption process," he explained. "They're supposedly paying a social worker to bypass all the bureaucracy."

"Is there something wrong with that? I mean, it is okay to do it that way, isn't it?" she asked.

"I think Gerald has some concerns. I wanted a legal opinion, so I asked Mark about it. He said the only way a person can legally get around the bureaucracy of any adoption would be through an attorney. Even with an attorney's involvement, they could bypass some of the paper work but they would still have to involve the adoption agency or biological parents. I know Gerald and Charlene are not dealing with an attorney but conducting all their business with a social worker."

"Have you spoken to Gerald about any of this?" she asked.

"I've tried. I really have. Just last night he was torn to pieces by it all. Now, today he's fine. I'm confused. We need to pray for them, Andrea. I think what they're doing is against the law. If it is, I can't just sit back and let them do that."

# Chapter 21

## Pull the String

Ms Dire was glad that she came into work early. She immediately noticed the yellow sticky note attached to her office door. It read... *Ms. Dire, one of your clients, Ms. Monica Gold, came by to see you to get an update on her case. I attempted to find her file but was unable to locate it. She gave me a brief report of her progress and I was really impressed. When you get a moment, please give me the file so that I can document what I've learned from her. I will also validate what she told me so that we can make certain that her progress is authenticated. Thanks. Brittany.*

She tore the note into shreds and threw it hard into the trash. Brittany had no business interfering, she thought. After all the trouble she'd caused with twin B, that she was responsible for straightening out, she should stay as far away from this case as possible.

"Ms. Prater, I mean, Ms. Gains, I need to talk with you before you go out this morning."

"Oh, hi, Ms. Dire. Did you get my note?"

"Yes, I did and I must say you have obviously been duped by Ms. Gold, like we all have at one time or another. She's really convincing, isn't she? I can understand why you would want to validate what she's saying. Let me save you the legwork on this girl. All the secondary caseworkers assigned to her case have had the same experience. Here's what she does time after time. She'll get herself together and stay away from drugs for about two weeks. That's when she'll come hanging around the office. We buy into this, I've gotten my act together this time for real routine. We let her see the children and they all cry like babies when they see each other. Then the next week, we don't hear from her and she's right back out there doing drugs again and hanging around her same old druggie friends. Do you know how hard that must be on her children? Sometimes I believe she really is sincere but she just can't stay away from the drugs. It's such a sad case, Brittany. I think if she would go away, perhaps leave the city, she may have a better chance. You can go ahead and look into Ms. Gold's case if you want to, but you'll find what I'm saying is true. Besides, I've been doing this line of work at least three times longer than you. I can tell you how it's all going to end up each time."

She wanted to believe Ms. Dire. She'd always been so conscientious about her work and never had anything but the highest praise from everyone.

"Well, Ms. Dire, I guess Ms. Gold fooled me as well. She should have gotten an Oscar for her performance when she saw her child."

"What do you mean, when she saw her child?"

"I forgot to mention that I went and got her oldest daughter so she could at least see her. I know you can understand why I did that, Ms. Dire. My goodness, she was quite convincing."

"That's okay, Brittany. You'll get used to that kind of behavior. In the mean time, I'll make certain everything is taken care of and documented appropriately in the file."

"By the way, where is her file? I couldn't find it," Brittany asked.

"It's in the file room. Maybe you over looked it." Ms
Dire actually stared at her as if she didn't understand why
she'd even asked such a foolish question.

Brittany spoke slowly. "Perhaps I did. I'll see you
later and thanks for the update on Ms. Gold."

Brittany was deeply concerned. She knew the record
had not been in the file room. She'd searched that room
from top to bottom. Something else troubled her. If
Monica hung around the office like she said, the receptionist would have known her. Judy had manned that
desk for well over fifteen years and knew the cases better
than the caseworkers did. When she came to find
someone to see Ms. Gold, she described her as a young
lady she'd never met before. Something wasn't adding up
and she was about to find out what it was. In the morning her first stop would be the rehabilitation center where
Monica had been. If they didn't give a favorable report,
she would stop and note that Ms. Dire had been right as
usual. If not, then her investigation would have only just
begun.

~~~

It was bright and early the next morning, Brittany
headed for *A Healthy Place*. Monica was her priority case
for the day.

"Good morning," Brittany said as she introduced herself to the receptionist. She displayed her ID and asked
to see the counselor in charge of Monica's case.

The receptionist was happy to see her. Monica had
forewarned them that Brittany would be coming by to get
an update on her progress.

"Come this way, Ms. Gaines. Ms. Elkridge will see
you now."

"Monica is one of our shining stars," Ms Elkridge said beaming with pride. "When she first came to the center, she was a total wreck and we had our doubts about her even making it. However, she had a motivation that many of our clients don't have. Monica has a strong and sincere love for her children. She wanted them back home with her in the worst way. The counselors used that to help keep her focused. When things would get rough for her in here, all we had to say, "I guess you don't want your children back." Those words could make that young lady do anything we wanted her to do. We were wondering why no one from your agency had been around so we could tell them all of this."

"Ms. Dire hasn't been here at all to check on Monica's progress?" Brittany asked.

She shook her head. "The last time we saw Ms. Dire was when she checked her into the facility. We haven't seen a caseworker since. You're the first to come by. Anyway, Monica is doing very well. I'm proud to say she is now one of our group leaders, occasionally accompanying us on speaking engagements. The second month Monica was in rehab, she found herself a job. It's a very nice position I might add. We didn't have to help her find employment, or convince her that she needed to work. She went out there and made it happen for herself. The last point I'd like to make is that Monica goes to the same church as one of our counselors. She sees her there each Sunday with her mother and grandmother. Those two women are very strong influences in her life. I know this is a lot to update you on, but I feel obligated to let you know everything. Especially since this is the first time we've been able to report it all."

Brittany walked slowly to her car. A sickening feeling rumbled inside. She could smell the rancid odor of misconduct looming in the air. She had been thrown into something that wasn't right and now it was resting on her shoulders to figure out what it was. Whatever Ms. Dire was doing, Brittany knew she couldn't be trusted with the welfare of children.

After speaking with Monica's employer and receiving another glowing report, Brittany sat alone in a nearby restaurant. She needed time to think. All that Monica told her was true and nothing about Ms. Dire's report added up. What was she up to?

The longer she sat, the more things began to unravel. The neon signs of questionable behavior flashed all over the place. Even though she had been assigned as the secondary caseworker, Ms. Dire always insisted that she never needed her help with this case. When actually, she was extremely overloaded and really did need her assistance. That's how she got involved in the first place. The hospital had called for the third time about needing someone to discharge Monica's baby. She ended up squeezing the case into her list of files for the day. Then the mix up happened. Once all the controversy began swirling around about the missing twin, Ms. Dire became the only one with access to the records.

Suddenly, Brittany felt a tremendous sense of guilt. Had she been so clueless that she'd missed many of the obvious signs? If so, she was just as much at fault for all that was happening to Monica as Ms. Dire was. How could she have been so naïve, she thought. The complex child protective system had her frustrated. She was disheartened by the number of cases where she discovered irresponsible adults and neighbors, who sat back and watched child abuse take place and never reported it. It had to stop, she thought. Now, her fellow caseworkers were complicating matters also. Well, it may be too late to do anything about the past she thought, but it certainly wasn't too late to help Monica create a better future. She just had to figure out how.

She knew she was no match for a woman who knew the system like the back of her hand and everybody in the city seemed to trust. Ms. Dire had been in and out of court so much with custody cases, she was on a first name basis with many of the judges and attorneys. She was invited to all the influential Christmas parties hosted by high ranking governmental officials and she definitely made her rounds. Although, she wasn't necessarily friendly in the office, she still got along with everyone. It was just quietly understood that she ran things around there. She was very helpful to the new caseworkers and gave great advice. She was definitely admired.

Then, there was her own personal track record. Being as checkered as it was, who would ever believe her story? To further complicate matters, she hadn't been there long enough to know who she could trust.

Perhaps the only person she could trust at this point was Monica. If that was the case, she needed to start taking action immediately.

"Hello, Monica? This is Brittany Gaines your caseworker. I need to speak with you as soon I can." She spoke softly into her cell phone. The restaurant's tables were too close and she didn't know who might be listening.

"I figured you would come to that conclusion," Monica replied. "There's something strange going on about my case, isn't it?"

"Can you meet me somewhere?  I'd prefer not to talk over the phone," Brittany whispered.

After she gave Monica directions, she left the restaurant and headed to the office.

She went to find her file.

~~~

"Are you certain the file is missing, Brittany?" Robert asked closing the door.  He understood what a serious offence that was.

"Yes, I've searched everywhere for that record and I can't find it."

"You, didn't lose it did you?"

"No-o-o.   Ms. Dire had Ms. Gold's file."  She kept her voice low.

"Let's go to the file room one more time to make certain that it hasn't mysteriously returned," he said.

They searched everywhere the record should have been.

"See, I told you… nothing."

"You need to get the supervisor in on this one," Robert suggested.  "Larry doesn't need to be kept in the dark about it."

She knew he was right.  She would eventually tell Larry, but had a few other things to settle first.  She headed out to meet Monica.

~~~

"You have a very nice place," Monica said.

"Thanks.   Come on into the sunroom, I've made us some sandwiches."

Brittany couldn't think of a safer place to meet, so, her condo had to do.   She didn't know how she was going to tell Monica all that she'd discovered.  Surprisingly, she didn't have to.

"You have a problem in your agency, Brittany," Monica said biting into her sandwich. "Ms Dire is up to no good. The only thing I can think she could possibly want from me are my girls. Why would a caseworker, someone who's supposed to protect my children, hurt them? I don't understand."

"I wish I could give you some answers. Perhaps once I find your file, I'll be able to. I may even be able to dispute what's in it if necessary. We need to think about what our next move should be."

They continued eating—mostly, in silence.

"Brittany! We have the solution right in our hands," Monica said wiping her mouth with the floral napkin. "You can't find my file, right?"

"Yes..."

"That's it! You don't need that file. I'll bet it's full of lies anyway. What if you started a file? A new one. Only this time, you'll write all that I've been telling you in it."

"Hmmm... You might be onto something. So, when they request your record, I'd be there to make certain I give them the right one!"

Monica threw her hands in the air, twirling around.

Chewing the last bite of her sandwich, Brittany smiled.

"We have a lot of work to do," she said. "Let's get started. I don't want to forget any of the wonderful things you've done."

The next day, Brittany was concentrating so hard on Monica's new file she didn't notice Ms Dire standing in her office door.

Glimpsing up, she jumped. "Ms. Dire, how may I help you?" She eased the record closed.

"I didn't mean to startle you, but I heard you've been looking for a missing file. Mr. Washington told me about it."

*She could have killed Robert.* She wasn't ready for her to know about the missing file just yet.

"I've been so busy with this case, the missing twin and all, I may have had the file with me the day you searched," Ms. Dire explained. "I know that's against the policy and I'm truly sorry but due to the extreme set of circumstances, I felt it would be all right this time. Here, jot down your notes," she said, handing her a blank intervention form. "I'll get it later and put it in her file."

"Thanks," Brittany said, reaching for the form. As usual, she was thoroughly convincing.

"I'll be here until six," Ms. Dire said, turning and walking swiftly down the hall.

Brittany took the empty sheet and documented exactly what she was writing in the new record. When she finished, she took it to Ms. Dire's office. This time, Ms. Dire didn't realize she was standing there. She took that opportunity to gaze over her shoulder. It was definitely Monica's file. She fought an intense urge to snatch it right out of her hands.

Patience, Brittany. Patience, she thought.

She went back to her office and continued working on the new file. She was determined to stay longer than Ms Dire to see if she would place the original file back where it belonged.

Seven 'o clock came and the shadow of Ms. Dire's office light shone into the hall. Brittany watched the clock. She had already written the last line in Monica's new file several hours ago.

At last, she saw the light in Ms. Dire's office go out. She listened as the door clicked close, her footsteps fading. When she knew she was alone, she gently pushed her chair back and eased out from behind the desk.

The entire office was dimly lit. The old building creaked as the wind blew. Brittany never liked being the last to leave. It had been well known that security extricated vagrants who'd made themselves homes in the crevasses of the building's basement. It definitely wasn't a place to be left alone late at night. It didn't matter Brittany thought, she had to go to the file room.

The heels on her shoes clicked along the hall making way too much noise. She didn't want anyone hearing her that shouldn't have, so she tip-toed the rest of the way. Slowly turning the knob, she entered the massive room lined with metal cabinets. She'd always been easily spooked and the large creepy room did little to help. She immediately went to work, heading for the section highlighted, GA-GO. Opening the drawer, she thumbed through the alphabetized files until she reached, Gold. Again, no file. Maybe it was best to come back in the morning. The large room made her uneasy.

She turned to leave when suddenly, she froze. Were those footsteps? She stood completely still as she strained to listen. Those were footsteps and whoever it was, was heading her way! She knew when she left for the file room, the office was empty. Skirting across the room she pressed in between two large metal cabinets. Holding her breath, she listened as the hinges of the door squeaked open. She watched the shadow fill the room—catching occasional glimpses of the silhouette moving towards the files along the walls. Clutching her purse to her chest, the muscles in her neck twitched. She knew it was too late to make her presence known without a confrontation. She eyed a door that led to the outer hall. Counting to three, she dashed through it accidentally bumping its side, causing it to sway back and forth. Racing down the hall, she never looked back, not even to see if the shadow in the room was following.

# Chapter 22

## Trapped

Joy always walked home from school the same way. Myles had to talk to one of his teachers and said he would catch up with her later. She slowed and turned as the strange looking man followed. She noticed him the moment she left campus. Picking up her pace, she darted into a convenience store. Browsing the aisles, she picked up a bag of chips and paid for them. Peeking outside, good, she thought. He was gone. She stepped out with a sigh of relief. While opening the bag of chips, she looked up and spotted the same thin man staring at her.

Poised to run, she heard Myles call out. "Hey Joy, wait up!"

"I think that man is following me," she said rushing to him. When she tried pointing the stranger out, he'd disappeared.

"*Where*?" Myles looked up and down the street.

"Come on. Maybe it was all my imagination," she said pushing him along. "Let's just get out of here,"

Myles always had a way of making her laugh. By the time they'd walked home, she'd forgotten all about the stranger. She ran ahead, grabbing his cap, placing it on her head. He caught up with her and tickled her until she gushed. "Stop it," she laughed.

Seconds later, her eyes grew large.

"There he is!"

Myles jumped off the porch, barely missing the banister and headed straight for the guy.

"No-oo, Myles!  Come back."

"What's all the noise about?" Grandmamma said, almost stumbling as she reached the door.

When Joy told her, she dialed 911.

Yeah, right, Joy thought.  She knew better.  The police would always promise to come into their neighborhood and never show up.  That's exactly what happened.

Joy paced back and forth on the sidewalk.

"Come up closer to the house honey, it may not be safe out there," grandmamma called to her.

Joy walked slowly to the house when the phone rang. She raced to answer it.

"It's me.  I lost him," Myles said panting.  "I chased him pretty far.  I'm going on home from here.  I'll call you when I get there.  From now on, you don't need to walk home by yourself."

She knew he was right.  She was used to all the drama in Monica's, life, but never thought it would spill over into her own.

When Monica drove up, she panicked when she saw both Grandmamma and Joy standing in the door.  She ran inside praying all was well.

Joy told her what happened as she paced back and forth.

"Did you recognize him at all?" Monica asked.

"I've never seen him before in my life.  He was weird and looked totally scary."

When mamma came home, she repeated the story.

"That's it!  From now on, we'll be picking you up from school," mamma said.  "This neighborhood is worse than it's ever been."  So, she mapped out a schedule of the days she would be picking Joy up.  That did little to calm her, though. She knew having only one car was still a problem, and the tires on it were wearing thin.

Once they'd all gathered around the dinner table, Monica felt it was time to share her news.

"There's something I think all of you should know," she said. "Brittany has finally figured out that Ms. Dire and her plans have corruption written all over it."

"Do you think you can even trust Brittany?" mamma asked. "Ms. Dire seems to be such a loser. I'm beginning to think they're all crooked down there at that agency."

"Relax mamma. Brittany's going to help us," Monica said. "The one thing I do know for sure is that Ms Dire is not on our side. She's trying desperately to make everyone believe that I'm an unfit mother."

"I think it's bigger than even that," Joy spoke softly.

Her response was unexpected and took them all by surprise. She'd never freely expressed her thoughts before and when she did, she had their undivided attention.

"They have the power and authority to take your girls away from you Monica and they're doing just that," she said. "If something doesn't happen real soon, we will all lose. You, your daughters, I'll lose my nieces and you two, your granddaughters."

~~~

"Miss G-A-I-L, is that you?"

"Who is this?" she snapped.

"It's me-e-e, Cray!" he said gasping for air.

"What have I told you about calling me on my cell phone, boy?"

"Whoa… who you calling bo-o-oy, baby cakes?"

"*Look*, tell me what you have for me, Cray."

"He-e-e-y, I followed the pigeon today."

"Oh, you did? What happened?"

"N-o-ow... you want to talk to ba-a-a-d boy, Cray, don't ya?"

"Don't give me that crap Cray, just talk to me. If you want your money, you'd better talk up."

"Okay, ok-k-kay. I followed her home, Miss Gail, but some guy spo-o-tted me. Started chasing me-e-e and everything. Hey, but you know 'ole Cray's just too-o-o fast for any young buck to try and run down. I shook him like this and I ditched him like, tha-a-at...you know wha-a-a-t I mean?"

"Right, Cray, like I can see you with my x-ray vision right through the phone."

"Go-o-d, Miss Gail. Now, when I sho-o-ok him off, Ka-POW, ba-a-ad boy Cray came and called you. What you got to-o-o say about that Lady G!"

Gail hated dealing with Cray. She knew he was one of the sharpest and trickiest heroin addicts around and that's why she solicited his help. He would do anything for drugs.

"Will you be able to do what we talked about, Cray?" Gail asked.

"It's as good as done. I know exactly what ba-a-ad boy Cray has to do. I'm going to get her to ..."

"Are you crazy! You know better than to talk like that on my cell phone," she shouted.

"O-o-o-h, no you didn't just call ba-a-ad boy, crazy? I can't work with that la-a-ady G."

Gail knew she had to treat him better. Ever since she'd been back on her feet again, it seemed she was growing more and more impatient with normal people, let alone nuts like Cray. She was ready for it all to be over.

She took a deep breath. "I'm sorry, Cray. I didn't mean to upset you. I won't call you that again."

He took a deep breath. "You're such a sweet la-a-ady. What about you and me-e-e going out some times? I think you'll like ole, ba-a-a-d boy Cray."

"Let's talk about that at another time, Cray, can we?" At that point, she was tapping her foot almost uncontrollably.

Gail didn't know if she was going to be able to deal with Cray much longer. This time, her plan for Monica had to work.

# Chapter 23

## Brittany

The offices were vacant as Brittany entered the building. She'd gotten there early, to give herself enough time to search for Monica's file. It had to be there. She just needed to figure out where. Ms Dire was way too smart to take the file off the premises. She headed back to the file room, a much safer place in the day time. Again, she searched the boxes and shelves and every file cabinet. Nothing.

What if she filed it under "M" instead of "G"? That would be the perfect excuse for misplacing it if she were ever questioned. She looked under the "M's" and again, no luck. Ms Dire was foolish enough to take the file with her. Turning to leave, she eyed something resembling an old wooden cabinet resting in the corner. It was almost completely covered with dusty artificial plants, a box of old Christmas decorations and other office junk someone perhaps believed would be useful some day.

Brittany pushed the clutter aside and opened the rusty, file cabinet. She blew the dust from the aging files. Immediately, she flipped until she reached the "G's".

It was time to call it quits, she thought. The file wasn't there. She didn't know what her next move should be. Casually, almost absent-mindedly, she thumbed until she reached the "M's." Suddenly, the blood rushed her face. In her hands, was Monica Gold's file. She quickly leafed through it. Inside, the notes confirmed everything she'd suspected. Speed reading, she tried to absorb it all.  Glancing at her watch, she had fifteen minutes before anyone was scheduled to arrive. She needed more information and the only way to get it all was to have the file copied.  The thought of it made her ill.

Fumbling, she gathered the papers and raced to the copier.  She copied fast, eyeing the door.  Grabbing the next to the last page, the office door opened as she caught a glimpse of the navy blue jacket.  Reaching for the sheets that were threatening to fall, she stuffed the disorderly file back together.  She skirted to the file room, placing the file in the old wooden cabinet and quickly rearranged the plants and other items over it.  Taking a deep breath, she walked back down the hall.

Brittany willed her hands to stop shaking.  It didn't work.  Her legs immediately joined in.  Ms. Dire stood at the end of the hall.

~~~

She regrouped in the bathroom using the paper towel to dab away the moisture that had accumulated over her lip.  She headed straight for her office, careful not to run into Ms. Dire again.

"Monica, I know you're getting ready for work but I have some very important information I must share with you," Brittany whispered into the phone.  "We need to get together as soon as possible.  Meet me at my house."

The rest of the morning, Brittany tried focusing on her other clients.  She felt dealing with them may somehow reel her scattered thoughts in.

At twelve noon, she watched as Monica parked in front of her building and climbed the steps.

She opened the door before she had the opportunity to knock, waving the manila folder in the air. "I found your file."

"You did it!  Oh my goodness."

They both stood in the middle of her living room floor doing a little shuffle. Brittany slowed her moves.

"Here's the bad news. It's everything we thought and more. Ms Dire is painting a grim picture of you. All fingers are pointing to her having your children taken away and adopted. I'm not allowed to let you read your file, but I am going to try and paint as a clear picture as I can. We now have the names and addresses of where all your children are."

They moved to the sun room and immediately began working. Flipping through the file, she read the dates Monica's children were placed in each home. Some information she read out loud. Some of it, she didn't. It was way too inflammatory. Brittany read the part about Sergeant Foley... *"He stated the client is a suspect in the brutal death of James Fort, a notorious heroin and crack dealer. Ms. Gold will be questioned about her involvement in this murder. She was on the scene when the shooting occurred. A place called "the hole" where drug deals are often conducted. Mr. Fort had been under surveillance, for the last several months for drug trafficking. The deceased drug dealer was a close associate of Ms. Gold. She was also..."* Brittany reached for the next page and realized there was no more. It dawned on her in her rush, she'd left the last sheet on the copier. The expression on her face told the story.

"What's wrong?" Monica asked.

"I can't remember if I took the last page of your file off the copier. What if Ms. Dire found it?" She took two quick breaths and her head cleared.

When had she ever been that afraid of anybody, she asked herself? *She* wasn't doing anything wrong. If anybody needed to be shaking, it should be Ms. Dire.

Brittany pulled herself together.

"Monica, Ms Dire has painted a picture of you that will easily allow the couples to take permanent custody of your children. So, it's time we take some pretty bold steps of our own."

"Trust me, I'm ready," Monica said.

"I think we should start by setting up supervised visitation with each of your girls. The first one we'll start with is Gerald and Charlene Brown. Then you'll get to see at least one of your twins. You know this is going to cause a real stir with Ms. Dire and the agency. Hey, but it's about time she starts to feel the pressure. Wouldn't you agree?"

Jotting down the address, Brittany headed straight for the Brown's. When she arrived she couldn't believe the home the child had been placed in. She'd never known a foster child to be taken in by a family that lived in an upscale neighborhood as beautiful as this.

She rang the doorbell and announced who she was. It was Charlene's face that told the story.

"What's wrong? Who's at the door?" Gerald asked.

"It's the caseworker from the Child Protection agency. She wants to take Geraldene to see her mother. I'm not going to allow her to take my baby anywhere," she said spreading her body across the nursery door.

"Calm down, Charlene," Gerald said lowering his voice. "Where is she?"

"I left her standing there. She can't come in here. Tell her to go away. I asked to see some identification. When I looked at it, I told her that it could be fake. She gave me this number to call and told me to phone her supervisor." She handed him the business card. "It's the same number to where Ms. Dire works. Gerald, she's in one of those agency cars."

"Hello… Hello." Brittany called from the front door.

"Just one minute please," Gerald said. "I'm going down to talk to her."

"Don't go down there. Maybe she'll just leave." She tried blocking him.

"Move, Charlene! Let me handle this."

"Gerald, what are you going to say to her?"

Before she received an answer, he'd already moved her aside and headed down the steps.

"Hi, I'm Gerald," he said inviting her inside.

"I gave your wife my card. I know you normally deal with Ms. Dire, but I am also assigned to this case. I've spent a lot of time with the mother of the child you have in your home. I feel it's time for her to have supervised visitation with her daughter. She has made tremendous progress."

Gerald could feel the color slowly drain from his face.

Brittany noticed his expression too, but continued. "I will have her back in a couple of hours."

Gerald's mind was racing. The thought of Charlene crossed it. At this point, he had no idea what she would do if he let the baby go with the case worker. Gerald knew he had little choice. He couldn't afford any more attention brought to the case.

"Are you sure the baby will be okay with the mother?"

"Oh, I'm positive about that. I'll be with them the whole time."

"Come in and have a seat while we get the baby ready," he said.

Brittany sat on the couch, breathing a sigh of relief. She was glad she'd driven the agency's car today.

Gerald went upstairs to Charlene. She clung to the baby, shifting her from one arm to the other.

"Honey, we're going to have to let her go and see her mother," he whispered. "It seems as though Ms. Dire hasn't been quite honest with us. The lady downstairs says the mother is doing well."

"No, Gerald, you can't let her take Geraldene."

"We have to. We don't want them to find out how we're going about the adoption, do we?"

"No, Gerald. No."

"You want to take the risk of losing Geraldene forever? Let her go! She'll only be gone for a couple of hours."

She gave him the baby, ran into the bedroom and slammed the door. He could hear her wailing from where he stood. He took a moment to allow the tears in his own eyes to dry. He kissed the baby's soft cheeks, gently cuddling her in his arms as he slowly descended the steps.

"Here she is," Gerald said.

"Oh, my, she's absolutely adorable," Brittany said, admiring the curly head, bright eyed bundle, dressed in a pink and white lacy jumper. "Come here, little one. Her mother will be so happy to see her. I'll call you when we're on our way back. Will you be home or should I look for your wife?"

"No," Gerald said. "We'll both be here."

He'd already made up his mind that he would not be going anywhere. Not until he found Ms. Dire.

~~~

Monica rushed home from work. Brittany had been so persistent. She finally agreed to let her bring the baby to their home. The only reason she gave in, she knew the other twin would be napping during that time. It was still a chance but one she had to take.

She was just around the corner and Monica could hear the excitement in her voice. "This will be the first time you'll actually hold one of your twins," Brittany said.

As Monica slowly opened the door, she couldn't believe her eyes. Brittany cuddled an exact replica of the other twin. Her heart melted as she reached for her baby. She kissed and laid her face gently against the tiny cheek. She did everything to keep the fresh tears from falling onto her baby girl.

"Isn't she beautiful," Monica said, kissing her baby's hands. She knew she would need both babies, side-by-side, to tell the difference between the two.

She sat and rocked her child. No one else in the room mattered. She paid little attention to Brittany's nervousness, completely unaware of the alarm raging inside.

Brittany knew that as of today, Ms. Dire would definitely know the extent of her involvement in the case.

They all sat admiring the baby when suddenly, whimpers from the bedroom flowed into the room. Monica stared at her grandmother as she gave a slight nod towards the noise. Grandmamma excused herself and left for the other stirring baby.

Monica shook her head *no*, as grandmamma walked into the living room with the sleepy-eyed twin.

"I didn't know you had another baby in the house with you," Brittany said.

Monica didn't say a word. She continued staring at her grandmamma, not believing any of what was happening right then. *What was she doing?*

"Wait a minute," Brittany said. "Let me take a look at that baby."

Grandmamma gently placed the other baby in Monica's arms. "You've been without your girls far too long."

Brittany sat with her mouth opened wide. Her hand covered her heart. She looked at Monica, her eyes instantly saddened. Finally, she whispered, "I trusted you. Why didn't you tell me *you* had the other twin? Do you know how much trouble I've been in because of this baby?"

"Brittany, please...just listen. You can still trust me. I didn't know what to do. I mean... we..." Monica looked over at her grandmamma for help.

Grandmamma walked over to Brittany, sat beside her, reached for her hand and held it gently.

"I believe God sent you to help us young lady, and you deserved to know that we had the other twin." She told her the story of how they ended up with the baby.

Brittany leaned her head back and closed her eyes. She tried recalling everything that happened the day Twin B was discharged. "I remember the lady standing there crying as she stared at your twin. In fact, she told me she was the child's aunt. She had a look of compassion that you'd expect only a close relative to have. So, I interviewed her. Quite frankly, she was quite impressive. She knew a great deal about you. Her address was almost identical to yours...so I just assumed... Boy have I learned a lot from this case. Due to this *one* incident, my co-workers have labeled me incompetent and my supervisor relieved me of some of my cases. How long have you had the baby?"

"A couple of months."

Brittany shook her head. "This is unreal."

"Listen, Brittany. I know I should have said some-thing to you. I'm so-o-o sorry. I just didn't know who I could trust. It's as if I've been stuck in the middle of a horrible dream and I can't wake up. Only in this night-mare, I feel the pain. *I* hurt when I think of how I used to leave my kids alone." She gazed softly into her babies' faces. "Brittany, *I* hurt when I replay over and over the night my babies were taken from me. When I think that I almost killed, Julia and Countess. Oh boy, you can't imagine the feeling. When I think that my children are all separated and in foster homes with people they don't even know, all because of me... I can't make the pain go away." With tears streaming down her cheeks, she continued. "Then I think of the moment you will take my baby out of my arms and walk away with her, I ache...and...I ache all over again. So, you see, it's not a dream," she said, through the tears. "Many times I tell myself, I don't deserve another chance. I was a horrible mother and a horrible person. That's when I hear my grandmamma saying, "Monica our God is a God of a second chance." Brittany, can you find it in your heart to give me another chance too. I really do need to hear those words right now."

At last Brittany spoke. "Monica, your life is amazing. I also believe God gives us chances to get it right. So, who am I to deny anyone else that opportunity. I will give you the chance to get it together and make things right for yourself. Hey, but let's not push it. Let's all agree today, no more secrets, okay."

"Thank you! Thank you!" Monica said, lifting her hand. "I promise. No more secrets."

"I almost wish I hadn't found out about this baby being in your home," Brittany said. "Since I have, I must deal with it. It's my professional obligation to let the agency know I've found the twin. You know what, Monica? This just may be the time for us to reveal all that we know about Ms. Dire and her schemes," Brittany said with a gleam in her eye.

"Will they believe you?"

"I'll have to take that chance but I have proof of everything now. Your new file has the correct account of your life. I've even asked your counselors and others if they would be willing to testify on your behalf, if necessary. No one refused. Not even your pastor."

"My pastor," Monica said.

Grandmamma smiled.

"Yes, your pastor. He said he sees you at church with your mamma and grandmamma each Sunday. He also says that he's heard nothing but good reports about you."

Brittany sat back, taking it all in. She knew genuine love when she saw it. The way Monica caressed her twins—she was witnessing it right then.

"It's time for me to take the baby back to her foster parents, Monica," Brittany said, hating to say those words. "I'll be back in a little while to get the other twin also."

Taking the baby from Monica was one of the hardest things she had ever done.

~~~

Ms. Dire had been all over the city looking for Gail, when her cell phone rang. She recognized Gerald's number.

"She did what!" she shouted. "What reason did she give for coming to get the baby, Gerald?" She took several deep breaths trying to maintain the little composure she had left.

"The caseworker said the mother was doing very well and deserved to see her child," he fumed.

She knew Brittany had made contact with Monica when she caught her in the file room, the first time. After she'd left a sheet of Monica's record on the copier, she also knew Brittany was aware of what was in the file she'd created. She never dreamed she would be so foolish as to go and get the child. That's why she had to find Gail. Something needed to be done about this trouble-maker, she thought. Today!

Right now, she needed to calm Gerald down.

If he was this upset, she couldn't imagine how Charlene was coping. He kept repeating, "I don't think your plan is working, Ms. Dire."

"Gerald, I know you're upset but you have to trust me. This girl doesn't know what she's talking about. She's young and very inexperienced. When a mother tells her they've decided to give up drugs, she believes them right away. She hasn't been burned yet. It's unfortunate that Brittany has to find out the hard way," she told him. "Monica is not clean Gerald and she will not be clean any time soon. Brittany will make certain that Geraldene is okay. It's our policy to never leave children alone with known drug offenders, and that's exactly what Monica Gold is! I'm going to stop by the attorney's office to make certain our court date is still on the books next week. I need to be sure they know this case is a high priority."

"Are you sure things will be okay?"

She could hear the tiredness in his voice.

"Absolutely," she said.

After they hung up, she floored the accelerator. She needed to find Gail.

When she finally found her, she was with Cray. That was perfect.

~~~

When Brittany arrived at the Brown's, they both came to the door. Charlene took the baby from her, never saying a word.

"Will you be back any time soon?" Gerald asked.

"I'm sure I will, Mr. Brown. We had a very good meeting today with the child's mother."

"Have a good day," he said, closing the door.

Brittany got in the car and headed straight for the agency. First, she had to report she'd found the missing twin, but more important, she had to stop Ms. Dire. Maybe since she'd located the twin, it would help him to believe what she was about to tell him. With the bizarre behavior of the Brown's, she knew the adoption was scheduled soon. She began rehearsing what she would say to her supervisor. *Mr. Brandon, you don't know what Ms. Dire is doing.* No, no, no, that's not it. *Mr. Brandon, I've found...*Suddenly, her car swerved. She could hear the flapping of the rubber as it pounded against the pavement. A flat tire! This had to be the worst timing ever. She reached for the triple A card in her wallet. Maybe they won't take too long, she thought. She had to make it to the agency before her supervisor left.

She got out of the car to check the tire. Stooping down she fingered the head of two huge nails fully emerged in it. She was about to stand, when a sudden burst of light exploded in her head. As she reached for the spot that caused the most pain, she realized she was having difficulty standing. It was then that the sticky dark blood oozed into her eyes. The strange quietness helped rock her to sleep. She never even remembered slumping down beside her car onto the rough pavement as she slowly slipped unconscious.

He took her cell phone, purse and briefcase, jumped on the motorcycle and sped away.

# Chapter 24

## Miracles

Sheila noticed a significant change in Peaches. Ever since she'd visited her mom, she seemed happier and her grades were back to normal. She hadn't seen Mr. Craft lately either. Whenever she saw that man, it made her skin crawl. Mrs. Craft had started picking Peaches up from school.

Sheila wanted to ask Peaches a few questions. She just needed to find the right time.

The twelve fifteen bell rang. "Settle down. Settle down, class." She watched as Peaches lined up beside her good friend Tiffany. It was a beautiful day. All the teachers and students would be outside.

"Slow down ladies. No running," she said, as they exited the rear door.

"Come here Peaches, let me tie your shoe before you trip."

"Thanks, Miss Tate. I can do it."

She bent down beside her. "Peaches, I talked to your mommy yesterday."

A huge smile lit up her face.

"How are things at home with your foster parents?" Sheila asked.

"A lot better, Miss Tate. Besides, Mr. Craft has been gone." She struggled with the shoelace.

"Gone?"

"Yep. Away on a trip for his work. Can I go now?" she said, snapping to attention.

"Okay. Don't run…" It was too late. Peaches took out like a flash.

Suddenly she stopped and ran back. "Miss Tate, I forgot something. Mr. Craft will be back so he can take us to court next week. Will I go with my mommy then?"

~~~

Chris was proud of Brooke. While in Italy, she'd landed one of the largest accounts in the company's history. He was closing one himself but it didn't come near the amount Brooke negotiated. He headed for his parent's estate to share the good news.

His father rarely visited the office anymore always reminding him the company was in good hands. His parents were proud of them. Their only regrets, they had no grandchildren. When Brooke married, she'd told them they had decided not to have children. He knew how disappointing that was for them.

Chris admired the magnificent scenery as he entered the gates of his parent's estate. Sprawled on one hundred fifty acres of an immaculately trimmed lawn, the pink azaleas were in full bloom growing perfectly alongside the white and pink roses planted throughout. The estate he'd called home his teenage years was now only occupied by his parents along with their four Alaskan huskies and three thoroughbred horses.

"Good afternoon, Mr. Chris, how are you?" Brent greeted him as he opened the door.

"Fine, Brent. I haven't seen you in quite a while."

He had been the family's butler for over twenty years and had always proven loyal.

"Your mother is in the library and your dad is napping."

"I'll go in and see her. It's good seeing you."

"Same here, sir."

Chris walked into the library where he found his mother reading.

"You need more light?" he said, bending down kissing her on the cheek.

They both laughed. She'd always said that to him whenever he studied.

"Well, what a welcomed surprise." She removed her glasses.

"How ya feeling, mom?"

"Fine, dear."

"How's dad?" he asked picking up the paper.

"Great. It's his naptime. He'll hate he missed you. Why don't you stay for dinner?"

"Good idea. I'm starving."

"I'll let Brent know you'll be joining us. By the way, have you spoken with Brookie today?"

"I talked to her earlier. My sister is amazing. You know, she pulled off a deal I didn't think could happen."

"Haven't you realized by now I have the smartest children in the world?" she beamed. "She called and told me about it. In fact, I'm going to join her in Italy next week."

"Then the two of you can do what you love to do most, huh!" he said. "Shop!"

He always enjoyed talking to his mother. She had an unusually dry sense of humor that practically made her famous. It drew people to her from all over the world and she had countless speaking engagements as a result. He was proud of her—an avid and skilled rider who absolutely adored her thoroughbred, Midnight.

He relaxed his head back on the thick leather couch, as he read the Wall Street Journal.

"Chris, Camille called me this morning," she said turning the page to her book.

He never looked up from the paper.

"Quite frankly, I was surprised to hear from her. She was extremely upset and asked my advice."

He kept right on reading.

"She told me you called off the wedding. You don't want to see her anymore? Is that true, dear?" She casually turned the page to her book.

"Yes, mom, it is," he said skimming the paper.

"What happened? I thought she was the one. I mean, I really liked her. What went wrong?"

He knew his mom. He wasn't leaving there until she found out what she wanted. He took a deep breath and tried explaining. "Mom, when I look at you and dad, I love what I see. That special something the two of you have is what I want. I don't want to be like my friends, all on their second or third marriages. I could never marry Camille. I wouldn't be happy and neither would she."

"Chris, listen to me. I love your father with all my heart and I know he loves me. Son, it hasn't always been that way. I once considered divorcing him."

Chris silently pleaded for her to stop but she continued.

"The night I would have signed the divorce papers, he showed up at my door and we talked all night. By the time the sun came up, we both realized that commitment and forgiveness would always play a key role in our relationship no matter what challenges we faced. From that day on, we renewed our life time commitment and decided that we would forgive each other's faux pas. That's how we've made it all these years, dear."

"I know I'll be committed to the woman I marry, mom and be able to forgive her if I ever have to. I just need to find the right one. That's all."

"What's all this noise about the right one?" his dad said entering the room.

"Hi, pop, how are you?" Chris said, sighing with relief. Perfect timing—the conversation with his mom was now officially over.

"I talked to Brookie today," his dad said. "She's pulled off a honey of a deal. What about those Yankees, they'll surely walk away with it all this time."

That was his cue. Father and son, they engaged in their lively, customary debate.

At a quarter to six, Brent called them all for dinner.

Before Chris went into the dining area, he picked up the phone and called Monica.

~~~

Monica had reluctantly accepted Chris' dinner invitation for tomorrow. Again, she had a lot on her mind but found it difficult telling him no. Brittany was not answering her cell and wasn't returning her calls from all the messages she'd left. She was extremely worried. Was she still angry with her? She was expecting her to come and take the other twin away any day now. Where was she!

Joy insisted that she get a new dress for her date with Chris this time. Grabbing the keys, she dangled them in front of her. "Come on, let's get out of here for a while. I've got a couple of places I want to take you. Besides, you never spend any money on yourself."

Joy navigated the city like a pro, taking her to a few boutiques located right outside the city limits. "How do you know about these shops?" Monica asked.

"My friends and I always go to places like these. Retail all the way, baby! No, seriously. Erica's mom is a buyer for a few of the owners. There's this one dress I'm dying for you to see. I wanted it for myself but it was just a little too expensive." She pulled the car in front of the quaint little dress shop. The display window was arrayed with trendy, chic clothing. As soon as they went inside, Joy headed straight for the dress and pressed it against her. "Isn't it the bomb!"

"That is nice. Pretty color too." Monica flipped the price tag over. "Now, I see why you love it and I also see why you didn't get it."

"No, try it on, Monica. I just want to see how you look in it."

"Let's go, we can't afford that dress."

"It's another 25% off the sale price, ladies. Isn't that just absolutely gorgeous," the saleslady said, approaching.

"Yes, she wants to try this on." Joy handed the dress to Monica.

"Sure, right this way." She took the dress from Monica and headed for the dressing room area.

Monica looked back at Joy and mouthed, "you're in trouble."

When she came out with the dress on, Joy whistled. She knew Monica would look good. She had no idea she would look *that* good.

"That's your dress, hon!" The salesladies swarmed around her making her turn around again and again.

"Are you a model?" one of them asked.

"I wish."

Monica went to take the dress off. She turned and admired herself for the last time in the mirror. She was glad she'd come. Even if she didn't buy anything, she had to admit shopping had been the distraction she needed.

"I'll hang it up for you," the sales lady said through the dressing room door.

After Monica finished dressing she walked towards the counter where Joy stood. "Let's get out of here before it's too late to look for another outfit."

"Thank you ladies for shopping with us and please come again," the sales lady said smiling, handing Joy the dress.

Monica was about to object. Joy grabbed her arm, took the package, and led her out of the store.

"What are you doing, Joy?"

"I was going to buy the dress for myself, but when I saw you in it, I knew it was yours. From the money you and mamma have been giving me, I saved enough to get it today. In fact, with 25% off, I actually got a few bucks back."

The next afternoon, Monica enjoyed the attention as Joy bustled around with the new dress in her hand. She held everybody's earrings in the house up to it until she found the perfect pair. Joy applied her makeup and helped style her hair. After one last look in the mirror, Monica knew Chris would be proud to have her as his date.

"Chris is going to die when he sees you!" Joy said. "You look gorgeous…so elegant, Monica."

"This is your second date with this young man, isn't it?" grandmamma said coming into the bedroom.

"Yes, but he's just a friend, grandmamma."

"Okay, I'll accept that for now."

When she walked into the living room, Monica peeked out to see if the limo had arrived. She couldn't believe her eyes when a black Mercedes pulled up. She hadn't thought about Chris coming to pick her up. The last time, he'd just sent his driver.

When she opened the door, she tried muttering a few words that actually made sense. "Well, hello… umm, guys, this is Chris."

Introductions made, he shook hands with everyone except Joy. Pinching her on both cheeks, Joy blushed. Monica couldn't believe any of what was happening. He sat down, crossed his legs and made himself right at home.

"Can I get you something to drink?" grandmamma asked.

"I could use some water if you don't mind."

Mamma sat quietly, taking it all in.

Monica was mesmerized at how well Chris worked the room.

"Congratulations, Joy on all your success," he said. "Salutatorian, now that's an accomplishment. Have you selected the college you want to attend?"

She told him how difficult the decision had been for her. They discussed the pros and cons of each school. Monica was blown away. Mamma was now engaged in the conversation. When Chris invited them to his office to see pictures of several of the campuses, he had them all eating out his hands!

*Finally*, Monica thought, as he stood. They were ready to go.

Right before they were about to get into his car, Chris drew her close. "I didn't want to say this in front of your folks, but you look amazing!"

"Thanks. Now, can we get in the car so my neighbors can quit staring?" She smiled, gracefully sliding inside.

Chris was glad he selected this restaurant. Driving along the cobble stone streets, he knew the hidden inn offered the privacy he desired. The special dining area was always reserved for him at a moment's notice, his favorite portrait of Venus Rising from the Sea, tastefully decorated the small cozy, private room.

As they climbed the stairs, he gently held her arm.

"Mr. Blankenship, we have prepared for you and your guest an exquisite steak diane, avec salade niçoise," the maitre d' said in his thick French accent.

"Ce son délicieux," Chris responded as he completed the order.

Chris couldn't take his eyes off Monica. Her skin was flawless, her face radiant. Her slender five foot nine frame allowed the teal colored dress to cling as if it were designed with only her in mind. Chris looked into her eyes as they drew him in. Instinctively, he reached for her hand. He was glad she didn't pull away. He was happy to finally be alone with her again and wanted to tell her so.

"I really enjoy your company, Monica," he said.

"Thanks." She looked away.

The unexpected, brief comment left him uncomfortable. "Are you all right?" he asked, releasing her hand.

"I'm fine." She didn't know how to tell him what was on her mind, but knew she needed to.

"Okay, come clean," he said smiling. "What's wrong?"

"Chris, I really do enjoy your company." She hesitated. "My concern is the people at work. I love my job and most of all I love working for Brooke. I don't want anything jeopardizing that. If they even suspected I was going out with the boss, boy oh boy."

"Is that it," he said playfully hitting his head. "Listen, I should have been more sensitive. I'm sorry," he said gently reaching for her hand again. "I've never asked anyone out in the company before. Never. I also understand what position that puts you in. Unfortunately, you caught my eye before you worked for Brooke. I knew this had the potential of happening, even at Expresso's. When I first met you I wanted to ask you out. It's just that you needed the job more and I had almost decided to leave it alone. When I bumped into you on your way from lunch, well, the smile...the flowers...the birds...the perfect day..." he said smiling. "There was too much going against me. I had to ask you out."

She laughed, tilting her head as the reflection of the candle's light softly touched her face. "It's amazing how things worked out. Let's still be careful."

Chuckling, he said, "You don't have to worry. I have... a plan."

She sat back and enjoyed the rest of the wonderful-fun filled-romantic, evening.

On the way home, the sky roof offered a view of the city lights that seemed to give an extra special sparkle. The stars glistened in the crystal, clear sky—a bright and wonderful night.

She thought of her girls.

~~~

As soon as Brooke returned, the office was chaotic. The meeting with the Australian clients called for the entire senior executive team. They all chatted as they sat around the boardroom table waiting for the boss to arrive. Brooke wanted her there to take minutes and assist.

As he entered, she noticed how sharp Chris looked in his tailored suit—crisp. It was all business between the two of them and Monica now understood why he was CEO. She had never seen him so alluringly confident. Even Brooke responded differently. It was if they had their own secret language. He would nod, she would react and vice versa. Their timing was impeccable as they both worked the room. The clients along with their attorneys showed a level of respect that only a veteran business man could demand. They negotiated long and hard but it seemed Chris was always the one in control.

Monica had once overheard several of his colleagues describe him as a very shrewd business associate with the negotiating skills of a pit bull. He'd graduated the top of his class at Yale's Law School.

Monica had never worked so hard but she didn't mind. She welcomed the hustle. It took her mind off the girls. Her feet were beginning to object though. Walking the long halls of the executive suite was a challenge in her two inch heels.

When the meeting finally ended, she was grateful. She sat at her desk, immediately kicked off her shoes and began massaging her feet.

"Excuse me, but no one introduced us tonight," a young man said. "I wanted to thank you for all your help."

"Oh, hi," Monica said, putting her bare feet under the desk and out of view.

"My name is Robert Brownlee. I wondered who Brooke would get to take Sophie's place. I'm really impressed. How long have you been with the Blankenship's?"

"Almost three months now."

"That's great. I conduct a lot of business with your company so I'll probably be seeing you around quite a bit. I must say again, how thoroughly impressed I am with how you managed to keep everything so organized in there. That's very difficult to do, especially with a group like us. I hope they're paying you well. Firms would pay top dollar to get that kind of help. Well, it's nice meeting you," he said, handing her a card.

He leaned in and whispered. "If you ever get tired of working for the Blankenship's, give me a call."

She looked at the business card. Robert Brownlee Esq.—Brownlee and Brownlee Law Firm.

# Chapter 25

## Unknown Trauma

Brittany was rushed through the doors of the Trauma Center with a name tag that read, "unknown". They found her lying on the side of the road and someone had called 911. Fortunately she was breathing on her own. Batteries of neurological tests were quickly performed to determine the extent of her injuries. They rushed her on the gurney for a MRI and once the scan was complete, she was placed in the neuro intensive care unit.

Brittany could hear someone in the far distance calling her name but her eyes felt like lead. She held up her hand to try and let whoever it was calling know she heard them.

"Good. Now open your eyes," a faint voice said.

She was really trying and finally, she managed to open one eye. When she did, there was no one at the bedside. The room was bright with all kinds of machines around. She drifted back to sleep and again she managed to open her eyes. This time there were people at her bedside. She tried talking but nothing came out.

She must have fallen asleep again. "Stop it! That hurts!" she croaked. Someone was sticking a needle into her arm.

"She's awake," the blood collector announced.

Two nurses came rushing into the room. "Good morning," they said. "You're awake! Do you know where you are?"

She'd just managed to get the other eye open. "No, I don't," she whispered.

"Does your head hurt?"

"It really hurts," Brittany said, feeling the bandage. "Where am I?" She tried sitting up but couldn't.

The nurses gently lifted her up in the bed, fluffing her pillow.

"You're in the hospital. You've got yourself one large bump on your head there. I'm Carmen and this is Brandi."

"Hi, I'm Brittany," her voice cracked.

They laughed. "We know. It's nice meeting you, Brittany."

"How did I get here?"

"You were mugged. Whoever it was, gave you a really hard lick. We were worried about you," Carmen said as she adjusted her IV. "Are you in pain? They had to put a few stitches in your head."

"I can tell," Brittany said, feeling the bandages again. "It seems like more than a few. It really hurts."

"How about I give you something to ease the pain? On a scale of one to ten, how bad is it?" Carmen asked.

"Ten." She coughed. The bright lights made her head feel like mud. She longed for anything that would take the pain away. Brittany had never believed in taking drugs of any kind but this was an exception. As the drug flushed through her IV, she wanted to ask a few more questions, but forgot what they were. She was positioned in just the right spot and slept late into the night.

Hours later, she stirred. She looked into her nurse's face.

"Hi, I'm Craig, and I'll be your nurse tonight," he said entering her room with a tray in his hands. "Would you like a little broth and jello for dinner?"

"Not really." Her words slurred.

"Let's try a few sips," he insisted.

Surprisingly, the broth made her feel better. Still, the sleep made her feel even better.

The pain medication was beginning to wear off and the discomfort became intolerable. With the next dose of medication on board, Brittany knew she had something important to do but couldn't think of what it was. It didn't matter at that point. She tucked the blanket under her chin, turned over and eased into a much needed sleep.

The bright morning light greeted her as soon as she opened her eyes. While it usually gave her the lift she needed to start the day, today it caused her pain. "Could you please close those blinds?" she asked squinting.

"Sure. Is your head feeling any better Brittany?" her nurse asked.

"Not at all. Is it suppose to hurt this much?"

"You have a sizable lump on there. The doctors are watching it closely. It should start feeling better soon."

The pain medicine had her so groggy. Work…she hadn't called in to work. Did they know where she was?

"Excuse me, but could you help me make a phone call? I need to call my supervisor."

"That's all taken care of. It's a good thing you were in the company's car," Carmen said. "Everybody in your office is concerned about you."

~~~

Ms. Dire hoped the sincerity on her face seemed genuine. She wanted them to believe she was just as concerned about Brittany as they were. She needed to get to

Robert Washington because he had the most information regarding her condition. The latest update he'd given was that she was still in a coma, but breathing on her on. That was the best news ever, she thought. She didn't want her to die—but if that happened... oh, well. Gail told her she didn't know if she was dead or alive but did know one thing for sure—she was out like a light. The women in the office talked about it nonstop.

Usually the longer you stay unconscious from a blow like that, the greater are your chances are of never waking up again, she'd heard one of them say.

"Robert, this is so unusual. That's not the kind of neighborhood you'd expect something like that to happen," Ms. Dire said, pulling up a chair next to him.

"I know. Apparently she had a flat and was checking things out when it happened."

"Do you think she'll pull through?"

"I have a friend that's a nurse. She says if they can just get her to wake up, her chances would be better."

"Please keep me informed about her progress, Robert. I want to make sure everything turns out okay for that young lady. I've really grown fond of her."

"I will," he said. "I know the two of you were working together pretty closely. If there's anything I can do to help, let me know. They've assigned me to her cases while she's out."

"Don't worry about one of them—the Gold case. It's a little complex but I have a handle on it. I know what a heavy load you already have. Just concentrate on Brittany's other cases," she said with all the sympathy she could muster.

"Will do," Robert said.

Ms. Dire couldn't believe how well things were turning out. Finally! Brittany was out of the picture. This was definitely going to give her enough time to get the twin adopted. They were going to court in two days.

~~~

Robert went over the names of each of Brittany's cases. He'd forgotten about the file Brittany was so upset about until Ms. Dire mentioned it. He headed straight for the file room. He located all of Brittany's cases except Monica Gold. Ah-h…the missing file, he thought. Robert went to Brittany's desk to see if it was there. To his surprise, it was sitting right on top. Puzzled, he opened it, and read Brittany's notes. His trademark furrowed brow, etched his face. Her first comments took him off guard. *This second record has been developed due to the inability to locate the original file. Monica Gold has made tremendous progress.* He read further. *There was obvious lack of follow up on the client's progress. As a result, it had been determined that she should not be allowed parental visitation. It was the agency's impression that she was still at risk. I am unable to validate any of this because of the glowing remarks I've received from her rehabilitation counselors, pastor and employer. Therefore, I have arranged parental visitation for my client under some duress.*

What did she mean *duress*? Robert had been around the agency for a long time and had seen just about everything. His instincts were keen and he always followed them. They were screaming to him at this point. When he read Brittany's closing remarks, he knew he would have to be involved in this case whether he wanted to or not. *Ms. Dire has arranged adoption proceedings for two of Monica Gold's children. It is obvious she is unaware of the progress this mother has made and her sincere desire to regain full parental rights of all of her children. It is the recommendation of this caseworker that any adoption proceedings be immediately postponed and that the agency takes a "true" and closer review of this client's progress and her entire case.*

Robert collected the rest of Brittany's case files and prioritized them. Monica Gold was placed on top.

His first stop had to be at the hospital to check in on Brittany. He wanted to see how she was doing and if at all possible, talk to her about this case. He copied a few notes, grabbed his keys and headed for the hospital.

Robert was nervous about what he would find when he got there. Walking in, he noticed Brittany lying peacefully in bed. Looking down at her he thought she was still in a coma. Introducing himself to her mother, their conversation caused Brittany to stir.

"Oh, hi, Robert," she said wiping her eyes.

It almost startled him. "I am so glad to see you are awake. How are you feeling, young lady?"

"Like someone's beaten me with a bat. Other than that, I'm fine."

He laughed. "You're one tough cookie. I wanted to come by and see for myself how you were doing. You know how information like this gets around in that office of ours. They still had you in a coma this morning."

She managed to smile.

They chatted for a few minutes, but Robert could tell her head bothered her.

The nurse came to check her bandage. "How's your head feeling?" she asked.

"Awful."

"The doctor wants to try you on a different pain reliever. Would you like it now?"

"Yes, I could really use something now."

"I'll be right back with it," she said leaving the room.

"I know you need your rest and I hate to bother you about work, but I was wondering if there was anything you wanted me to know about any of your cases," Robert said lowering his voice.

She frowned.   "I'm sure there is, I just can't remember right now."

He was disappointed but knew pushing her to recall would not be a good idea. "Well if you think of it later, just call."   He jotted his cell phone number down and handed it to her mother.

"Thanks for coming by.   Tell everyone hello and I hope to be back at work soon."

"I'll check on you later," he said patting her hand.

The nurse came in with the pain medication.   She helped her freshen up while the pain reliever took effect. Just as she was about to doze off, she thought of Robert. She had been trying hard to remember what it was she had to tell him.   She closed her eyes and listened as the nurses chatted in the hall.   The new pain medication was more powerful than the other.   She'd closed her eyes briefly to just enjoy it for a moment.

She slept the rest of the day.

Tossing and turning, the medication caused her to have strange - weird dreams.   She was chasing Monica down a long-winding road while pulling Peaches along with her as she ran.   The faster Monica ran the further behind they became.   If only Monica would stop running, she could give her the child.

It was too late.   A car sped up blocking her from moving forward.   An extremely thin arm reached out, opened the door and with a long crooked finger, gestured for the child to get in.   She had no strength what so ever to keep her from climbing inside the car.   Peaches peered out the rear window, waving her tiny hand as they slowly drove away.

"*Stop*," she cried, sitting up in bed.

Brittany could feel her heart pounding.

*Monica!* She had to help her.

The force of the pain shooting through her head forced her to lie back down. What time was it? How long had she slept? She needed to talk to Robert as soon as possible. She reached for the number her mom had placed beside the phone. She needed help to dial and time was ticking away.

She promised never to take the new pain medication again. After five attempts, she finally managed to dial his number.

"Robert, this is Brittany. I need you to come back to the hospital as soon as possible, while I'm awake. I have something very important to discuss with you about one of my clients."

"I'm on my way," he said.

She vowed to stay awake no matter how much her head ached. She tried not to think of the nauseous feeling inching its way up.

At last Robert walked through the door.

"I'm warning you. I have something to tell you that I know you'll find difficult to believe."

Even though her sentences were disjointed and she kept repeating herself, she finally got the story out. When she got to the part of the "lost twin" being with Monica, it was the first time she saw the expression on his face change. She knew exactly what he was thinking.

"Robert," Brittany said. "You've got to trust me. You don't have time to check things out like you normally do. They are going to court real soon about this case.

If something doesn't happen tonight…well…it might be too late."

"I did hear Ms. Dire tell Larry she would see him in court tomorrow," Robert said. "I'm going back to the office to find out which case they're talking about."

"Be careful Robert, he believes Ms. Dire can do no wrong. You're going to need some pretty hard proof to intervene on this one."

"Let me think it through a little more. I'll call you later."

Robert left the hospital, his thoughts racing. He'd prided himself for being one of the most dependable and competent case workers in the agency. All of his evaluations indicated as much. The only person in the agency that had been given higher accolades than he—was Ms. Dire. She was the *one* person he'd go to when he didn't know what to do about a difficult case. He couldn't make any sense of what Brittany was trying to tell him. He had so much respect for Ms. Dire, he forced away the thoughts that kept trying to pry their way in. It had to be poor judgment, a misunderstanding, even poor communication— something other than what he was beginning to think.

He was in luck. His supervisor's and Ms. Dire's cars were still on the lot when he drove up.

"I thought you were gone for the day," Ms. Dire said, as he passed her office.

"I forgot to remind Larry about something."

He headed straight for the supervisor's office. "Hey man, I was wondering if you're not too busy, we could have lunch tomorrow? I need to run something by you about one of Brittany's cases."

"Let's try another day. I have to be in court most of the morning on a couple of cases."

"Adoptions, I assume."

"Yeah. The mom is a real loser."

"Brittany wasn't involved with either one of these adoptions was she?"

"No. These two are Ms. Dire's. Wait a sec. Brittany did play a small role in one of the cases. This is the mother of the missing twin."

"I remember that case. I thought Brittany said the mother was making pretty good progress."

"As usual, she must have the cases mixed up. In fact the mother will probably be arrested soon for trying to sell drugs and in connection with a murder."

"Wow, *I* must have the wrong case. I'll check back with you later this week to see about lunch."

Stunned, Robert turned and headed for his office.

When he called Brittany, the words just spilled out. "Did you know Monica is going to be arrested…something to do with drugs and a murder."

"*Oh, no, Robert, you've got to find her!*" She forgot to tell him what Monica said about being set up by one of her friends. She tried explaining.

"Slow down, Brittany, I'm not following you. A set up?"

Brittany held her head. "Robert, I've failed her. It's too late. She'll never get her children back!" Her head throbbed. Laying the phone beside her, she threw up.

# Chapter 26

## Keep the Faith

Monica was worried. It was so unlike Brittany not to answer her calls. She phoned the agency out of desperation.

"Is Brittany available please?" she asked.

"No, she isn't," the receptionist said.

"Can you please tell me when she'll be in?"

"Right now, I'm not sure, ma'am. Brittany may not be back for a while."

Monica couldn't get any more information about Brittany's whereabouts from the receptionist. She tried her cell phone and her home once again and still, no luck.

Then she replayed her mother's words. "All of them may be crooked at that agency." Shaking her head, she thought—not Brittany. No one could ever make her believe that. She wanted to take the time to go and look for her, but couldn't leave the office. It was busier than ever. *Think, Monica!* she said to herself.

Looking up, she didn't realize Brooke had been standing there.

"I'm sorry, did you need anything?" she asked.

Brooke smiled. "In deep thought?

"I'm sorry. I have a lot on my mind."

"That's okay. Would you please take this to Chris' office?" She handed her the contract. "I need him to review this right away if we're going to get it signed."

Monica took the shuttle to his office. This was the first time Brooke had ever asked her to go there and she had to admit, she was nervous. Exiting the shuttle, she walked into the glass covered building.

"Hi, Dorothy. This is the document Brooke sent to Mr. Blankenship."

"Thanks. I'll take it in to him right away. May I get you something to drink?" she asked, leaving her desk.

"No thanks, but I do need to use your phone if that's okay."

"Sure, right this way."

Monica phoned grandmamma as she sat in the corner office.

"I can't find Brittany anywhere," she whispered.

"I haven't heard from Jessica either," grandmamma said. "She would tell us if anything was going on at the agency."

"This isn't the Brittany we know. She always answers my calls. You don't think something happened to her do you grandmamma?"

"I hope not. She sure has been a lot of help."

She heard Chris' voice in the hall. "I've got to go. I'll call you later." She stood just as Chris and Dorothy entered the room.

"Hello, Monica," Chris said. "Tell Brooke that everything seems to be in order. This is the only modification I would like her to make." He pointed to the changes.

"I'll make certain she sees that."

"Thanks and ask her to give me a call around five this afternoon. I'll have some free time then."

"Will do," Monica said politely. With those words she realized she wasn't nervous anymore.

Arriving back at the office, she worked non-stop, having to skip lunch. She had so much to do today. The list seemed endless. She had to pick Joy up from school, get the baby to the doctor and check on Brittany.

Glancing at the clock, she knew Joy was already waiting on her. School had been out for over an hour. She needed to hurry.

~~~

Joy waited out front of the school with her friends. After the incident of the *creepy man*, she didn't like being left alone. She wished her mother would pick her up, she was always on time. Monica was always late. Mamma had agreed to let her keep the car today in case she needed to go to the agency about the children.

Joy checked her watch again. *Come on, Monica, where are you?* Pacing back and forth she looked up the street for any sign of mamma's car. Her friend's parents had long since picked them up. One of her best friend Karen had a car and would have offered her a ride home but the tire was almost flat. Her dad had come to fix it and made her drive straight home.

"Hey, you want my dad to take you home?" she offered.

"Nah. My sister should be here any second." Joy waved as her last friend left.

She decided to wait inside the building while some of the teachers were still around.

"Hi Joy, how's everything?" It was her Calculus teacher.

"Great, Mr. Sylvester."

"Keep up the good work and congratulations on being Salutatorian."

Joy looked at her watch again. Monica was an hour and twenty minutes late.

Finally! She saw the maroon Ford swerve around the corner. As soon as Joy opened the door and walked towards the car, the creepy man jumped out. She screamed and tried running. He blocked her, greeting her with a wide toothless grin. Joy could see Monica getting out of the car running towards her.

*"Hey, what are you doing?"* Monica yelled. *"Get away from her!"* She reached for Joy and swung her behind her.

"I know you! What are you doing?" Monica yelled.

"I need my fix, Joy, sell this junkie his fix, ma-a-an." He reached and brushed her hair.

Joy screamed.

"Where's my stuuuff," he yelled.

With the heel of her hand Monica slammed it into his face.

The hit did little to faze him. "Just give me my-y-y-y stuff," he yelled louder.

"What's going on here?" the security guard shouted, running up.

Cray pretended to run but the guard snatched him by his collar.

"What's going on?" he demanded.

"Nothing, ma-a-an."

Cray reached in his pocket for the small vial of white powdery substance, slipping it to the ground.

The guard saw it and picked it up.

"What's this?"

"That belongs to them, ma-a-an," he pointed.

"They were trying to sell it to me and cheat me out of my-y-y money!"

*"He's crazy,"* Joy yelled.

The guard looked up, immediately recognizing her. "What is this joker talking about, Joy?"

"I don't know, but he's lying."

"No, she's lying.  They both are trying to-o-o take my-y-y money.  Her sister is a known crack-head, ma-a-an, ask anybody!"

Monica hadn't said a word.  She was standing there feeling as if she'd just entered part two of her series of bad dreams.  The security officer escorted them all into the principal's office.

"What's going on, Officer Robinson?" Mr. Cash asked.

"We have a serious problem, sir.  I'm going to have to call the police on this one."

Joy watched as Mr. Cash spoke with the security officer.  She could not hear what they said, but noticed the grim expression on her principal's face.

"What's going on, Joy?" he asked, walking towards her.

"I don't know, Mr. Cash.  I have no idea who this man is."

They turned and looked at Cray.  He sat with his head in his hands rocking from side to side.

Mr. Cash left her, walking over to Cray.

Joy whispered, "Do you know that man, Monica?"

"He's a known junkie and lives at The Hole.  I've never said two words to him.  He seemed harmless, just a little crazy.  I think this has to do with me, Joy," Monica whispered.  "They're trying to set me up.  No one is ever going to believe that I didn't sell him drugs.  Oh, Joy, can't you see, they'll do anything to take my babies away."

"Stop it, Monica.  That's not going to happen.  This man is just mad!  They'll believe us...I know... they'll believe us."

"They've done it this time. I would never let them think you had anything to do with drugs. I've got to protect you no matter what," Monica whispered.

"No, listen to me. You've got to get your babies back. You can't be associated with drugs and you know it."

"Joy, you have to…."

"Young people, we have a very serious matter," Mr. Cash said marching towards them. "Joy, we are calling the police and also calling your mother. She should meet you at the police station."

"Mr. Cash, I promise, neither my sister nor I know anything about this or what he's up to. You've got to believe me, sir."

"I know, Joy" he said, his voice much softer. "The police will sort this situation out,"

"No, Mr. Cash, you don't understand! We can't go down there! Can't you just believe me? He's lying!"

"I wish none of this was happening. Illegal drugs have been found on the school's property. It's the policy to always contact the police in cases like these. I'm sure everything will work out for you and your sister," Mr. Cash said as security led them away.

When the two police officers drove up, Joy cried, "*no-o-o-o.*" They put them into one car. Cray got in the other.

By the time they arrived at the police station, their mother was sitting, waiting. They noticed her tear stained face as they passed by. The officer took Joy and Monica straight to the back and placed them in separate rooms.

For two and a half hours, they were questioned. Afterwards, Joy was released.

Monica looked up as a heavy set, balding man walked into the room. Sergeant Foley introduced himself.

"I'm sorry, but you're going to be with us a little while longer.  We need to ask you a few more questions regarding the murder of a James Fort, better known as Jay Jay."

Monica laid her head on the table.  She knew it was time to give up the idea of getting her daughters back.  Maybe it was God's will for them to be in other homes and not with her.  She knew any association with drugs would see to that.  Now, they were talking murder!  That would definitely put an end to it all.

Sergeant Foley was relentless.  He questioned her hard.  "What were you doing at The Hole if you are clean?  Why do you continue to associate with known drug addicts if you're not selling anymore?  How long have you been a drug addict?"  The final blow came when she'd explained to him about her church, her job and even school.  He stared at her never blinking and said, "Wall Street executives use cocaine."

"What can I do to convince you that I'm telling the truth?" she tried explaining.  "I'm tired and I need to go home."  She laid her head back on the table.

"Let's go over it one more time, Miss Gold."  He kept her another two hours.

Monica never deviated from her story.  She kept hearing her grandmamma say, *"The truth will make you free, baby."*  If indeed it would, then she needed it to work on her behalf right now.

Finally, Sergeant Foley got up from the table and left the room.  She had no strength to cry.  Monica sat in the metal chair, and whispered a prayer.  *"Father, I reach out to You today.  I truly am thankful for all You've done in my life.*  She prayed, *but now Lord, I need to ask You something maybe I've never been able to ask You before.  That is, please help me to accept Your Will. When it comes to my girls, only You and I know what they truly mean to me. So, from this point on, I give each of my girls completely to You. A kind and loving Father like Yourself will give them the best life has to offer. Take care of them like only You know how. In Jesus Name I pray."* It was at that point she resolved that whatever the Lord did with her girls would be good. Even if it meant they weren't with her.

Sergeant Foley came back into the room and sat facing her. "We're releasing you for now, Miss Gold. You may want to get a lawyer. It seems people are connecting you with Mr. Fort's murder and we need to rule that out. Have a good night," he said, pushing the chair back as its metal legs screeched across the concrete floor.

Mamma was leaning against the car when she came out. She fell into her comforting arms.

Grandmamma and Joy were standing in the door, holding it open when they drove up.

"It's been a very hard day," mamma said as they walked in.

They all sat quietly. It was clear they were all trying to make sense of everything that was happening.

"What's really going on?" mamma finally whispered. "There must be a good reason they are claiming you two were involved in a drug deal and Monica with a murder. It sounds as if everything Big Man said about Gail is true. She has to be conspiring with Ms. Dire. The two of them are behind all of this."

"What can we do about it now, mamma?" Joy said softly.

"Where is Brittany? I knew she was up to no good," mamma shot out before anyone could answer.

"Monica has been trying to find her for the past four days! She was our only hope!" Joy said. "What's going on grandmamma?"

Grandmamma sat still. She stared at Monica.

"I'm not worried about any of that," grandmamma finally said. "Brittany has been a great help, that's true, but she certainly isn't our only hope. Right now, I'm just a little more concerned about Monica."

"Are you okay?" Joy asked, sliding beside her sister.

Monica didn't answer. She kept her swollen eyes shut.

Grandmamma got up and sat on the other side of her. "Tell me what you're thinking, Monica. I know it's hard but we still need you to fight."

She didn't respond.

"Let's just leave her alone for now," mamma whispered.

"No!" grandmamma said, the intentional firmness now apparent in her voice. "I've got to know what you're thinking, Monica. Talk to me."

"It may be God's Will, grandmamma," Monica finally said.

"What may be God's Will?"

"That my children be placed in other loving homes. He may have found them a better place and its okay."

"Wait. Now, you listen to me real good. Your faith is being tested like never before, but here's what I want you to do. Remember, God is going to see you through all of this. Don't miss out on it by giving up now. You've come too far. Please hold on. Your help is just around the corner."

They all waited on her response.

"Do you really think God wants my children to come back home to us, grandmamma?"

"Indeed I do. That's what He told me and He's not like you and me Monica, changing His mind all the time. That's what He promised us and that's what I believe."

"I believe too," Joy said. "I'm not going to stop believing no matter what happens."

Monica glanced at Joy and smiled. "Grandmamma, what if I *really* believed that? I mean, deep down inside, believe it."

"Then sit back and watch God give you the victory."

They all sat quietly until the ringing phone broke the silence.

"Monica is busy right now. Would you like to leave a message?" mamma said. "Oh, hold a second. There's a man on the phone that says he's the case worker taking Brittany's place. It's really important that he talks to you."

She jumped from the couch. "Hello, hello, this is Monica."

"Hi, my name is Robert Washington. I have some critical information about your children and I need to talk to you right away. Is it too late for me to come by?"

"No, it's not too late at all."

"Then open the door," he said. "I'm sitting out front in the grey SUV."

Monica opened the door to a tall, stately gentleman. His voice resonated so deeply, she found it slightly intimidating.

"Did you know the agency was about to proceed with the final adoption of your two girls on tomorrow, Ms. Gold?" Robert asked. "They claim you were arrested today on a possible drug and murder charge. Is any of this true?"

"Let me explain," Monica said. "I don't know how much Brittany has told you, because what I'm about to tell you may not sound too believable."

"Talk to me," he said, never turning away. He knew he made her nervous but it didn't bother him one bit.

Monica told him everything Big Man shared with her about Gail. Repeating the entire story took all of twenty minutes but he never said a word. She described in detail how Cray followed Joy and how they all ended up in police custody.

"That's what happened, Mr. Washington," she said finishing.

Robert took off his glasses, blew on them and began wiping each lens with his cleaning cloth. The room was still.

"You need to get a lawyer. *Tonight!* Miss Gold." His booming voice made her jump. "Do you know anybody that could suggest a real good one for you?"

They all looked at each other. Monica got up and phoned Chris.

# Chapter 27

## Things in Order

Ms. Dire placed her savings account information on the dining room table. She took off her glasses, sat back in the lone recliner, and stretched. With the money the Browns had given her, even if the adoption of the other child didn't go through, it would be enough for her to retire. She closed her eyes and dreamed of her move to Florida. No more bad neighborhoods, junkies, snotty nosed kids and parents she could care less about. Next week seemed like an eternity. The only thing she had left to do was make certain Monica was picked up on a drug charge. Then no one would ever be able to doubt that she was exactly what she told them she was—a junky. A wide smile crossed her face.

The next morning when she returned to the office, she went over Monica's file again. She'd highlighted in great detail her first real encounter with her. *I met Ms. Gold when she was about to attempt suicide—possible postpartum depression after having premature twins. She now has a total of five children with no support from any of their fathers. With her welfare assistance cut off, she has no means of supporting them. She'd refused my repeated offers of much needed rehab due to her serious cocaine habit. She's ill-tempered and needs money desperately. She even asked me for some.*

Ms. Dire knew Monica had reached out to her for help on a real bad day. She actually had tears in her own eyes when she drove up to the projects. She was so tired of dealing with people like Monica, the bottom of society.

She desperately wanted to associate with only the Gerald's and Charlene's of the world.

It was ironic how she'd met Charlene and Monica during the time she wanted out of the profession the most. When she tried to convince Monica to go to rehab the first time, she resisted. It was at that point she knew she was not going to help this girl. She was going to save her girls though, and through it all, save herself. She sat there and listened to Monica as she cried and felt sorry for herself. When she asked her if she really wanted her children, she suggested again that she go to rehab. Monica actually caught her off guard when she agreed to do so. Ms. Dire knew about the reputations of all the rehab centers so she put her into a mediocre one. Her plan was for her to get lost in the system so she could work her retirement scheme.

Her thoughts were interrupted by the ringing phone. After answering, she shifted back in the chair. It was the news she had been waiting for. It almost brought her to tears. *Monica Gold had been in police custody.* Not only had she been questioned for possible drug charges, she was also questioned in connection with a murder.

Grabbing the coveted record, she documented all of Monica's misfortune in it. She faxed the information directly to the agency's attorney's to use in court tomorrow.

"Thanks for the fax. This should all but seal the adoption for the Brown's," the agency's attorney said. "Another bit of luck that's on our side, Judge Evanston will be hearing the case."

"*YES!*" Ms. Dire said. "I'll see you in court tomorrow."

When she hung up, she decided to go home early and finish packing. After tomorrow, she was going to have all the money she needed to shake this god-forsaken town. The other adoption should fall in place right after this one. The Crafts agreed to have the money in her account by the time she moved to Florida.

Opening the door to her house, she walked around the boxes she'd stacked in the middle of the floor. She had lived there twenty- five years and collected a whole lot of stuff, but now, she felt the house to be an empty, lifeless shell. She sat on top of one of the boxes and reminisced about her daughter, Antoinette. There was never a day that went by when she didn't think of her.

When her only child died, her whole world had fallen apart. She'd been a healthy, beautiful young lady who lived a vivacious and wonderful life. Antoinette's wedding had been an exciting time for them and the news that followed of her pregnancy a year later was a welcomed event. The pregnancy was an uncomplicated one and they had the baby shower right there in the room where she sat. They'd anticipated a smooth delivery but by the time they got to the hospital, suddenly, everything had gone wrong. Neither mother nor baby was expected to live. Her daughter died first and then the baby girl after a valiant fight. She rarely heard from her son-in-law anymore. Ms Dire could not understand why her beautiful daughter had to die. She didn't use drugs and basically did everything that was right. Why did God allow mothers who obviously didn't care for themselves, let alone their babies to live, and then take her only beautiful girl? It wasn't fair. For twelve long years she had been trying to understand that. Finally, she'd managed to push all the bad memories aside. Now, she was determined to take matters into her own hands. She would soon be leaving this cold city behind that offered her nothing but a heart full of sorrows—a place where she didn't have to associate with people like Monica and her family, Gail and Cray and even Robert and Brittany.

She just hadn't been able to afford to get out of town before. Now, all of that was about to change.

~~~

Ms. Dire was happy to see the two girls were getting along better with Ann when she phoned.

"The girls seem to be more content with you, Ann," Ms Dire said.

"I told you I could handle them. They don't cry near as much either, have you noticed?"

"Well, that's great. Your daughter and son seem to like having them around as well."

"It's the strangest thing. I can't keep my kids away from those two. They ignore the other kids and just spend their time with these fosters. Especially Clara. The girls cling to her like crazy. They'll sit and let her comb their hair and even dress 'em and all kinds of stuff."

"How old is your little girl, Ann?" Ms. Dire asked.

"She's eight, and my son is nine."

"You know, your little girl reminds me of the girl's older sister, Peaches."

Ann didn't ever want to hear that name again. She'd finally gotten the older girl to stop calling for her. In fact she'd had enough of these kids. Even though it was obvious her own kids were trying to keep the "two brats" away from her, it still wasn't working. She was tired of trying to hide the bruises and black eyes she had given each of them. She wanted Ms. Dire to come and get them.

"Even though the girls are getting along better here, it's still time for them to leave."

"You're going to have to deal with them for just a couple of more weeks."

"If you knew how tired I was, you would never ask me to do something like that, Dire."

"Now calm down, Ann," Ms Dire said.

"No, I'm tired and I need a break from all the children that are in my house—even my own."

She hated when she called her Dire but she needed her to keep the kids until the adoptions took place. After she was in the sunny state of Florida, she could do whatever she wanted to with the girls. In her heart she knew these two kids would end up as mere statistics, hopelessly lost in the complex foster care system. They would most likely go from home to home.

"I need the kids out and out of here now!"

"You are really making things extremely difficult for me. I need them to stay in your home for just two short weeks." Ms. Dire said.

"I don't know if my nerves can take anymore, Dire. Anyway, I think I already need to take the little one to the hospital again. If I take her there this time, they may just lock me up. Do you understand that?"

She was silent. Even Ms Dire was tired of her banging up on these kids.

"What's wrong with the child this time, Ann?"

"I think her arm is broken."

"Well, you can't take her to the hospital now can you?"

"Oh, I think you're finally getting the picture, Dire."

"Well, you're just going to have to set the arm yourself."

"How do you propose I set an arm, Dire?  I don't need to be playing doctor on that kid."

"Put her arm on a board and wrap it, Ann."

"Okay, okay, I'll try and do that.  Now, tell me when are you're going to have these two brats taken out of my home?"

"Like I said, give me two more weeks?  I promise I'll have them out of your house by then.  Now, please give me your word you won't kill one of them, Ann, before then," Ms. Dire said.

Ann knew in her heart she couldn't make that promise.

# Chapter 28

## Kink in the Plan

Gerald could tell whenever Charlene was nervous. She was always quiet. Any other time, she would be chattering away. Today, she simply dressed Geraldene.

This was the day they both had been waiting for. Ms. Dire assured them that everything was in order. All they had to do was get through the morning and Geraldene would be theirs. He was disappointed when Pastor Collins said they couldn't join them. He really did want them to share in one of the most important days of their lives.

Gerald thought of the day that he went in to invite Pastor Collins to the last of the adoption proceedings. He still voiced concern.

"I know this seems like a good idea to you," he'd said. "I wish you would do it the way your heart is telling you to. Things will work out for you and Charlene if you go about adopting Geraldene the right way."

Gerald had become slightly annoyed at that statement. Why did he keep using the phrase, "the right way?" He'd finally come to realize that they were doing it "the right way." Anything that would keep his baby out of the hands of an abusive mother, to him was "the only way." Pastor Collins is a good man, he thought. He'll come around in time.

"Are you okay?" he asked, wrapping his arms around Charlene.

"I'm fine. I guess I just can't wait until all of this is over."

She leaned her head against him. "I hate bringing this up but Ms. Dire's called yesterday. She asked me to remind you about the money."

"I have every penny of it. Honestly, I'll be glad when we don't have to deal with her anymore," he said releasing her. "Let's get going before we're late."

When they were summoned inside, Ms. Dire sat in the back of the courtroom. Charlene and Gerald joined hands as the judge began reading the adoption petition. After he completed it, he looked up. "A second petition has been issued to the court as well by the child's biological mother. She is requesting that the court restore full custodial rights of this infant to her. Is counsel here representing the mother?" the judge asked.

"Yes, your honor," he said approaching the bench. Monica, grandmamma, mamma, Joy and Jessica also walked in with him and took seats opposite the Browns. The lawyer representing Charlene and Gerald looked at the judge and lifted his hands to object. He decided against saying anything when he realized who the lawyer was. John T. Alexander was his name, one of the premier attorneys in the country. His prices were exorbitant and had a reputation of getting exactly what he wanted.

While the judge threw a barrage of questions at Monica's lawyer, Gerald squeezed Charlene's hand. He could tell she was about to lose it.

The judge listened and scratched his head. One side described the picture of a mother who was a hopeless drug abuser and linked to a murder. The other painted one of a mother who'd turned her life around.

"I'm ordering an hour recess," he said, vacating the bench.

When Gerald and Charlene turned, it was the first time they'd looked into the face of Geraldene's mother. Charlene wanted to scratch her eyes out. Gerald steered her outside. Ms. Dire met with them in the hall and tried consoling them both. She saw Brittany's name all over this. An officer in the courtroom called out her name.

"The judge needs to see you in his chambers," he said.

"You never followed up on this client. Is that true, Arlene?" the judge asked.

She sat in front of his desk and calmly explained. "I didn't follow up your honor because the centers would usually send *us* follow up notes on their clients. Whenever they didn't, that simply meant the client left the center and had not succeeded with rehabilitation. Plus, you know the case loads we have. I can't keep up with that level of detail on everybody."

She knew she was convincing. "I've been so concerned about these girls. I saw to it personally that they were placed in the best homes possible. Judge, this mother has been involved in a murder and…"

"They say she's gotten a job now," he said, interrupting.

"That's not too uncommon for drug abusers," she answered immediately. "They want to support their habits. She's been cut off from public assistant. She needs the money."

The judge nodded in agreement.

"You know I've been in this business a long time, Jimmy. Please, let's not make a mistake on this one. I know you remember the case of Baby Albert. The agency—no, the entire city can't afford another black eye like the one they received. I realize the judge thought she was doing the right thing—giving the baby back to the biological mother and all. The mother painted a wonderful picture of how she'd changed her life. I don't need to remind you it wasn't a month later the baby died a horrific death at her hands. We took him from a loving mother and father who would have given him the best life had to offer and gave him to a murderer. When the baby died, I knew then the judge that made the decision would never recover."

The adoption battle of Baby Albert made the front pages of every newspaper with the judge's name spread throughout.

"Your honor, this mother was seen at The Hole the exact time Mr. Fort was killed." She paused and took a deep breath.

"Thank you, Arlene. You've been very helpful."

The judge had all but made his decision. He remembered the Baby Albert case all too well. That one case had more influence on his decisions than any. He had a serious problem as it was with judges who removed babies from homes they knew to be safe, just to give them to biological mothers whose futures were uncertain. He also knew Ms. Arlene Dire. She'd appeared before his court many times. She was competent and dependable. He didn't care who the attorney was that came up against her. The evidence she presented was too convincing.

Even though he didn't want to, he knew he had no choice. He called for Monica.

Monica walked slowly into his office. She didn't understand any of the feelings she was experiencing. Something deep inside was telling her to give up. When she looked at the Browns, she really did believe they would be good parents. The mother looked a little angry, but that was all right. She knew she really loved her child. It was all so confusing. She desperately wanted her baby, but even if she lost, she knew the Browns would give her a happy home.

"Young lady, you need to tell me what's going on in your life. I don't like what I'm hearing."

She wanted to ask him, *"And exactly what is that, your honor"*—but she knew better.

"Sir, I don't know what anyone has told you. I know you have no reason to believe any of what I'm about to tell you either." She paused and swallowed hard. "I did some things no decent mother should have done to her children. Now that I know better, I am not proud of how I lived my life and exposed my children to such dangers. I just want the opportunity to make it up to them and I can do that now, sir. I've changed…boy have I changed. If you find it hard to believe me, there's only one request I have. I'd just ask that you find good people like the Browns to give my girls to if you want to give them away, your honor."

"Do you want your children given away Miss Gold?" he asked.

All the emotions of the past year, poured out. She knew he was finding it difficult to understand what she tried to say. The tears and gulps garbled her words.

"Take your time, Ms. Gold." He handed her his box of tissues.

"Sir, I'm so tired. I'm so-o very tired. I…love… my girls…more than anything… in this world," she forced out. "Please don't take them from me. *Please*…I'll do….right…I promise I will," she cried.

Monica had nothing left to say. She laid her head on the side of his desk and wept.

~~~

"Ms. Dire, are you sure the judge is on our side?" Charlene asked, biting the side of her nail.

"Charlene, this is Judge Jimmy Evanston. He knows me very well. Trust me."

She was tempted to tell Gerald to forget everything and implement Plan B but again, Miss Dire was convincing. Everything will be okay she told herself. Geraldene was going to be theirs no matter what. She thought about how Gerald wanted to call the whole adoption off at one point. Now that he was safely on her side, she wasn't going to allow anything else to stand in their way. Charlene motioned for Gerald as they huddled in the long hallway.

"I think we can believe Miss Dire, honey. She's been here for us all the time. She deserves every dime we promised her," Charlene said.

"I don't want to give her the rest of the money until this is over, Charlene."

"Come on, Gerald. Give her the money. She's gotten us this far. I feel that if we give her the rest now, she'll pull this off no matter what."

"What do you mean?"

"If we need her help to implement plan B, she'll be there for us. Please give it to her."

"Perhaps you're right."

Charlene saw the look on Miss Dire's face when Gerald handed her the rest of the cash. She couldn't hear what he said but did notice that Miss Dire shook her head, in firm agreement.

"All rise," the bailiff announced as the judge entered the room. Only the rustling sound of the people standing could be heard. An uncomfortable quietness filled the room.

"There is a serious breakdown in communication in this case," Judge Evanston said. "There are obviously two completely different stories and I'm not thoroughly convinced of either. What I do know is, this child is in a very safe environment at the present time. Therefore, it is the decision of the court to allow Gerald and Charlene Brown to maintain temporary custody of the child until we can sort through this matter. I will set a date in two weeks for counsels to return and present their cases."

The judge pointed his gavel at Monica and said, "*You,* young lady. I hope you will not be found *at* or *near* this place called The Hole during that time. That's all!" He pounded the gavel hard.

Charlene, Gerald, Miss Dire, along with their parents moved swiftly from the courtroom.

Monica looked at her lawyer. "I lost didn't I?"

"You'll only lose when he says he's giving permanent custody of your child to the Browns. So, today, you've won."

# Chapter 29

## Trial Time

Brittany was trying to convince her neurologist to discharge her from the hospital. He'd already transferred her to a regular room. Even though her head ached, she didn't ask for any pain medication. The follow up MRI showed that the bruise to her head was improving and she continued displaying no neurological deficits. He still wouldn't release her due to the pain.

Brittany knew another day would mean one less day of working on Monica's case. Not any of it was fair to Robert. He'd been thrown into the middle of this and was convinced he wasn't making any progress. He told her what happened in court today and was extremely disappointed and worried about the results. She tried her best to reassure him.

"Getting an attorney like John T. Alexander in one night was a miracle, Robert. Without that, we might be talking about how we could go about reversing a permanent placement decision."

Her pep talk wasn't working and she didn't have the energy to continue.

"I understand, but Monica's own lawyer admitted if she hadn't gone to The Hole, we'd be looking at a completely different case. Brittany, Monica's presence there has cast serious doubt on her credibility. In fact they are building their whole case around that."

"Even after everything else she's done to clean up her life.   What about all of that?" she said, her frustration mounting.

"Listen," he whispered in the phone.   "They found someone in the Rehab Center to say that she hadn't been checking in at night like she should have and that she was told to stay away from The Hole no matter what.  So her successful rehab is even being questioned.  Oh, by the way, the drug debacle at the school, they're doing a good job of making that situation even more believable.  Ms. Dire is good, Brittany.   She knows exactly what she's doing"

Brittany held onto the phone wishing her head wasn't throbbing.

"One more thing," Robert said.   "Even though I know you won't be surprised by this, her best friend Gail was expected to testify against her.  Since she's gone and gotten herself shot, she sent a taped message to the judge supposedly of Monica's involvement in Jay Jay's murder. Get this—she's now living in a nice house with some guy named Mike and they take care of foster children.  A real upright kind of girl, huh?"

~~~

John T. Alexander had great concerns about what was going to happen in the courtroom tomorrow.  The lawyer for the agency was doing a yeomen's job of discrediting Monica's parental skills.  She had been an awful mother, he thought.   Judge Evanston was known for having absolutely no sympathy for parents like that.  He was even known for giving sole custody to father's who's wives worked outside the home and didn't spend enough time with their children.  Likewise, he would give mother's sole parental custody from fathers who refused to pay child support. His rulings were often viewed as controversial and he was proud of it.

He would do everything he could to show how well Monica was recovering but it was going to be difficult. When he got the phone call from Chris asking him this favor, he thought it would be a simple win. Even with the incident at The Hole, it was still a fifty—fifty chance of him winning this case. His inside sources said they thought the police now had witnesses that could confirm Monica plotted to have Jay Jay killed. If that were the case, she would be looking at a bigger charge against her. He tried to keep Monica encouraged. He didn't need her too distraught on the witness stand.

He'd already spent more hours than planned going over her case. His gut was telling him Ms. Dire was the culprit behind it all. If his hunches were right—and they usually were—money was at the root of it. It was a sad case. The way things were going, she may actually pull off her elaborate scheme.

He pushed back from his desk and yawned. He was tired and wanted to go home. Then it dawned on him, there was one more thing he needed to look at.

# Chapter 30

## Someone to Talk To

Monica didn't want to miss another day of work. Brooke had been more than understanding. Even though she felt she needed to spend more time with her attorney, going back to work at this point was a priority.

Monica arrived early. As usual Brooke was already there and quite surprised to see her when she walked in.

"I had to come in today. I know how busy we are. Besides, it takes my mind off all that I'm going through," Monica said.

"Sit down for a moment, Monica," Brooke said sliding the chair towards her.

Monica massaged her temples. Was this the end of her job? Had Brooke also heard about Jay Jays' murder? She took in a deep breath and tried to brace herself for what was about to come next.

"Tell me everything that's going on with your children. You seem different and quite frankly, I'm concerned about you."

Monica found Brooke's words comforting. While she enjoyed her businesslike manner, she was not quite use to this softer side she now displayed.

She never wanted her personal life to impact her job and until now, she had been successful. Her emotions were so fragile at this point, she wasn't at all surprised that Brooke had noticed a change in her demeanor. Her boss deserved an explanation. "Let me start from the beginning," she said. Monica told her a portion of what she was dealing with. She didn't leave out the nights she left her children alone—not even the night she lost all of her girls.

Typical Brooke style, she never changed her expression.

The ringing phones in the background were a distraction. Monica was about to answer when Brooke put up her hand. She reached over and dialed the intercom. "Tanya, transfer Monica's lines and reschedule all my appointments for this afternoon." She nodded. "Now, please finish."

Monica proceeded. "When I met Chris and he offered me this job, I knew it was my time to show everybody I had truly changed. That was important to me. I thought if I could make others see the change, then perhaps at some point I'd even be able to convince myself that I had. Little did I know I had that part backwards. Once I understood for myself how important it was to be a different person, then it was easy for others to see. I needed a lot of help to make that happen. I actually found it in the most unexpected places. A Healthy Place helped me work on my self-confidence but it wasn't until I moved into my mother's house that made the difference. I went to church with my grandmother one day and I haven't been the same since. To make a long story short, as a result, I now have a savings account, something I've never had before in my life. I've slowly regained the trust of my mother, which is a biggie. Yesterday, I opened my grades and officially have a 4.0 average at the Community College. All of these are first's in my life. I know without a shadow of a doubt, I'm a dependable and trustworthy person. The bottom line, I am able to take care of my children. I believe that deep in my heart."

"I believe you can too," Brooke said smiling. "Take care of yourself through all of this Monica. Tanya and I can handle the office until things get back to normal."

Monica hugged and thanked her for being so understanding.

Brooke watched Monica as she left the office. She picked up the phone and called her brother.

# Chapter 31

## Ann

Ann kept count of the days when Ms. Dire was coming to take the girls off her hands. She had less than a week. If she didn't come, she already had their belongings packed and planned to just drop them off at the agency. They couldn't force her to keep them. The younger girl's arm was not healing. She really needed to see a doctor. She'd asked Ms. Dire to come and get them. In fact she'd begged her to. So, it was Ms. Dire's fault they were all beaten up.

"Mommy, may I give the girls a bath?" Clara asked.

"Yeah, go ahead and then put them in the bed," Ann said.

"May I give them some milk and cookies before they go to bed?"

"Absolutely not."

She skipped upstairs with the girls close behind.

Ann knew Clara tried everything she could to take care of those two girls. They loved being around her. The most tense time for them all was when the girls cried. She didn't understand why but all the yelling would cause her to go into an uncontrollable rage. It wasn't normal and she recognized that and one day would seek help but for now, it was just best to keep the girls away from her. That's why she put them to bed early. They would go to bed so early that they would wake up at dawn. The baby girl would cry because she wanted to get out of bet. She'd dared her to get up, though. Once she got out of bed and she had to put her back. She beat her so badly that when she checked on Clara she found her with her head under her pillow—crying.

When she let Clara give the girls a bath, they stayed up a little longer. She played with them in the tub. That was getting on her nerves, too.

Ann walked into the bathroom to get a towel out of the closet.

"Get those girls out of the tub right now, Clara."

"Can we stay in a little longer?" Julia asked looking at Clara.

Ann knew that wasn't a reason to get upset—but she did. From out of nowhere, she reached down and held Julia under the water. She struggled but she was much too strong for her. She saw the horror in Clara's eyes as she watched Julia lose her struggle to fight. She was drowning and there was nothing she could do about it. Ann knew Countess was going to be next. She was screaming at the top of her lungs.

# Chapter 32

## Friends

Joy's first day at school after the incident was a nightmare. She could feel the stares. The word had spread everywhere that she was involved in selling drugs at school. Myles tried consoling her but it did little to help.

The girls that didn't like her before any of this happened—the ones that hated all cheerleaders, wanted to see her kicked off the squad. It worked. Early that morning the coach called her into the office.

"Please close the door behind you, Joy," she said. "I've heard some very disturbing news. Quite frankly, I'm finding it difficult to believe. I'm afraid we're going to have to suspend you from the squad until this drug matter can be sorted out," the coach said.

By the end of the day there were rumors that she could no longer represent them as the homecoming queen. Her student advisor was also threatening to inform the universities offering her scholarships of the incident.

Joy watched as two of her closest friends walked pass her without saying a word. She ran to catch them. "Hey wait up," she said.

They kept walking clutching their books without acknowledging her.

"I know you don't believe what they're saying about me, do you Karen?" Joy asked, pulling her aside.

She shrugged.

"So, you do believe them! I thought we were friends."

She pulled Joy closer. "We are friends, Joy. It's just…"

"It's just what!"

"My dad offered you a ride home when he finished fixing my tire and you turned him down. He thinks you wanted to stay there to sell your drugs. He told the principal that. Why didn't you come with us that day Joy?" she asked.

"My sister was coming to pick me up! You know that!"

"I know but, my dad thinks differently. He doesn't want me hanging around you anymore," she said tearfully, slowly, turning and walking away.

By the time her mother came to pick her, Joy had not talked to anyone most of the day.

"What's wrong?" mamma asked as soon as she saw her face.

She burst into tears.

~~~

Monica really couldn't explain to anyone how she felt as she entered the courtroom.

Her lawyer kept reaching over and telling her to relax. "Breathe," he said. "Just answer the questions honestly."

She was trying to relax. In fact she was trying to do anything that would muster up an emotion. In her heart she knew she had to pull herself together. There was one problem. She couldn't get her mind to cooperate.

Of all days, it appeared her emotions had decided to shut down for the day. She wanted to reach over and tell her lawyer that she simply couldn't do it. She couldn't testify and she didn't understand why. All her hopes, all her dreams and desires, everything she ever wanted were right before her. She just didn't have the will to fight anymore. She tried to pray, but that wasn't working. She tried thinking about the prayer grandmamma prayed just before they came, and that didn't help either. The fuse that lit her emotions had gone out. She couldn't generate a spark no matter how hard she tried. Her emotional shutdown intensified when she looked into the eyes of the *judge*. He seemed to be glaring at her with such disdain. *Gerald and Charlene* were sitting on the other side and looked over at her as if they wanted her dead. *The Brown's lawyer* was tapping his foot as if he could hardly wait to tear her apart. *Gerald and Charlene's church members and family* packed the courtroom. They would occasionally look at her as if they pitied her. Some even shook their heads. As for *Ms. Dire,* well, the sneer on her face made her nauseous—a look that epitomized evil. She sat next to a man Monica thought was her *supervisor.* He constantly looked at his watch as if he wanted to hurry it all along and take her children away. Then there was *Robert Washington.* The expression on his face was one of great concern. One that said, I'm so sorry Monica about how all this is going to turn out for you. Sitting next to him was *Brittany.* She had on dark glasses inside the courtroom and kept her head down. She was probably thinking the same thing. Monica wished she hadn't over heard Robert tell her lawyer how much trouble he thought he and Brittany were in as a result of this case. They could possibly lose their jobs, he'd said. He was worried. He had a family.

*Her own family's expression* caused her grief as well. Ever since Joy came home from her awful day at school, she'd grown more and more depressed. She wouldn't eat and didn't want to go back to school. *Mamma* had been crying all night. What happened to Joy really upset her. This was the one daughter she had hope for. Now, because of her, it was slowly being taken away. Mamma's expression didn't help matters either. Every day she would say how all of this was her fault. *"She should have gone and gotten her girls and brought them home."* She repeated that ten times a day.

*Grandmamma* sat there expressionless. Monica heard her tell Jessica that she'd been having bad dreams about Julia and Countess. What concerned Monica most was Grandmamma wasn't saying very much. That just meant she knew something she didn't want to share. It had to be really bad news if that were the case.

The unthinkable happened as they were leaving for court this morning. They finally came and got the other twin. Her lawyer informed her, they might be filing charges about that as well.

The slamming of the judge's gavel made her jump. She reached over to her lawyer, pulling the cuff of his shirt. "I can't do this."

"Calm down, you're going to be all right."

"No…listen…I can't do this anymore."

He leaned over and whispered in her ear. "You've got to get yourself together, Monica. I need you right now."

"I don't know what's happening to me. Maybe my baby is better off with this couple. Look at them. They look as if they could give her a better life than I ever could."

"What are you saying? Do you really want to give up and let them have your baby?"

"I think so.  I can't go up there and testify.  I can't make myself do it."

"At least try so you won't regret it later."

The agency's attorney had already started telling the judge what an outstanding job the Brown's had done caring for the baby.

"Monica I don't want you to give up.  Let's see how things turn out," he said reaching out to hold her hand.

After the agency's attorney finished calling one by one a list of character witnesses for the Brown's, he turned and called her name.

She could feel the battle raging in her mind.  It was pleading with her at this point.  *Give it all up.  It's over.*  With everything in her she forced her way to the stand.  As soon as she was sworn in, the questioning began.

"Have you ever left your children alone for an extended period of time, Ms. Gold?"

"Yes."

"For more than a couple of hours?" he asked.

"Yes."

"Speak up Ms. Gold.  I need you to speak up!"

"For more than a day?"

"Yes."

"More than two days!"

"Yes."

"How old was your youngest when you did that?"

"One."

"How old was the oldest?"

"Seven."

The questions got tougher.

She watched as the unfamiliar faces sat shaking their heads.  The attorney like a skilled artist, painted a vivid

masterpiece of the abusive mother for the entire courtroom to see.

Monica was numb.  She couldn't hear anything the
attorney was saying at some point.  She began to wonder
how it was going to feel to give birth to five children and
not be able to raise any of them.

"Miss Gold!  Will you answer my question please?"

Monica spoke at a murmur.  "Can you repeat the
question?"

"Were you at The Hole at the time of the death of a
James Fort?"

Monica cleared her throat.

"Will you speak up Miss Gold?  I repeat, were you at
The Hole at the time of the death of James Fort?  Miss
Gold are you going to answer the question?"

Monica never responded.

"Miss Gold, I need you to answer?"

"Yes."

Gasps could be heard throughout the courtroom.

"Are you okay young lady," the judge asked.

"Your honor, may I approach the bench?" Monica's
attorney asked.

"Please do."

They huddled.  "My client is overwhelmed your hon-
or.  I need to have a word with her."

"Tell her to get it together, John.  We can't be here all
day."

"Monica," he whispered approaching her.  "Please let
me help you.  Do you trust me?"

"No," she said.

"Then I can't help you.  Is there anyone you do trust
right now?"

"God."

"Why don't you let God use me to help you today, Monica? Relax and answer the questions. I know they're difficult but just tell the truth."

He returned to his seat as the agency's attorney resumed.

Shortly, it was his turn. John T. Alexander stepped forward.

"I must admit, my client has displayed some pretty horrendous behavior. Yet, we're not here to deny or defend any of that, your honor. We are here, however, to point out what Monica Gold has done to rectify all her ill deeds and turn her life around."

He enumerated one by one, each of her accomplishments, his voice rising and falling. The Browns squirmed. He was good at causing that reaction.

"Your honor, the first person I would like to call to the stand is Ms. Arlene Dire."

Ms. Dire casually walked up never taking her eyes off him.

That was okay. He couldn't wait to get her on the stand. Once she'd answered the preliminary questions, he then focused his attention on exposing her fraudulent behavior.

"Did you follow-up with the Rehab Center about Ms. Gold's progress?"

"Not in this case. No, I didn't follow up."

"Was this a high risk case for you, Ms. Dire?"

"Yes, it was."

"Could you explain to the court, why you didn't follow up on this high risk case like it required?"

"Even though Ms. Gold was a high priority, she joined twenty-five other mothers just like her that also deserved my undivided attention. Therefore, the methodology we have established around the city due to our heavy case load is as follows—if I don't hear from a facility, then I know the clients are no longer there and didn't have a successful rehabilitation," she said her eyes penetrating. Ms. Dire knew this brand new facility wasn't as familiar with all the unspoken rules the older centers had established. That's why she chose this one to put Monica in.

John T. realized he needed to switch his line of questioning. She was good.

Even though he'd given a stellar performance, Ms. Dire was just too believable. He hadn't covered up The Hole incident very well either. He'd been a lawyer for years. He knew when he'd lost.

After he finished his questioning, he sat beside Monica.

"Let them have her," she said. "Let's stop all of this and give these people my baby. I don't want the judge to *take* my children from me again. I wouldn't be able to stand that," she whispered. "They've taken my children from me too many times. I won't let them do that to me again. I'm going to *give* my child to them. I think I can live with that better. So please go and tell that judge this couple can have my baby," Monica said.

"Are you sure?"

"Yes. Hurry! Go up there and tell him. Please don't let him take my child away from me."

He stood and was about to ask permission to approach the bench when the officer handed him a note. Monica watched as John T. turned and looked in the back of the courtroom. When she turned to see what held his attention, she looked into Chris' face.

"Your honor, would you please allow me the opportunity to approach the bench regarding one more witness?"

"I object, your honor!" The other attorney interrupted.

"Come up here you two. What are you doing, counsel?"

"I have someone sir that could explain everything that's happening here."

"You have exactly five minutes. The clock is ticking, starting, *now*."

John T. hurried out the doors. Everyone in the courtroom began to whisper.

Monica gazed straight ahead. She was tired of all of the drama. Her mind was focused on her attorney telling the judge she would like to *give* her baby to the Browns.

Three minutes later, he skirted back into the courtroom.

"Your honor, please give me an opportunity to call another witness. I think we'll have the answers we've all been looking for."

"Go ahead, counsel," he said, peering over his reading glasses.

His voice rang out. "I would like to call a Mr. Marshall "Big Man" Scott to the stand."

Big Man walked into the courtroom with his unique stroll, a slight lean to the right. He appeared larger than ever, with his head held high. He made no eye contact with anyone. With his giant hand raised as he towered over the bailiff, Big Man was sworn in.

"How long have you known my client, Ms. Monica Gold?" the attorney asked, never lowering his voice. He paced back and forth in front of the witness stand.

"We grew up together. Say, about twenty years," Big Man said.

"During those twenty years, how much time did you spend with her?"

"We spent time together in elementary, junior high and high school. We hung out with the same friends until we got older."

"Would you consider her a close friend, Mr. Scott?"

"Yes, a very close friend."

Big Man answered each question as if he had rehearsed them.

"What can you tell us about the incident at The Hole?" he finally asked.

"Gail talked Jay Jay into getting Monica to The Hole. It was all a set up."

"I object," the agency's attorney said rising from his seat, lifting his hands in the air.

Big Man ignored the shouts of objections and the banging of the gavel. He kept on testifying.

"Gail was determined that she wouldn't help Jay Jay until he brought Monica there." Big Man's deep voice boomed over all the noise. "Monica was at the church on the altar when all of this was going on. When she did show up, the murder had already taken place."

A whirlwind of activity followed. Objections, sustains, and orders in the court, were hurled all around.

With much effort, the judge regained control of his courtroom.

Big Man took the opportunity to speak when everyone was quiet. "Your honor, the one person that can tell you better than I can is standing right outside those doors."

"Thank you Mr. Scott. It is time to call our final witness," John T. interrupted.

All eyes turned towards the double doors in the rear. In walked a thin, tall man with a white shirt and tie.

"Please state your name."

"Mr. Cra-a-ay Bedford."

Ms. Dire wouldn't have recognized him had he not stated who he was. The waning color in her face said it all. She jumped from her seat and charged towards the agency's attorney. "Can't you do something about this?"

The pounding of the judge's gavel, echoed in her ears.

"Order! Oder in my courtroom! Will both counsels please approach the bench?" All three men put their heads together. Monica's lawyer was obviously very passionate about something.

"I'm tired of this three ring circus in my courtroom, gentlemen. Continue your questioning John, but I'm warning you, you'd better wrap this up."

"Tell us about the shooting at The Hole, Mr. Bedford."

Ms. Dire's heart raced. Tiny beads of perspiration slowly surfaced when she heard the words that came out of the witness' mouth.

"I sa-aw the whole thing. Miss Monica there was ju-just pulling up when Jay Jay was shot. She-e-e wasn't even there yet. She was real sho-o-ok up man. She-e-e was the one screaming for he-e-lp and all."

He told them about his deal with Ms. Dire and Gail. How he was used to set up Monica and Joy.

"When you che-e-eck out the evidence, you gonna find tha-a-at fake cocaine was mostly a Goodie mixed with ba-a-aby powder. So do-o-n't be ge-e-tting no ideas about arresting me today."

Several people snickered.

Cray confessed to being the person to have followed Joy from school. "I've done some pre-e-etty messed up things, but I tha-a-ank God for Monica's grandma-a-a-amma and my mamma Jessica over there for finding me-e-e-e today. They helped me to understa-a-a-nd how important it is to do the ri-i-ight thing for once in m-m-my life. Gail didn't tell me they were trying to ta-a-ake away those kids. Cray don't mess with no-no-no-body's kids. Man, and I don't hit no wo-o-omen over the head either."

He sat back. They could all tell he felt good about what he'd just done.

Ms. Dire watched as the agency's attorney came forth and tried desperately to discredit him. He got Cray to reveal his drug history and all of his convictions. He did an excellent job again of proving that Cray may not be such a reliable witness. His past was even worse than Monica's and Jay Jays.

"Mr. Yo-o-ur Honor. Can I sho-o-w you something? If you don't believe me, ma-aybe you'll believe this," he said handing the judge a letter. "Jay Jay's mo-o-other, couldn't come down here to-o-o your courthouse today. She's in one of tho-o-se wheelchairs… you know. She sent this letter to you 'cause she-e-e thought it was something yo-o-ou needed to know. Her son wrote it the da-a-ay before they gunned him do-o-wn like a dog. I-I-I really liked Jay Jay. He was my friend."

The judge took the letter and read most of it. He looked at Monica's attorney and said, "I think you need to read this. ALOUD."

John T. took the letter and began to read. *"Dear Monica, I want to tell you how proud I am that you've turned your life around. It has to be magical to finally know where you're headed. I've watched you from afar and I've seen how full of life you are now. You're healthy, and you look real good. You're definitely a changed person and everybody can tell. What an excellent mother you are going to be to each of your five babies now that you've abandoned this crazy lifestyle. Even though you've decided not to hang around Gail and me anymore, I want you to know you're still my best friend, no matter what. I guess that's been the most difficult part of all this, not being able to hang out with you. That's why I'm asking you to help me get what you have. There is one thing my mother always told me, that if the Lord will do it for you, He'll do the same for me. Would you help me Monica? I've known you since grade school and I know what kind of heart you have. You will help me because that's the kind of person you are. So when I shake all this craziness, we'll be able to hang out together again. That will be a day I look forward to. There's one other thing I want you to watch out for. I don't know what Gail is up to but I get the feeling she's up to no good. She keeps trying to get me to bring you to The Hole. I've told her that you would never go there again. She still keeps trying. Just yesterday she told me to try and get you there. I don't know, maybe she really misses you. Well, I wanted you to know what's going on and what my thoughts were. Thanks Monica for being my friend. I'm excited about your future, as well as mine. They both look bright. Your friend, Jay Jay!"*

By the time he finished reading the letter—Monica was standing. Her best friend Jay Jay had somehow rescued her. When she turned around, she saw grand-mamma and Jessica smiling. Miss B. was also there sitting next to her grandmother with her lips pursed, nodding.

Judge Evanston recessed into his chambers. He looked at all the information in front of him. He needed a moment by himself to digest it all. The letter from the dead man was strange even for him. This was turning into one of the most complex adoption cases that had come into his courtroom in years. He'd never had a moment's hesitation of granting custody to the rightful parent based on the evidence. This time, however, he was having difficulty deciphering through this latest version of the story. If the biological mother lost, she could easily go to jail. It would establish the fact that the court still believed she was dealing hard core drugs and involved in a murder. On the other hand, he wondered if Ms. Dire had deliberately painted a negative picture of the mother. If that were the case, then she was in serious trouble as well, along with the adoptive parents.

It was time to find out some answers.

~ ~ ~

Gerald and Charlene decided to implement Plan B.

"If they don't give us Geraldene, we'll move away," he whispered. To a country we both love. It will be an excellent place to raise our daughter."

She squeezed his hand. "I think that's a great idea," she said calmly.

Ms. Dire wanted to get out of there. She scanned the room and weighed her options. There was only one way out and a large sheriff was standing in front of it. The judge had given instructions to let no one leave the courtroom. Then, she noticed her supervisor engaged in a vigorous conversation with Brittany and Robert.

Her only choice at that point was to sit down and wait.

Grandmamma was glad to have Jessica and Miss B by her side. It was Jessica that called her and told her about the letter Jay Jay's mother discovered. Nobody but the Lord had allowed them to see Cray on their way to retrieve the letter. Jessica hadn't seen her son in over a year. After they prayed for him, they were surprised at the story Cray told them.

Grandmamma also knew the two men she could count on to help her granddaughter. Big Man and Chris did what she expected them to do. They both handled the situation.

"All rise!" the bailiff's deep voice boomed.

As the courtroom settled, an eerie quietness again, rippled through the air. It seemed an eternity before the judge said anything. He readjusted his papers and calmly veered at all of them in the room.

"I've thoroughly reviewed this case and I've come to a firm conclusion along with a set of recommendations of my own. Anyone that knows anything about me is very much aware of how much I detest the use of illegal drugs or the sale of them in our communities." He peered over his glasses at Monica. "The Protective Services attorneys have done an outstanding job of thoroughly convincing me that both drug use and the sale of them have indeed taken place. How any of you could come into my courtroom knowing that you exposed five innocent children to such heinous behavior is beyond me?" he said, staring angrily at Monica. "I am also convinced that in the biological mother's custody, these five girls were at extreme risk and in fact, their very lives were in jeopardy. What you did to those beautiful girls was unforgivable. It was a wise and correct decision of the agency to take these at risk children and place them into stable and loving homes. When the agency did that, it allowed this out of control family the time it needed to either get it together or proceed with permanently taking these children away from such ominous living conditions. Miss Monica Gold, would you please stand."

The judge's eyes seemed to pierce right through her. Her attorney assisted her. She glanced back at her family. In all of her twenty four years she could never remember her grandmother's face so sad. Joy laid her head on their mother's shoulder and cried.

"I am convinced young lady, that you have conducted yourself in a way that saddens me. You have negatively impacted our community by infecting it with illegal drugs and all the evils associated with that kind of behavior. It is because of what you have done, that we are all here in the first place. Most of all, it grieves me to know that five innocent baby's worlds have been flipped upside down because of it all. I don't have to remind any adult what it does to a child when their home lives are unstable like the one you provided for them. They suffer both inside and out."

He glared and hesitated before he spoke again.

"Monica Gold, you've done a lot of damage and I know you are keenly aware of that. Not only were you about to lose your girls—you were about to squander away your own life. I am glad however, to hear that you had a change of heart and decided to turn your life around. You have come to your senses young lady and it couldn't have come soon enough. So that I could with all certainty know this about you, I took the liberty of talking with your rehab counselors myself. It is clear to me that you have done an outstanding job during your rehabilitation period. I also made a personal phone call to my friend and your pastor to corroborate your rehab success. He spoke highly of you and told me that you were actually at church with him on the day you witnessed your friend Jay Jay murdered and the wonderful experience you had there. The letter that was presented from the deceased, James Fort I must say was impressive. Many of your old neighbors are outside those doors and have attested to it all. I would also like to thank you Mr. Chris Blankenship," he nodded towards the rear of the courtroom. "I understand Miss Gold is an excellent employee of yours. It was good talking with Brooke." He smiled. He looked back at Monica. "Based on all the evidence presented, I believe you are no longer a danger to yourself or a threat to your child," he said peering hard at her. "You have been on the right track for quite some time now. I am convinced you understand how fortunate you are to have been given a second chance and right now you're taking full advantage of that. Therefore, it is the court's opinion that the child be returned immediately to her biological mother. All parental rights restored and full custody is awarded to Ms. Monica Gold."

"*NO!*" someone shouted out. The courtroom began to buzz.

"*Order. Order in the court room,*" he said banging his gavel. "You have until three pm tomorrow afternoon to return the child back to her mother," he continued.

"I am also advising that the agency take a very close look at the manner in which this case has been handled."

There were gasps all over the courtroom.

"I can't believe this," someone yelled.

"*I will have order in my court room,*" he yelled back, banging the gavel repeatedly. The guard made his presence known as he marched up and down the aisle. The courtroom became quiet again.

The judge turned his gaze from Monica and eyed Ms. Dire.

"I don't know why the agency failed to follow up on the progress of this young lady but to me it is inexcusable. Whatever the reason may have been, I would even advise you Miss Gold to ask your lawyer to find out why. There is obvious pain and suffering you've incurred as a result of all this manipulation. If you presented this case to me, I would award you the maximum amount young lady," he said shifting his attention between Monica and Miss Dire.

He paused. The court room remained quiet.

"In addition, it is the court's opinion that no drug deal took place at the school between the defendant and her sister. Miss Gold, I will personally send a letter to the school on behalf of your sister, clearing up that situation as well. Go home young lady and take good care of your child."

He slammed the gavel. "Court's dismissed."

The courtroom was in a frenzy.

Monica looked at her lawyer and smiled.

"Well, you won," he said. "You're going to get to keep your baby."

Monica's family rushed up to her and held on. Her lawyer tried to pull her aside to set up arrangements for getting the baby home tomorrow with the other attorney. He gave up. Many of her old neighbors had already flooded the courtroom. She was consumed by the crowd. Even a newspaper reporter was trying to interview her.

# Chapter 33

## Change

Gerald, Charlene and their parents exited the courtroom immediately after the judge's decision.

A church member tried grabbing Gerald's arm. "I'm so sorry," he said.

He rushed right past him steering Charlene out of the courtroom straight to the car. Once inside, Charlene screamed and cried. *"They can't do this to us. They can't take my baby away."*

"We're going to work through this." He had no other words of comfort.

Her mom and dad wanted to come over but they needed to be alone. Even though he talked about running away to another country he wasn't sure if he could go through with it. It would only be a matter of time and they'd find them and when they did, they would definitely be in more legal trouble than they were already in.

As he thought it through, he knew he was going to have to somehow convince Charlene of the unthinkable. She had to let Geraldene go.

When they arrived home, he immediately paid and dismissed the babysitter. He watched Charlene as she nestled the baby close, kissing her tiny head as she walked along the flowers in the garden area. He joined them, cuddling the two people who meant more to them than anyone could have imagined.

"Honey, I think we have to talk about what's happening," Gerald said.

"What's there to talk about?" she asked. "We need to pack our bags and get out of town with our baby."

"I know we talked about moving, but let's think logically about that option. If we get caught, we'll have to spend some time in jail. If that happens, not only will I lose Geraldene, I'll lose you too. You know I can't let that happen."

Charlene knew in her heart he was right. She put her head on his shoulder and cried.

"I don't know how to give my baby away Gerald."

"I know, honey. Perhaps we can talk to the mother. She seemed like a nice girl. Maybe she will let us come and see Geraldene every now and then."

"Ms. Dire lied to us!" she screamed.

~~~

Brittany and Robert finally got to Monica through the crowd outside. Monica pushed everyone aside when she saw Brittany. "I'm so thankful you are okay. I've been looking everywhere for you!" She yelled over the noise.

"I had a date with a bus," she laughed. "Congratulations, Monica," Brittany said.

Monica whispered in her ear as they hugged. "Thank you for everything you've done for me."

Brittany got in Robert's car. They went to meet their supervisor at his request. When they walked in the office, spontaneous applause erupted. All their co-workers surrounded them, giving them well deserved pats on the back. Above Brittany's desk was a huge sign. Welcome Back! On her desk were a dozen red roses.

"I just want the two of you to know how much I appreciate what you've done for the agency. It was because of your hard work and commitment that we were able to avert a catastrophic event from occurring in this office. I also want you to know that I understand why you couldn't come forth any time sooner than you did," their supervisor said.

Brittany squeezed Robert's arm.

"We are trying to locate Ms. Dire. She left the courtroom right after the judge's ruling. Another case worker went by her house and it's vacant. We will be looking deeper into the allegations about her connections with another client named, Gail Bonner. Ms. Dire should know that criminal charges could be filed against her by the agency," he said. "Again, I want to thank the two of you for such an outstanding job. Brittany, how are you feeling?"

"I'm actually feeling better then I've felt since the incident happened. I guess it may have been the tension that kept me with the headache. Suddenly my head feels one hundred percent better."

"I know this is your first day out of the hospital. So take it a little slow considering all you've been through."

"I will," she said. "I'd like to thank Robert for following up on my cases while I've been out. If he hadn't intervened, I'm afraid this wouldn't have ended the way it did."

"I agree," the supervisor said. "Brittany, Robert, the one case I do want the two of you to continue to follow, is Ms. Monica Gold's. I think we need to fix it so that she is able to get all of her children back home as soon as possible."

"Thank you so much," Brittany said. After leaving his office, she went to the file room and pulled Monica's real file.

~~~

The next day, grandmamma's house was filled with family and friends. While Monica enjoyed being with them all, her thoughts were on her child. She liked the sound of the five words that whirled inside her head...*her child was coming home*. Brittany also called and said she would be bringing the other twin back in a few hours.

"I can't wait until I get my hands on those little munchkins," her older sister said coming through the door. "I can't believe you've had one of them for three months and didn't tell me. I realize I haven't done my part by helping you, Monica. Hey, but I promise I'll be there for you from now on."

They hugged.

Monica watched her grandmamma wipe the kitchen table as she hummed. Every inch of her body language was saying, *I told you so*.

Monica pulled Big Man aside, putting her arms around him and squeezed tightly. "Why is it every time I'm at the very end of my rope, you're there to rescue me? How can I ever thank you, Big Man?"

"By the time your grandmamma called me, I was already on my way. My informant had already filled me in on everything. You need to thank God for giving you a grandmamma like that."

Monica went from room to room, talking with everybody and re-living the day. She heard the doorbell ring and ran to answer it. It was Joy's friends—practically the entire cheerleading team.

"We heard everything that happened today," Karen said holding a handful of colorful balloons floating in the air. "Do you think she'll ever forgive us?" someone asked. Myles was among them.

"Come on in. We've been taught to forgive," Monica said.

Plates were being passed with barbeque ribs, chicken, baked beans, slaw, spaghetti, homemade apple pie and ice cream. Monica couldn't eat a bite.

Big Man came in the house with several gigantic boxes. "YEAH!" All the kids yelled and tore into them.

While the celebration continued, the phone rang.

"Monica, this is Chris. Do you mind if we join the celebration?"

"I'd feel honored, but who's the we?"

"I have Brooke in the car with me. We're about fifteen minutes away."

All the kids squealed as the stretch limousine steered its way around the corner. Chris and Brook stepped out with teddy bears and loads of *Kids R Us* bags. The atmosphere was charged and the excitement palpable. Monica was a little nervous about having Brooke in her home but soon realized there was no need to be.

"Mmmmm….is that apple pie I smell," Brooke said.

"Yes it is. The best in the city. Come right this way, I have a piece just for you," grandmamma answered.

Later, loads of laughter spilled from the dining area where Brooke and the other women in her family sat eating pie and drinking her grandmother's specially brewed coffee.

The entire house was filled with fun and laughter. The kids gathered in the front yard playing games, as the women exchanged stories inside. The men slowly converged out back monitoring the meat that slowly simmered on the grill. Joy and her friends kept the music blasting. The tiny, little framed house rocked with happiness.

# Chapter 34

## Shock and Grief

The huge estate was dark and quiet. Tiny rays of sunlight seeped through the drawn curtains adding a small amount of diffuse light to an already dim room. It was one-forty-five pm. The hours seemed to tick away, two at a time.

Gerald looked up as Charlene walked into the room holding the baby, her face drawn with sorrow. She'd pulled all of her hair away from her face as it dangled in a long, ponytail.

"I'll be in the baby's room. I just need some time alone with her if that's all right with you." She spoke softly.

"That's a good idea," he said. He kissed and held them both tightly—watching as she took the baby into her nursery for the last time.

He took the steps two at a time and fell on the den floor next to the couch and began to pray. "God please take away our pain." As the tears rolled down his face, he knew he couldn't help Charlene because he was in too much pain himself.

Gerald stood when the doorbell rang. He really didn't want any guests today. Geraldene's grandparents had said their good byes on yesterday. Who could that be? He was surprised to see Pastor Collins and his wife standing there.

"We thought you could use some company right about now," Pastor Collins said when he opened the door.

He was actually glad to see his Pastor. He tried to fight back the tears but was finding it next to impossible to do so.

"It's going to be all right," Pastor Collins and Andrea kept repeating as they both hugged him.

"Where is Charlene?" Andrea asked wiping her eyes.

"She's upstairs in Geraldene's room. She probably needs someone to talk to right now."

Andrea took the back steps to the baby's nursery.

Gerald looked up at Pastor Collins. "I've been meaning to call your secretary to see if I could come and talk to you. I really wanted to apologize."

"There's no need to do that. I'm glad this is all over, Gerald. Now it's time for you and Charlene to begin healing."

"Would you and Andrea go with us to take the baby to her mother?"

"Of course we will."

They both watched as Andrea walked towards them and stood alone in the door.

"Where is Charlene?" they asked.

"No one is upstairs," Andrea said. "I've looked everywhere."

Gerald searched the house. He immediately knew Charlene had gone down the side steps and taken Gereldene with her. "Call her cell phone," Pastor Collins said.

Gerald paced back and forth. "She won't answer. I'll just have to wait until she decides to call."

"The judge said to have the baby to her mother by three, Gerald. It's already two 'o clock," Pastor Collins said.

He stood there helpless, drained and with a tremendous heart ache. He hung his head. "I don't know what to do. I don't want any more trouble."

"Call her cell phone, Gerald," Andrea urged, softly.

He dialed Charlene's number and was about to hang up, when he heard a soft voice—"Gerald."

"Charlene, where are you?" he asked. He couldn't understand what she said. "Stop crying, honey and tell me where you are."

"I don't know how to give our baby away…Gerald….I came here… so God could tell me… how to give our baby to her mother."

"You went where, honey?"

"Church, Gerald. Geraldene and I are here on the altar. I'm asking God to show me what to do."

Gerald mouthed to Pastor Collins where she was. They all headed out the door and climbed into Pastor Collins' SUV. Gerald continued talking to Charlene as they drove along.

"I'm sorry I caused you so much pain," she cried.

"You've never caused me any pain. I would go through anything as long as I have you. God is going to show us both how to handle this. You'll see. I don't know how to take away your pain, Charlene but He sure does. Maybe we should have gone there together."

He kept on talking until at last she looked up into his eyes. Gerald dropped to his knees at the altar and held his wife. *"Father, help us. Help us,"* he cried.

Pastor Collins and Andrea waited a few minutes before they joined them. For a while, no one said a word.

"I'm okay," Charlene said, looking into Gerald's eyes. "I love you and I'm sorry. I hope you'll forgive me someday." Then she turned to Pastor Collins and Andrea. "I'd also like to apologize to the both of you for everything I've done. I truly am sorry."

They all put their arms around her as Pastor Collins led them in prayer.

"It's time to take Geraldene home to her mother." It was Charlene who'd finally said those painful words.

"Wait, before we go, I have something I need to tell the both of you," Pastor Collins said.

Andrea looked at him and nodded.

"We were going to wait until after you gave Geraldene back to her mother. Somehow, I believe this is the right time to tell you. There's a young college student in our congregation that's found herself in a very awkward position. This is her first year in college and she's pregnant. She's decided the best thing to do is place the baby up for adoption. I've counseled her ever since she found out about the pregnancy. She wanted to have an abortion at first, but we've spent countless hours on that subject and she now sees the wisdom of adoption. Andrea and I took the liberty of welcoming her into our home until she delivers. We also told her about a wonderful couple that could raise her child in the best home imaginable. She's gained our trust and says she would love to have her child adopted by any couple we would recommend. We would like to recommend the two of you."

Gerald and Charlene sat stunned.

"We don't know what to say," Gerald said.

"Say yes," Charlene laughed, wiping away the tears. "Say, yes."

"There's one more thing I need to tell you," Pastor Collins said.

"She's having a girl."

~~~

"One more hour," someone yelled. Monica looked at her watch again, two o' five. She looked at her grandmamma.

"It's going to be all right. We've waited a long time for this moment," grandmamma said. "Come and sit down. Are you hungry?"

"I can't eat a thing. I'm not used to these many butterflies in my stomach. I'm just ready for my daughter to get here, and then I'll know it's all real."

Monica looked up and down the street to see if they were in sight. As the next hour passed, Monica bit down on her lip. She couldn't take it anymore. She picked up her cell phone and went outside.

"Brittany, it's four 'o clock and they're not here!" she said. "Where are they?"

"These things can take more time than expected. They'll show up, Monica. They are probably just saying their good byes."

"Wait a minute," Monica said. "There's a SUV pulling up now. This may be them."

She watched as four adults got out of the car. Finally, Gerald removed the baby from her car seat as Pastor Collins held the bags.

Grandmamma, mamma and Joy, joined Monica.

"Hello, everybody, I'm Pastor Collins," he said as they walked up. "We're sorry to be so late. It was just very difficult to say goodbye. I hope you understand."

"We do," grandmamma said. "Thank you for bringing her home."

Gerald and Charlene kissed Geraldene over and over. "I hope one day you'll know how much we love you," she cried as she handed the baby to Monica.

"I want to thank you for taking such wonderful care of Geraldene. You don't have anything to worry about. I promise I'll take care of her just like I know you would have," Monica said. She kissed Charlene on the cheek.

"I believe you will, Monica."

Charlene kissed the baby softly for the last time. "Maybe someday you'll let us see her. Perhaps bring some Christmas gifts to all your kids. I hear Geraldene has an identical twin sister," she said smiling through the tears.

"We love you, sweetheart," Charlene said, holding on to her tiny hand.

Monica's heart was breaking for them. She looked at the tremendous sadness in Gerald's eyes. He couldn't speak as he drowned in a stream of tears. He continued to gently hold the baby's hand.

It was good their pastor came along, Monica thought. He needed the support.

"I can't do this," Gerald cried. "This is too hard," he said.

Monica had never seen a man cry so hard. His wife seemed so much stronger than he did, she thought.

The four of them headed back towards the car, turning for the last time to say good bye.

~~~

Brooke was thankful she and Chris came to welcome the twin home. She had never witnessed such an emotional scene. Her heart was breaking for the Browns. However, once the Brown's departed and the other twin arrived, it became a tremendous family celebration.

The next day when Monica came back to the office, she was a different person. She was talkative, cheerful, with a sparkle in her eye.

After she'd spoken with Brittany, she was expecting all of her girls home in a few days. The judge was completing the necessary paper work.

"Monica, do you think you could join me for lunch today," Brooke said.

"Sure. Any place special you'd like to go?"

They went to Brooke's favorite, The Chalet. After they'd finished eating, Brooke pulled out two sets of papers from her bag.

"Monica, I have something I would like for you to consider. Several of my rental properties are vacant at the moment. I have been looking for a reliable tenant to lease this wonderful home to. The layout of the place is spectacular. It even has a pool. It's in a perfect location and the schools in the area are some of the best. It would be totally right for five little girls to enjoy....."

"Wait a minute Brooke, what are you saying?"

Brooke smiled.

"Are you serious....I mean... can I afford it...I believe I would be a reliable tenant."

"Slow down a minute," Brooke said laughing. "I think you would be a reliable tenant as well. First things first. Do you think you would like to rent it?"

"YES," she yelled. "I mean yes," she said lowering her voice, looking around the restaurant a bit embarrassed. "Yes, indeed Brooke but how much are you talking about a month. I haven't saved quite enough money, yet."

Brooke smiled. "If you agree to take care of all the up keep on the property and oh yeah, take care of those beautiful girls, I could let you rent it for…say, one hundred a month."

Monica tried to speak but the words wouldn't come out. The tears welled in her eyes.

"Before you answer," Brooke said holding up one finger. "There's something else I need to say. I know how close you are to your grandmamma, mamma and sister. I have another home in the same neighborhood. I would love for someone like your grandmother to have."

"No-o-o Brooke…"

"Tell me—would you be willing to consider my offer?"

"I don't know what to say," Monica said. "How could I ever repay you?"

"Taking care of your family would be payment enough."

"I promise to do that." Monica set back, clutching the papers to her chest.

She sat up. "Brooke, my grandmamma has been in that neighborhood for years. I hope I don't have to tie her down to get her to move."

"It's funny you should mention that. While I was at your home the other day, she was telling me how much she disliked the neighborhood now. At one point when it was really crowded, it was touching the way she kept apologizing for not having enough space. I believe she'll move in a heartbeat, Monica."

"This is wonderful. As awful as my life was just a week ago—it's that good today," Monica said.

Brooke dangled two sets of keys in front of her. "So, I assume the answer is, yes. You can move in any time you're ready," Brooke said.

"YES…A thousand times, yes!"

"Do you want to go and see your new home?"

"Brooke!" Monica said almost tipping over her glass. "Let's go."

When they drove up, Monica couldn't believe her eyes. The house was even prettier than she'd dreamed. With four spacious bedrooms, a huge den, dining area, an eat-in kitchen, game room, plenty of walk-in closets and their own private baths, Monica stood in shock. The backyard had a very large play area with swings and a beautiful in-ground pool.

"Brooke, this is too much. I…can't…"

"Yes, you can. It's your time Monica. It's your season."

Monica went from room to room. She did that over and over again.

Brooke decided to wait before she would tell Monica that both houses had already been purchased in their names.

# Chapter 35

## Oh, No...

Brittany had been given clearance to expedite the process of getting the rest of Monica's girls home with her. She was concerned about Julia and Countess. She observed multiple hospital visitations in their records, so she decided to pay a surprise visit to the home.

"Oh, I wasn't expecting you," Ann said speaking through the crack in the door.

"Can you please get the girls ready, we're taking them to their mother today," Brittany said.

"Well...they have...uh...really bad colds. Why don't you come back tomorrow? They'll probably be better by then. Where's Ms. Dire?"

Brittany silently took in the environment and noted the untidy conditions. "I'm sorry to hear they're sick but I need to get them today."

"No. Come back tomorrow, like I asked you to!"

"Is there a problem, Brittany?" Robert said getting out of the car. His strong voice caught Ann by surprise.

"I don't think so. Ann was about to take me to the girls." Brittany put her foot in the door.

When Brittany saw the girls, she dialed 911.

~~~

Monica parked in a no parking area and ran into the emergency room. "They're both being admitted into the hospital," the nurse said.

The doctor came around the corner. "Who's the children's mother?" he asked.

"I am," Monica said holding her breath.

'Ma'am, both girls have fluid in their lungs. They are having a very difficult time breathing. We are going to do everything possible to make them better. The little one has a broken arm and they both are badly bruised."

Monica swayed as they grabbed her to keep from falling.

"Have a seat Miss Gold."

"Take me to my girls. I need to see them."

"Are you sure you're okay? You're awfully pale," the doctor said.

"Yes. I'll be fine."

Monica did everything in her power not to pass out when she looked at Julia and Countess.

"Grandmamma, are you praying," she said turning to her. She wasn't there.

"She went in there." The housekeeper buffing the floor pointed to the chapel.

She found her grandmamma stretched out on the altar.

Monica never left the hospital. After the first two nights, she was glad to finally receive the report the doctor gave her.

"Miss Gold, your girls are making remarkable progress," Dr. Grove said. "Overnight their breathing has improved. I will be transferring them out of the Stepdown unit to a regular room today. We're still watching them very closely."

She hated to ask for any more time off, but again, Brooke understood.

Monica was glad when all of grandmamma's prayer partners showed up and joined her in the chapel. They were now very special to her and their faith and loyalty was something she cherished.

Their prayers were answered. The girls were almost back to normal.

"Knock, knock," Brittany said, peeking through the door. "May I come in?"

Monica was always glad to see Brittany.

She opened the door wide with Teddy bears in her arms, both girl's names engraved on each. "They look like two different little girls, Monica," Brittany whispered. "They are so beautiful."

"I know. They really are doing very well. The doctor's talking about discharging them tomorrow if their lab work comes back normal again."

"That's great. Do you think you can get away for a second while they nap?"

"I hate to leave them, Brittany. When they wake up, I'm the first person they look for. They don't want me to leave them."

"We'll hurry right back. I promise."

Monica rang the nurses' desk. "If I decided to leave for a moment, would somebody watch the girls for me?"

"You don't have anything to worry about Miss Gold. They're in good hands. You need to get out of here for a few hours anyway," the nurse said.

"Hurry," Monica said, grabbing her purse.

Brittany drove and at last pulled up in front of Peaches' school.

"What are we doing, Brittany?"

"Come with me," she said grabbing her hand. They stood outside the classroom's door. Sheila looked up with a gigantic smile on her face.

"Peaches, please come here," Miss Tate said.

She walked up to the desk.

"Look over there."

Peaches looked straight into her mother's eyes. She walked slowly over to where she stood.

Monica picked her child up. "Are you ready to go home with mommy?"

"Yes," she said softly.

"Miss Tate, can Peaches go home a little early today?" Brittany asked.

"She sure can."

Miss Tate reached up, tears in her eyes, and kissed Peaches. "See you're going home with your mommy just like Miss Tate told you."

# Chapter 36

## Oh, Yes...

Monica turned and watched as Chris drove up. She couldn't believe the difference a few years had made.

"Hey, Chris, look at what I can do!" Peaches did a swan dive off the diving board. "Watch me too, Chris." Julia jumped into the shallow end.

"Julia, be careful," Monica said. "She tries to do everything her big sister does. Girls wipe your feet before you go inside. Wait for Countess."

"I bought all of us tickets to the aquarium in Atlanta next week," Chris said. "The girls have been begging to go. My mom wants to join us. She loves having the girls around. She says they are so lady like, whatever that means."

"You are a remarkable person Chris Blankenship and so is your family."

"Monica do you think you'll ever be able to forgive them for all they put you through?"

"It's weird. I already have. I really do feel sorry for all of them. I spoke with Big Man and Jessica the other day. They both told me Gail has lost her home and is back in the projects. They kept such close watch on her she had to stay squeaky clean. Her friend Mike had to let her go and she's really struggling taking care of her kids. They still can't seem to find Ms. Dire. I do have some good news, though. I spoke with the girl's counselors today and she's given them all a great report. I don't know if Ann is still in jail or out on parole. They are in the middle of investigating the Crafts, however. In the meantime, I'm glad they've made the decision not to let another child be placed in their homes."

"Enough about that, are you hungry? Grandmamma has just taken the food off the grill."

"Which house does your grandmother stay at the most?" Chris asked smiling. "She seems to always be at yours."

"Both! It's wonderful. Often times grandmamma, Joy and I are at my house alone while mamma and the girls are having a fantastic time with each other in her home. The girls have grown extremely attached to her."

"Look at all you've accomplished Monica. At the end of the month you'll graduate with your associate degree. Considering you're now Mr. Brownlee's legal aid, what's *the plan* after graduation?" he asked.

"You know, I really miss working for Brooke but I'm thankful the two of you encouraged me to accept this position. So, I have a wonderful surprise for you. I've being dying to tell you this, but I wanted to get my official notice." She waved a white envelope in the air. "Here it is! I just received my acceptance letter into the University this fall. I'll be majoring in political science. I'm going to be a lawyer. They really need my help in the Family Courts, don't you think. I have the right experience for it." As usual, her classic smile brightened the place.

"I want to make certain nothing ever happens to any-one else like what happened to me."

"I'm proud of you," he said, kissing her softly.

# About the Author

A native Memphian, author Rhonda Nelson attended Hamilton High School. After graduation, she attended the University of Tennessee at Knoxville, where she obtained a Bachelor's Degree in Nursing. She continued her education at the University of Memphis, and received a Master's degree in Public Administration. Presently, she is pursuing a Masters of Arts in Religion.

Professionally, Nelson has been a Joint Commission surveyor for the Hospital Accreditation Program and Chief Nursing Officer of several hospitals. In the community, Nelson has been members of various boards. She is a member of Temple of Deliverance Church of God in Christ. Being called to do the work of the ministry, she is a licensed Evangelist.

In the community, Nelson has served in many capacities and on various boards throughout the city of Memphis including: Girls Incorporated of Memphis, Memphis City Beautiful Commissioner, and the Advisory Board for Nurse Executives. She is a graduating member of Leadership Memphis, and a member of the Alpha Kappa Alpha Sorority, Inc. Nelson is also a member of Temple of Deliverance Church of God in Christ, a church under the former leadership of Bishop G.E. Patterson and now under the leadership of Superintendent Milton R. Hawkins.

Being called to do the work of the ministry, she is a licensed Evangelist in the Church of God in Christ and has made several mission trips to Africa.

Nelson signed with RiverHouse Publishing, LLC in March of 2011 and her first book, *No Other Help I know*, a Christian motivational novel will be released in April of this year.

Despite her numerous accomplishments, her primary goal and focus in life is based on the scripture given to us in Matthew 6:33 …. *"But seek ye first the kingdom of God, and his righteousness; and all these things shall be added unto you.*